Archie Weller is the author of two novels: *The Day of the Dog*, which was runner-up in the first Vogel Award and was made into the film *Blackfellas*, and *Land of the Golden Clouds*, which won the Human Rights Award in 1998 and was presented by Sir William Dean. His stories have been widely anthologised and collected in *Going Home*. He has published a volume of poetry, *The Unknown Soldier and Other Poems*, and he has written a number of plays and a film script. He currently lives in Western Australia.

First Nations Classics

THE WINDOW SEAT

ARCHIE WELLER

First published 2009 by University of Queensland Press
PO Box 6042, St Lucia, Queensland 4067 Australia
Reprinted 2017
This First Nations Classics edition published 2023

University of Queensland Press (UQP) acknowledges the Traditional Owners
and their custodianship of the lands on which UQP operates. We pay our
respects to their Ancestors and their descendants, who continue cultural and
spiritual connections to Country. We recognise their valuable contributions
to Australian and global society.

uqp.com.au
reception@uqp.com.au

Cover design by Jenna Lee
Typeset in 11.5/16 pt Bembo Std by Post Pre-press Group, Brisbane
Printed in Australia by McPherson's Printing Group

First Nations Classics are assisted
by the Australian Government through
the Australia Council, its arts funding
and advisory body.

This project is supported by the Copyright Agency's Cultural Fund.

C⊚PYRIGHTAGENCY
CULTURAL FUND

A catalogue record for this book is available from the National Library of Australia.

ISBN 978 0 7022 6601 0 (pbk)
ISBN 978 0 7022 6793 2 (epdf)
ISBN 978 0 7022 6794 9 (epub)

University of Queensland Press uses papers that are natural, renewable and
recyclable products made from wood grown in well-managed forests and
other controlled sources. The logging and manufacturing processes conform
to the environmental regulations of the country of origin.

Contents

INTRODUCTION
by Ernie Dingo

We love Archie, what's not to love? He has this uncanny knack of planting an old seed in your mind, feeding it and making it Weller – then it grows around you from within.

Kirky was a quiet bloke; you never heard him come and sit down – he was just there. I can't remember why I called him Kirky; he was Archie Weller to most people, and he is my Brother. A quiet and unassuming bloke – didn't say much – he wasn't the competitive type; he never spoke over us at all. In fact, he hardly ever spoke.

When we were all together we were loud – just black teens trying to find a way to impress the Wujbullas without stamping our feet and getting angry. Laughing and big-noting ourselves, wanting to be different – laughing with each other, at each other – finding a better story to tell. Yeah, we wanted to be different but the same, but different in a funny sort of way that was the same but different. The old people had taught us to be resilient and resourceful, for you don't get old being silly and if you were going to spin a yarn make it a bloody good yarn that will be remembered.

Kirky would listen to us — wry grin, cheeky laugh — but he never big-noted himself like we did, yet his presence was a part of us like a leveller. When the laughter would take its breath and turn our thoughts to a better way of surviving — in dealing with the gibes, the names, the attitudes and the insults that would again raise their ugly heads — our cultural heritage would rise higher: our sharing, our Brotherhood. We would talk about where we come from, what our old people would say to our minds, what they have done, what they have seen to remain mentally strong in all their turmoil. We spoke about twisting it back to the other foot rather than turn the other cheek. After all, they were paying us to assimilate to be like them and we didn't have any money to educate them about us and they were the ones missing out. Yet we played basketball and, when we did, we needed to be deadly — and I mean deadly — not cheeky and have the Monaych (the police) down on us but DEADLY.

When we would think about the issues we have gone through thus far, we would agitate ourselves up into a crescendo that would go silent and only our thoughts would fume as the last outlet. That's when Kirky would glow. 'Brother Ernie, I wrote some stories,' he said. He may have been quiet but he had impeccable timing as he fumbled with a notepad he always had in his mustard-coloured corduroy jacket — yeah, Kirk was a fashion icon in the late 1970s. *Ha ha ha!*

Kirk had a presence about him and his swagger created his space; his voice was soft, dotted with cheeky laughs in his preparation, always adjusting his glasses. He may have stumbled verbally to get his words out but he knew it was his moment for he had written it all down. He had prepared the space, even the silence had respect; it told the wind to tell everything and everyone to listen, and we did. Listening to his stories, being transported on his journeys, smiling at his cheekiness, holding our breaths – inhaling short and sharp – following his story, forgetting to exhale, breathing in the wrong places, and then finding the rhythm of his tale and breathing gently and travelling with him with pride.

It was beautiful to listen to his stories as he told them, feeling every emotion, imagining every smell, picturing every frame and riding every word. No-one said anything at story's end; his stories just tailed off into the silence – it wasn't as if there were more to come. You just had to sit there and watch the last of his words travel into the distance. He had painted pictures in our heads and coloured them the way that only he could have as he has done before and still does. Our greatest collective intelligent response was simple: 'Moorditj.' After all he was the writer, he has the words, and just look at him – nothing flash, nothing outlandish – and we have just been schooled and he was quite happy with that.

We love Archie, what's not to love? He has this uncanny knack of planting an old seed in your mind, feeding it and making it Weller – then it grows around you from within.

Once he had asked me to read 'Watson's Pool' and that was it; unashamedly, it is my favourite as I thought of a pool I know called Mungunumbi where young men are tied up (symbolising their youth and silliness) and thrown into Mungunumbi Pool. When they resurface they have, as their rite of passage, become Bunaba Men. I think of his words in 'Watson's Pool': of its beautiful names that sang sweetly on Black lips that Watson – bringing his stench forever inland – had stumbled upon this pool and named it after himself.

Archie Weller writes words that resonate throughout my entirety. I have travelled journeys on his words, I enjoy the colours he paints and I have taken his colours on my journey. I am in readiness for this new *The Window Seat* – it's like sitting inside as an early morning sun bathes the spring garden, waiting to swing open the French doors to a bouquet of words to match the symphony of ancient music still singing softly in the background.

Yes, Archie Weller is a quiet bloke. He don't say much at all. He doesn't have to; he don't have to stamp his feet. He can tell a bloody good yarn, and you can go and stamp your own bloody feet … in admiration.

I dedicate this collection of my stories to all those who played a part in my life and have now passed on, especially my foster brother David Wallam and my good, wise friend Errol Binder, but also Oodgeroo Noonuccal and her son Kabul, Bob Mazza, Jack Davis, Justine Saunders, Michael Riley and Byron Syron, and not forgetting Irwin Jones, Annette Jones, Eric 'Drakie' Mourish, Phyllis Bropho, Vanessa Howard, Florrie Kickett, Brian Garlett – to name just a very few. Because without friends you are lost – a nobody. On earth your presence lit up my world with your jokes and smiles and now, as stars above, you light the path I travel today with memories of your friendship and love, muted laughter and wise words.

Stolen Car

He was eighteen years old, thin and dark as an ancient snag, hidden in a river. Golden laughter of the sun shone from his yellow eyes and melted into his blond curly hair.

His eyes were the first thing anyone noticed about him. Gentle, in half crescents of laughter, sometimes wide with interest, sometimes sad. But the colour was quite strange, and within them if one was kind or quick enough, one could see a spirit of restless searching and unsureness that was the very soul of the boy.

He had hitched a ride with a truckie that morning from the country to the ragged outskirts of the city. Red and white houses pimpled the hills that circled it like a sleeping snake. Orchards have tamed the crude wilderness, but now a new savageness, the city itself, squirmed like the awakening pupae of some cruel, giant insect, between the hills and the ocean.

He stood under the tree trying to thumb a lift. A grotesquely ugly, yet beautiful old red gum, covered in clusters of sweet smelling blossom, clinging tenaciously to the edge of the rushing highway.

But the tree and he are the same, out of place in this brick and bitumen world. None of the cars stop until an old Holden skids to a screeching stop beside him. A grinning dark face, minus one front tooth, peers out the window.

''Op in mate,' a nasal voice croaks. 'Ya won't get a lift 'ere mate, unless a Nyoongah comes along. Them white bastards too good for us,' continues Gap-tooth conversationally.

He wrenches the gear stick around, pushing the accelerator down. They spin off in a cloud of flying gravel and dirt, howling along the grey intestine leading into the bulging stomach of the city.

They swap names. Johnny Moydan, lived all his life on a farm near Katanning, come up for his first look at the big smoke. Benny Wallah, known as Wallaby. Brags about the girls he knows and the 'breaks' he has done.

Dusk. They shoot up onto the top of the hill in Shepperton Road and Johnny takes his first look at Perth.

Buildings scar the purple, pregnant sky. Anguished, tortured silhouettes, rearing from the darker mass below. Holding the diving sky and the living city apart. The claws of the city rip open the clouds. Blood pours from the wound and night comes slipping over the too truthfully cruel city, sending the day people scurrying for home and dragging the night people from their holes and ditches. Park the car in a dark, dead-end lane in an empty industrial area. Streets full of people, flat black shadows, dancing in the lighter grey of the night. Fluttering dank, dirty moths gathering in little clusters in pools of light on street corners.

'We'll go up to Zigi's first, see if me woman's there,' says Wallaby. 'Might even get you a moony too. Plenty of women 'ere for ya.'

City youth, wise in the ways of his world, treading the streets surely. Johnny follows, shy and confused. The sun, his sun, has quite gone now, and he is cold and a little afraid in this dead place that seems so alive.

Music from the nightclub throbs hypnotically, escaping through its gaping red mouth and crawling painfully across the air, beaten out on drums and lacerated by whining electric guitars. The club's pale face shows neither pleasure nor annoyance, only suffering blankly. An air conditioner protrudes like a grey wart, dribbling into a pool on the street. People are spewed out of the fluffy red mouth, gathering in chattering groups on the street. Stumbling people, happy people, angry people. Aboriginal people. This is the Nyoongah hang-out.

Around the corner, dark and full of lanes, Aboriginal people talk quietly and laugh softly. Sometimes voices rise in a family quarrel that erupts into a brawl. Then the police move in like a pack of hungry dogs.

Police car always squatting in the road outside Zigi's. Big cold-eyed policemen striding the streets, pushing the stray people around.

Wallaby leans against the glass window of the pizza bar next to Zigi's and fishes in his pocket for a smoke. A voice from the dark cries out.

'Hey, Wall, when you get out of 'illston?' and they are surrounded by a crowd of boys with a few girls clinging to muscular arms, afraid they will be swept away if they let go.

Dirty, sly, wary children, with eyes that look at, yet away from strangers.

Where is the soil that spawned their ancestors? Only bitumen and cement here now. These are not spirits from the bush who hide in the bodies of humans, or trees, or rocks, or bound joyously to the stars. They are like the leaves of yesterday's yellowed newspaper, with yesterday's news, whirling aimlessly in dirty streets.

'When ya get out, well? Ya only bin in 'illston a coupla munce, unna?' asks a slouching youth, paler than the others, blank, humble eyes and a twisted smile. A kicked, stray dog, tail between dusty, dungareed legs, and a whine.

'I ran away, Billy. Me an' Taiquan Moore. Taiquan got caught, but.'

'Well, what ya standin' on the streets for, Wall? Bloody demons 'll 'ave ya d'rectly. Flog piss outa ya then,' rasps a bedraggled boy, cheerfully.

'Not me, Eddie. This is th' Wallaby 'ere, look!'

Bursting into the cocoon of male security, two short solid girls push their way. They are sisters with blonde streaked hair, lively flat faces, and happy brown eyes.

'Wallaby, *darling*. Where ya been, ya stroppy bastard?'

'Ah, just 'angin' around, Junie.' A wink at the others, an arm over her plump shoulder and he has found his woman.

4

Her sister Jody looks at Johnny. Big, warm eyes and fleshy boldness. Shy Johnny looks away.

'Well,' Wallaby hitches up his trousers, ''oo wants a ride in me car?'

'Go on! Where's ya car, ya bullshitter? Ya just run off from 'illston an' buy a car like that or what?' sneers a youth on the outskirts.

'Don't believe me then,' cries Wallaby, ego shattered. 'Ya c'n ask me mate, Johnny 'ere, if ya wanna, Charlie Moran.'

To own a car is the dream of all of them. In a car one is king of the roads, going anywhere. Down to Albany, up to Geraldton, even across the Nullarbor. A car opens up limitless boundaries of adventure. Squeal around the dull streets, impressing the girls. Shout out to lesser mates who have to walk. A car is a throne for royalty to sit in and observe, in arrogant splendour.

'If none of ya wanna come, me an' Johnny's goin' up to Balga to roll some drunks.'

'Truth is ya jus' wanna show off, Wallah. Ya c'n roll drunks jus' as easy in Supreme Court Gardens,' jeers Charlie.

And Wallaby thinks it's time to be going. The Morans are enemies of the Wallahs, through some longstanding family feud. It would be just his luck to get in a brawl with drunk Charlie, be arrested, and returned to Riverbank for escaping custody.

He swaggers off, Johnny and the two sisters in attendance. Back to the car, lurking in the shadows. Scramble in, happily anticipating adventure.

'All of ya ready for one ride ya never goin' t' forget,' Wallaby cries. 'Orright, then, 'ere we go.'

Let out the clutch. Slam foot on accelerator. Alley fills with smoke and the smell of burning rubber, wheels spin on the spot, car leaps out of its cave, glad to be free.

'Jus' leave me trademark,' Wallaby laughs. 'Now, you mob, this car's 'ot, so if we get caught jus' say ya 'itch 'ikers, orright?'

'Let me out, Wallaby ya mad bugger. Ya drive too fast, an' in a stolen car too. That's askin' for trouble,' cries Jody, then shrieks as they just miss a bus.

'You shut up, ya stupid bitch. I'm a good driver.'

Then they hear the triumphant, maniacal wailing of a police car behind them.

Spin the car around the corner where the bridge sags over the line, near the station. Wallaby is out and running as it jerks to a stop. As though he is a magnet, the girls cling close behind, Johnny last. Up towards Zigi's they belt, desperate and afraid. Round the corner into James Street. Wallaby is out of sight. The girls run up a lane that opens bedraggled arms for them. It is the same as them, used only when needed. Johnny follows.

He catches up with Jody, leaning against a wall, out of breath. She gasps.

'Give up, Johnny, they'll only catch us anyhow.'

A thin, sharp-featured policeman runs up beside them.

'Come on,' he orders.

A van speeds swiftly and smoothly down the rutted lane.

Bundled in the door.

Before he can even sit down a torch probes in. The beam rests on him. A finger of doom.

'Come here, son. The sergeant would like a word with you.'

Torchbeam hauling him out, like a fish on a line. Pushed into the back of a sleek police car. Hunches into the corner, miserable, confused. The young driver's face, pale, humourless, looks around at him.

'Steal a car, did you?'

'No,' he mutters.

'Hah,' Face laughs, nastily. 'I'll bet you didn't.'

Then the sergeant gets in.

Middle-aged and thin. Greyish hair, a little curly. A hard, lean, bony face. A slit for a mouth, and cruel, dark eyes boring into the youth, alight with a madness that frightens and paralyses him. The sergeant leans close and speaks in short, hissing bursts.

'Right, sonny. Now you're going to tell me a little story, aren't you?'

'Me name's Johnny Moydan, an' I never knew th' car was stolen,' stammers Johnny.

The sergeant leans closer. The excitement in his eyes whips the quivering youth.

'Now listen, I haven't been a demon for ten years for nothing. I'm giving you five seconds.'

'What ... what ya wanna know? I never done nuthin'.'

Poor Johnny. Confused, terribly alone. Peaceful, gentle Johnny, who liked to muster sheep and breathe in their greasy smell; who liked to pick the first blossoms of the red gum, or Christmas trees for his mother; who liked to listen to the magpie's carol, or the parrot's cheeky whistle.

A fist slams into his face, just under his left eye. He doubles up in shock and pain, covering his head. He is pummelled in the side of the stomach, and punches thud on his thin back. Then the sergeant is savagely pulling his blond hair, his gift from his sun. All the time the hissing voice continues.

'You stole the car, didn't you? You stole it from Innaloo last night. Come on, who were your mates?'

'No, no! I didn't steal it,' cries Johnny.

'Don't lie, you little black bastard. You stole it, didn't you? Speak up.'

Jerks his head up and down. Johnny's brain snaps. He becomes a loose, ragged, spineless wreck.

'No, no! God's honour, mate. It was Wall 'oo stole it,' he blubbers.

'You said you didn't know it was stolen!' comes the driver's triumphant jeer, and Johnny hates him as he has never hated before.

The sergeant seems to love the feel of Johnny's hair between his fingers. He pulls it more and jerks Johnny's head up and down as though trying to break it off.

'Wall who? Where's he live?'

'I don't know. Oh, I don't know. Please don't hit me any more, boss. I'll never get into trouble again.'

'Hit you,' says the sergeant, surprised. 'Listen, I've only just started. By the time I've finished with you, you'll be stretched out on the ground. And when I get tired there's a younger bloke waiting to take over.'

The car rolls to a menacing stop in a vacant block and the sergeant suddenly opens the door and pulls Johnny out by the hair. The boy collapses onto the cold, earthy-smelling soil, his soil. A green, untidy vine stares sadly at him from the fence. A light winks in the old CATS building beside the empty army barracks.

Scream and bring people running. But nothing except a sick grunt, and another as he is kicked in the stomach.

'Too many houses and people here,' one of them says.

Pushed back into the car. It is too late. His chance of escape is gone and his soul dies.

The sergeant gleams at him, triumphant and victorious.

'Have you got your baton there?' he asks the driver, watching Johnny's face.

But Johnny has learnt in these last few minutes what he should have known since the day he was born, to keep a shutter always between himself and the white man. He stares blankly at the floor. Face expressionless. Only his mind knows the weak terror within him, which will stay there forever.

'Yeah,' comes the driver's flat reply.

'Well, we'll find some dark lane. I'll hold him down while you give him a few whacks in the crutch. Might help his memory.'

Move off slowly and surely around the corner and down the hill. Turn left into a lane of grey dirt, bordered by grey fences. Rubbish bins, startled awake by the stark, harsh glare of the headlights.

Turn them and the engine off.

Silence.

The two men stare at the youth, hungrily, with their not quite human eyes. Then a voice crackles over the car's intercom.

'Detective-Sergeant Maxwell would like to see the prisoners now.'

Hesitation. Then the car starts up, slides like a snake out of its hole.

The sergeant leans over Johnny.

'Listen, sonny. This Sergeant Maxwell is a big man, and a friend of mine. If I find out later you told him anything you haven't told me, I'll come looking for you. You understand, you little black bastard?'

Out in the main road again. Cars and lights, people and reality.

Past Zigi's.

Johnny looks up with his new, dead eyes, and sees two Aboriginal youths leaning against a car watching him with the same dead eyes. He is truly one of them now.

Drive to Central, a towering glassy building that curves beside the Swan River, like a scorpion's tail.

Statements, fingerprints, photograph, then led off to the cells.

Iron bars, flat yellow walls and floors. Pale light from the passage gently brushes his face. Lie on the hard mattress, smelling of vomit and other people. Pull the grey blankets up over him and momentarily stare at the hump in the next bed, wondering who it is.

The feeling that it is all a nightmare slowly dies away.

Shiver with shock, exhaustion and the reality of it all.

He had always been a 'good boy'. It had been like a medal for him and a trophy for his parents. The Moydan family had worked for Mr Williamson on his farm for years. Betty Moydan was proud of her neat little house and the whole district knew and liked quiet, gentle Johnny, a good worker and a good footballer.

Fall into an uneasy sleep, and dream his ordeal all over again.

Next morning. Thin and afraid in this wooden, shiny, court, before the bored, bespectacled eyes of the magistrate. Only the Legal Aid man isn't his enemy. Even him he doesn't really trust.

Gape around the room, while the lawyer speaks.

'... good boy ... up from the country ... never been in trouble ...'

What is the use? He's speaking out-of-date words.

Pompous, mechanical voice of the magistrate discharging him. Led out, signs book, receives his envelope of belongings.

Then he runs from the building.

Wallaby and Billy in a pool room. Wallaby grins at him.

'G'day, Johnny. They catch you, unna?'

'Yeah,' flatly.

'I was watchin' ya from behind a tree. Them demons flashed their torches at me, but they never seen me, look. I 'ad one big piece of pipe there. I'd 'ave given it to them monaych bastards too,' he growls.

Empty bragging. A pitiful attempt to prove a manhood that doesn't exist. Stamped out of existence by generations of white men. Roll a cigarette and silently offer his tobacco to the others. Slit his eyes against the smoke, gaze around the room.

This is what he had come to Perth for. Enjoy himself, then go home. But he can't go home now. Restless, uneasy and bitter like the city that has adopted him.

''oo give ya th' black eye, cood?' asks Billy.

''oo d'ya – well think?' snarls Johnny.

The two boys stare at him, shocked by the hate in his voice.

'I'm complaining about them two –' he continues.

'Hey, look out, Johnny,' Wallaby whispers, scared yet awed, while Billy looks fearfully around. 'Don't drag me into it, anyrate. I'm on th' run, remember.'

'Nor me,' says Billy. 'More better if you just forget about it, cood?'

'No.' Johnny's voice is flat. 'But you don't 'ave t' worry, you two. Only me. All by myself.'

Ring up the Legal Aid man who helps him write out a complaint. Two weeks pass. Watching TV with dark, happy Raymond and Wallaby's sister Ethel. A knock on the door. A deep voice.

'Johnny Moydan home?'

'Dunno. Might be.' Mrs Wallah flusters.

Walks into the hall, followed by Raymond and Ethel.

'I'm Johnny Moydan.'

A giant Inspector, shiny cap, snowy white shirt, row of coloured ribbons displayed on his jacket. He senses the other Aboriginals staring at him and knows he is alone.

'You made a complaint, I believe?'

'Yeah.' Johnny shuffles.

'I'd like you to come to the station with me. Make a statement. You understand?'

So he has begun. Can't stop now. Wallaby is angry.

'Ya too simple, Johnny. Jeez, ya can't tell ya nuthin! Now ya got th' cops sniffin' around Mum's 'ouse, gettin' 'er upset. An' what about me, ay?'

Night. Billy and Johnny ambling home. Billy spots the slowly moving car, pulling to a threatening stop and nudges Johnny. They lean against the charcoal-coloured wall, while three plain clothes men descend upon them.

Two of them close around the fearful Billy, eyes opened wide so the moon reflects the whites. Third one beckons to Johnny who follows warily. Pushed into a corner. Big red face leers down at him.

'Where's your switch wires?'

'What ya talkin' about? I got no switch wires.'

'Yeah! Supposing I search you, then?'

Beefy hands whip over his thin frame then the man straightens up and takes out his notebook.

'What places has your mate broken into tonight?'

'None, 'e was with me.'

'Well, what breaks have *you* done?'

'None. Leave me alone.'

A sudden slap across the face breaks his lip. The detective's mate calls from the alley entrance. 'Righto Wal. This one's clean.'

'Right, Allen.' Luminous eyes peer down at him. 'What's your name anyhow, smart arse?'

'Johnny Moydan.'

'Yeah?' the man stares at him a minute longer. 'Well, piss off.' Raises his hand. Johnny cringes. Hates himself and the man. Hurries away with Billy.

Next day. Rings up the same Legal Aid officer and complains. Can't understand Billy's fear and that of the other Aboriginals. He sees it as his right. Urges the others to complain too. Talks loudly to the lawyer about the wrongs his friends suffer. Advised in apathetic tones to get them to put it in writing. Other Aboriginals frightened of him. He is different. Begin to drift away from him until only cheeky Wallaby and Billy are his friends.

One evening, they wander aimlessly and happily down the street. Once again a police car slides to a halt. Two uniformed men get out, relaxed in their confident authority. One points to Johnny.

'You! Come here.'

Johnny is spat out of the group. Shambles forward.

'All right – . What's your name?'

'Moydan. Johnny Moydan,' he pouts.

'You mean you're the smart little nigger who's been rubbishing the force?'

Johnny says nothing. Digs thin hands into pockets. Where will he be flogged this time? The words of his friends drum in his mind. *Look, cooda, if ya black ya got no chance. It's natural ain't it? Monaych blame us for most anything, then beat piss outa us, but aint nothin' ya c'n do 'bout it, 'cept keep outa their way. Can't even take a slap in th' face look. That Moydan is one wild boy, 'e's mad I reckon.*

Glances into the policeman's face, then his eyes slip sideways.

Murky eyes, dull, muddy-coloured as a river in winter. Angry as one too. So much dirt in the water now, no-one can see the ugly snags that will impale a man.

The policeman's mate wanders over to Johnny's side.

'Listen Johnny,' he says gently, 'you may as well own up and give up.'

'What ya want with me, well? Ya always pickin' on me.' For a moment his eyes flash fire before the flood puts it out.

'No, Johnny, you've got it all wrong. You were identified, see?' Brings a pad from the car and reads from it. 'Young Aboriginal, blond hair, thin, brown coat, bare feet. Fits you exactly, Johnny.'

'So where's the purse, sonny?' growls his mate.

'I never got no purse.'

The quiet policeman treads on Johnny's bare foot, squashing it into the pavement.

'Johnny, you don't want us to flog you, do you?'

Remain silent, staring at the ground. Keep the pain in his foot from showing in his face.

The policeman sighs and removes his boot.

'Well, suppose we show you to the old man you robbed?'

The old man looks him over and shakes his head.

'You can go then. You were lucky tonight, Johnny, but just keep out of trouble in future, see,' says the disappointed policeman.

How can he keep out of trouble, when trouble waits around each corner to seize and roll him in the filthy mud of petty persecution.

Then Wallaby is recognised, picked up and returned to Hillston. For a week Johnny stays indoors at the Wallahs', brooding.

Wander back down town at last. Long, low pool room, glass windows staring onto street. Red door, gaping stupidly open like a lipstick mouth. Juke box mumbling words of love. Pool tables, flat and green – plateaus of dreams where a man becomes a hero or a loser, able to spin the balls into ideas of his very own. Around the walls pinball machines clack and tinkle.

He is about to spend his last twenty-cent piece on a game when he is hailed.

'Me ole cooda, Johnny. 'Ow are ya then, mate?'

'Goodoh. Run outa money, but, Billy.'

'Come out 'ere, bud' Billy hisses. Around the corner into the covered car park. Hands the startled boy a handful of crumpled notes.

'What's this then, Billy?'

'Well it ain't shit,' Billy grins. He is high and happy. He and Crabby Unkel have busted the easiest store of all, and stolen over a thousand dollars. Billy thinks of all the clothes he will buy, the wine he will drink to forget what he is, the friends he will have. But his laugh is sliced in half by a blinding spotlight.

'Hold it right there, you two,' a voice shouts.

Billy gets nine months, and despite his denials and Billy's insistence that he was not involved, Johnny gets six.

He is released in the autumn.

His face is thinner than ever, hard and angry, picked bare by experience. Quieter than ever, with bitter golden eyes staring like a savage dog. Catches a train from Fremantle into Perth to slide his body into the tepid, stagnant swamp of people.

No-one he knows anywhere. Wallaby inside again, Billy still in Bunbury. The girls like fat little brown moths have fluttered off to other lights. Wander down to Supreme Court Gardens. No-one there. Coloured leaves dance frantically in the wet wind, drying, dying. Perhaps like him they wish they still had something to cling to.

Squeeze into a corner by a brick wall. Roll a cigarette. He shivers and wonders where he'll sleep tonight.

A car pulls up beside him. But it isn't the police. A boy gets out of the car. His own age, in a neat clean suit, warm ruby-coloured shirt and white tie. Gold cufflinks show as he straightens his immaculate hair. An expensive watch circles his wrist. A chain shackling him to the rich life he leads.

'Come on, darl. We're running late.'

Now a slim girl gets out. Beautifully dressed. The prettiest girl Johnny has ever seen. They clasp hands and hurry up the street, leaving the keys in the lock.

Something deep down in Johnny's tortured heart breaks. The strange white boy has so much, while all he has is a bad name, lying among the weeds of society like rotten fruit, eaten away by white maggots.

The car is a smooth blue sports type. A prostitute, flaunting her body sensually. Teasing and tempting him. He desires her. Be as good as the boy who owns her.

Out of the shadows, into the comfort of the car. Turn the keys. The car purrs instantly to life. A good clean engine, just like the owner.

Squeal down the street and around the corner, past the immaculate boy and his beautiful girl. Honk the horn, laughing, leaving them standing there stupidly. He wishes Billy and Wallaby were there, to see him commit his first crime, and share with him the joy and beauty of his car.

Drive out to the ocean. Whirling around corners and up straight stretches. Push the car until it whines in agony. Rejoice in the speed and power he controls. Turn on the heater, to warm his frozen body. He finds a packet of cigars and sticks one jauntily in his mouth. Turns on the radio.

He reaches West Coast Highway and turns up it. Black and mysterious ocean. The light from Rottnest flashes regularly across its dark, oily, undulating back. The sea is his father, the earth his mother. He is remote from man. Safe and warm and sheltered in the pulsating body of the machine.

The police find him near Scarborough. He sees the light coming up behind him, hears the murderous howling. Thin face pulls into a dingo grin, hard angry eyes shine with excitement. He feels no fear. He has no feelings at all. They were beaten out of him in prison.

Slender hands grip the wheel and he pushes his beautiful blue being to its limit. The police car's blue Cyclops eye flashes into the blue-black night. People get out of the way to watch. For the first time in a long while Johnny Moydan isn't being pushed around. He is in control, he is free, he is supreme – he is someone.

But at the corner he couldn't control the creature he had created.

He was touching 120 mph when they hit the sand dune.

Someone?

Pathetic Johnny. The shadowy, formless people watch from the footpath. Watched you and the banshee-wailing police car rush past and away, leaving just a wind in your wake.

And who remembers a wind?

Dead Dingo

The gates close behind him and he's free.

Free? Ha, that's a laugh. In some ways it's more free in there than out in this crap.

Nothing to do, nowhere to go. But better move on.

The ex-con moves down the grey, dark, streets. No-one is his friend, the moon glares coldly down at him, the stars wink at him mockingly.

Mock him, Universe. Laugh at the boy who belongs to no race at all. Lost to the traditions of his mother's people, but black to the white race of his father.

And the Earth and all mankind laughs.

He acts like the big tough, but anyone looking at him would see only a thin, weedy half-caste with short, prison-cut hair and ill-fitting shoes.

Nothing to do. Get out, bust a safe, get caught and back in again. That's his life.

But no. Not jail again he thinks. No good, that place. Tin cabinets with crims, filed away, out of sight, out of mind. Bareness, coldness, greyness.

The boy, only nineteen, comes to a scratched, drab,

black and brown block of flats with a 'vacancies' sign staring down at him, daring him to come in. Who wants a dirty yella fella for a neighbour? But even a con's got to have a place to live and it looks cheap, so he plucks up courage and goes in.

Night, and the gay blazing neon lights flash off and on, lighting up the bare room and the rare cross-breed fauna crouching on the hard bed. Tough con has become lonely lost boy, country boy, nothing to do, no friends.

Go to Greaser's, look up some old acquaintances.

Greaser Symes' Pool Parlour. Up the faded, dirty stairs, into the cavernous black mouth swallowing idle youths, chewing them up and spitting them, penniless and idle once more, back into the streets to rob another factory or mug an old man.

Inside all dark, with white staring electric eyes hanging from nothing, hanging from a fly-spotted ceiling, air full of smoke fumes and cheap perfume. In between blares of bawdy music from the juke box by the door, the sounds from the pool tables, and laughter, as the moronic juveniles enjoy themselves.

The half-caste stands in the doorway. In a minute he is seen.

'Hi, man.'

'G'day, mate.'

''ow's it goin', sport?'

The hero has returned. He gets a Coke and pizza – on the house, of course, as Greaser doesn't want trouble. Then walks over to a couple at a table: Nicky Mulligan, a lame half-caste whom he's known all his life; and George Bondi, a dumb confederate in the gang.

'Well, Nick. What's goin' cooda?'

George, a typical moron, grunts, deep like.

'We got a job lined up,' answers Nick. 'Been waiting four weeks to break it. Dead easy, George reckons, no alarms or nothing and about five thousand in cash. Tonight.'

He thinks. With his short hair and square clothes he's out of place in this bunch and he could do with some money and flash clothes. But not now, not right after jail. At least a few days' freedom before taking any risks.

He looks up.

'Aw, jeez, Nick, not so soon. Maybe next week, unna?'

Nick grins and butts out his Winny. He shakes his head and black curls fall over his quiet brown eyes.

'No, we gotta do it tonight. It's a dead moon and going to be cloudy, look.'

'Righto. Well, count me out. But good luck, cooda.' And the boy starts to move off.

'Well don't go, Charlie. Me an' Nicky's goin' aroun' t' Muddy Jenny's'.

It's George, suddenly speaking up. All he can talk about with any knowledge is football and Jenny Kelly.

Why not go along? Free booze and some spunky girls. Better than hanging around here like one of those swinging light globes, tolerated until used up then thrown out.

They leave. Bursting out of the tawdry parlour into the grey street.

The neon lights, the flowers of this jungle, flicker around them, pulsating with their hypnotic messages – buy this, buy that, come here, go there, do this, do that. The boys are caught up in the wild dance of colour that turns their faces from green to red to white and back to green.

Nicky runs his fingers through his long curly hair and whistles at some chicks in a car. George checks the two cops in the mall. Charlie drinks in the freedom of his first night 'out'.

Cars honking, people shouting and pushing, a river of wonderful moving noise. He pushes into people for the joy of contact, breathes in the air full of petrol smoke and human smells, the freshest air he'll ever know.

Through an empty, ugly car park, stagnant puddles, footsteps sounding eerily in the blackness of the unlit back street.

'Sounds like she's got visitors,' George reasons stupidly as he sees the lighted windows and hears the stereo.

A knock on the faded door, a suspicious answer from Muddy Jenny.

Nothing's changed. Just like that big stagnant puddle, back in the car park. That's what life's like.

A typical night at Muddy Jenny's. Lying around on faded cushions, discussing their faded lives

'... Wally Coyne 'ad a blue wiv a skin ... caught th' clap off Annie ... dough's run out, 'ave t' do somethin' soon ... aw, Josephine's turned lesbian, I reckon ... so 'e got stuck on th' roof, when th' fuzz come they jus' took 'im ... dobbed in fer sellin' smack ... ten years fer rape ...'

Stuffing falling out of the holes in the cushions. Drink more beer from the stomach of the ugly, yellow fridge. Cold, refreshing, stimulating.

They smoke joints and get high. The room becomes filled with the sweet smell of grass, symbol of youth.

He cons up a spunky, unknown girl, and they kiss and cuddle on the thin, stained carpet. The boy is lonely no longer, for tonight anyway.

Goes for a walk through town, noisily, drunkenly, made brave by beer. George and Nicky higher than the rest with the excitement of the planned break-in.

Jimmy Davis pretends to be a dog and lifts his leg against parking meters. Much laughter for Jimmy the clown. Sally Gordon walks unsteadily along a high, thin, brick wall. Her brother Darrell tries, and falls off. George and Muddy Jenny stagger along together, shouting out, in slurred tones, some pop song.

'Department of Youth. Ooh! Ooh! We got th' power.'

The ex-con smiles down at his newfound girl. He'll have some fun with her, he thinks, before it's off to jail again.

The group pools its money and buys some fish and chips, and up into a dark unwanted alley the dark unwanted people go to squat and eat. People passing mutter 'drunken boongs' or 'poor homeless Aborigines'. But, either way, who really cares.

Police cars idle up and down the street, evil blue dingoes hunting their game. Every once in a while, the triumphant wailing howl of a car on a trail. The youths huddle instinctively together, wondering if it's one of their mates.

So passes his first night out. Aimless wandering with cobweb friends – not really wanted, but impossible to brush off, and a new girl to be forgotten soon, as she will forget him.

Next day. Same sun, same sky, same city. Rent to be paid next week and no money. Gotta get a job before then.

He tramps around all morning. But no-one wants an ex-con half-caste on his payroll.

Scab some cash off me mate Nick, perhaps. Wonder how th' job went last night.

About midday he gives up job hunting and goes down to Greaser's, but George and Nick aren't there, so he buys a Coke and hunches out.

Go to the zoo. Nothing else to do. He stares moodily in at the monkeys, who stare back, laughing and chattering. Jeez, th' zoo's going down deadville, all right.

Bored giraffe, mangy lions in small cages and the elephant who reminds him of the head warder. Bears ambling around, putting up a show of importance, looking like fat alcoholics in tattered brown coats.

Then he comes across the wild dogs, the jackals, coyotes, foxes – and the dingoes. Yes, arrogant Australia had to get in on the act.

He looks down at the yellow and red dingoes, one of which returns his stare in a lordly manner, just like one of the elders back home.

'You, dingo. Ha, you hate being in jail, too, just like me, ay? Only thing is I never had nobody staring at me. Yeah, mister king dingo, stare like a god, show th' white crap they can't beat us. We'll go out together in th' end though. Dead dingo an' mangled dog, broken by th' white man. But not beaten, ay dingo?'

He goes back to Greaser's and waits a bit. He's just going to leave when Nick bursts in. Any mug can see he's dead scared.

'Struth, where th' fucking hell you been all day? Bloody George ballsed it up. "No alarm" th' dumb coot says. But it's there all right an' me an' him got seen. I bashed th' white buggers, ain't no-one good enough to catch ole Nick, but they got that big oaf an' no tellin' what they'll do to make 'im talk, an' …'

He breaks off, sudden like and everything goes still as these two cops come in acting the real men. They come over to the table and Nick looks slowly up at them.

'Your name Nicholas Mulligan?'

'Nope, Joe Biggs is me number, cobber.'

'No cheek, Mulligan. You know George Bondi?'

'Mulligan? Who's Mulligan? An' who's this George Bondi you talkin' about?'

'All right, son, I'm arresting you for attempted robbery.'

'But I been with me mate 'ere, all day an' las' night, unna cood?'

'Just get a move on. You'd better come along too, son.'

★

26

In the court the fat-arsed judge lectures him on associating with criminals and tells him to get a job. Ha, the jokes are here today all right. Charlie Boomer *is* a criminal.

Nicky gets six months and the last Charlie sees of him is his face peering through the barred pig van on his way to Fremantle. Like that dingo in the zoo.

Black dingo. Dead dingo.

Charlie goes home to bed. As he stares at the dirty brown wall and feels a broken spring jabbing him through the thin mattress he remembers home. So far away, and such a long time ago.

The lop-sided tin humpy, the dirty, half-naked Wundi kids, his mother whom he has almost forgotten and his father whom he doesn't want to remember.

And the small country school. *Boomer, haven't you got any shoes? Boomer, your homework is not done again. Get down to the office. Boomer and Mulligan, you're not at home now, kindly be quiet or I shall send you to the office.*

Black man, black man,
Catch him, if you can,
If you can get past his smell,
Then you're doing very well.

All them big dumb farmers' kids, with faces the colour of sheep's wool and voices like sick cows.

'Hey, Charlie Boomer, you're a blackman. Get down on your knees an' say "Jim Burke is th' white boss!"'

'Go t' flamin' hell, y' white tuppy.'

'Cheeky coot. C'mon boys, let's belt *it* up.'

A full-scale fight. Charlie, his brother Luke, Joey Harris a cousin who lives with them, Nicky and others, belting crap out of the white punks but then ...

'Here, you hooligans. Break it up. Boomer, Mulligan, Harris, Stretch, down to my office.'

'But Sir ...'

'Don't answer me back, Boomer. You're a larrikin. Your tribe is always causing trouble.'

Caned six. Black loses, white wins.

A dark night. The usual drunken fight going on between the Boomer parents. But this fight is serious. Jake Boomer is stone drunk. He grabs a knife and goes for Rose who screams and throws a saucepan at him. Blood spurts from a cut on Jake's forehead and he goes mad. The Boomer kids and Joey Harris, all under ten years old, see their first murder.

The next day the police came and took Jake, Luke and Joey away. Charlie himself ran off. No white man was going to touch him and that night he and Nicky Mulligan ran away, heading for the big smoke, for Perth.

They were caught of course and Charlie was sent to join Luke and cousin Joey in mission school.

When Nick was fourteen he caught his foot in a harvester while working on a farm, so he got the sack, and that's all he did get. There was no compo for boong kids working as casuals. He would ever afterwards walk with a limp. And who wants to employ a crippled darkie.

So at sixteen Nicky got Jolly Stretch who was seventeen and Charlie – who was fourteen and had just been kicked out of mission school to find work – to help bust a store, and on a starless night they all went to do it.

As their first job it was a balls up. Jolly let go of the jemmy and smashed a window. Nick cut himself climbing through and inside they got bushed as they crept about whispering and flashing the torch on and off. As they left Charlie went arse over head into the arms of the waiting pig.

Caught. And this time it's for real. Not just getting caned or slapped across the face, but in the cell with a bullying pig who fancied he was Lionel Rose.

Next morning. Three thin weedy Aboriginals, one a full-blood, frightened dark eyes and the solemn, deep, voice.

'Six months in a reform school, and let this be a lesson to you.'

Well, they learnt their lesson all right. When they came out they were really experienced criminals.

Next time he went inside was when he and his cousin were picked up for stealing blankets. They had been sleeping in Supreme Court Gardens – weeds no gardener could get rid of.

Soon after they came out he was picked up on a car stealing charge and this time he got a year in Freo. He was to get to know that place real well, as do most Aborigines who drift to the city.

Bloody car. The girl wasn't even worth it either, too flat and tight and a borrie anyhow.

He gazes up at the cracked ceiling, remembering. But right now there's the problem of the rent and a bit of cash for tucker. He flings himself over on the hard bed.

'Aw, Jesus Christ, I'll have to bust a store. But this'll be me last job, I just gotta get regular work.'

And Charlie Boomer falls asleep, as away over the Swan River in South Perth, another native Australian, the dingo, also captive of the white foreigner, lays his lordly head down and closes his yellow eyes.

Sandcastles

Hello. My name is Tommy. I don't write too good, but I got all these things I want to say.

You know, when I walk down the street everybody stares at me. That's shame, like I was an escaped animal from the zoo, or a spaceman or something. I'm just a coloured boy. Maybe that is why they all stare at me, because they imagine I might steal their car, or knock them down and take their money.

I think of money a lot, when I don't have any. When I got it, I don't think of anything except having my piece of fun. When I got money then I'm someone, but when I'm broke I'm just Tommy Caylun, the boong, shuffling down the street, with an eye out for the monaych – coppers. With money in my pocket I can pretend I'm a main actor, you know? I walk around like Marlon Brando, big tough Tommy.

But their scornful stares, that look right through me, show me what I really am.

I hate white people – or maybe I hate myself because I'm almost white. And that is all I'll ever be – an almost man. Whenever I start becoming good and try to settle down, something always happens and I'm back where I come from. Like last time, when I had a wadgula girlfriend, and a Monaro, and a steady job. I told myself: Tommy, this is it. You right now.

But my cousin, Clemmy – who was on the run – come around home, one night, with a carload of stolen beer.

We all got blue-drunk and gang-raped this girl Clem brought along. Well, not really rape because she was drunk too, and asking for it. But, when police busted through the door, it looked like rape. You can't tell police nothing, when it's part-Aboriginals involved.

So I got three years in Fremantle, I was only seventeen. It hurt me; that's the truth.

Down the Central Station, five CIB blokes punched me and Clemmy and the two Harrison boys up and down the room. But we give them our best because we only got our pride; when that's gone we may as well go out to some park to drink and die.

Any rate, I'm out now. I tell myself I will settle down now. But I am what I am. Or rather, I am what the white people want me to be.

That white girlfriend of mine, she was pretty. She understood me, too. I met her at the tech school I was going to, where I was learning mechanics. One good thing about my dad (and about the only good thing) was how he could fix up any old car. I learnt all I knew off him. I remember dusty days in the hot sun, and rainy nights with the electric light dancing with the wind. I would huddle into my hand–me–down clothes and watch every move his stubby, greasy fingers would make. I reckon he could of fixed an engine blindfold, he was that good. Every now and then he would glance down at me and explain in his gravelly voice what was where. Sometimes, he would raise a rare laugh and say I looked like a little joey 'roo. That was when he would forget the black skin my mother had given me and just remember I was his son and I could love him then.

He used to say him and me would go into partnership, when I got old enough and passed tech. He was proud of me, you know.

Then Clemmy Jackson and Olman and Eli Harrison had to come along. So, that was the finish of that; all Dad's dreams, I mean. It was the beginning for me. You might say I'd finally busted out of my white cocoon, hanging on a tree. But I wasn't a butterfly, you see. I was something bad and black, and unsightly in my real world.

But I was telling you about my girl I was going to marry.

One night, she and me took these pills. I learnt if you take pills with Coke, it makes you like you was drunk – well, happy really. Plastic joy, you might say. These wadgulas have got funny tricks. Well anyway, we was rolling around on the floor, laughing at nothing much, thinking about nothing much – at this party. Somehow, me and her got together. Kissing and cuddling, you know? Then we made love, and it was like nothing that had ever happened to me. She was so soft and gentle, and she gave everything. That's what got me, because most wadgulas take everything off my kind. She quietened me down and showed me where I was going.

All that summer, me and her went everywhere together. I had this Monaro I bought off Uncle Butch for five hundred. Brother, she could move, all right! It made me feel like God or something, you know, to roar and rush up and down the streets. I hotted it up with floor shift, and foot-on-the-floor power, and mags, and bucket seats. I put a radio and cassette in it and, with my knowledge, I kept the engine in good shape.

But you can't get away from nothing. One night, outside this pizza hut, these demons pulled us up. They tried to say I stole my Monaro, and shamed me in front of my girl. They had a good look at her too, with a what-the-hell-are-you-doing-with-*him* sneer. They pulled me out and trod on my toes and scared the shits out of me. They made me look a fool, just to prove to themselves they was the men.

The people in the pizza hut stared, with hooded eyes, at another boong being picked up; the sluts in the one darkened car on the street (for it was past midnight) giggled at the two coppers who promised, silently, to come back this way, later on, and pick them up for a quick free one some place. The one Nyoongah there melted away into the shadows, not wanting to know about it. He knew that where there was monaych there was trouble: for him, or me, or any poor black bastard

34

like us. You live and learn and live. The lights blinked down on me, bored like. Even the jukebox couldn't give a damn, shouting out happily as I went through the third degree, on the hot street.

I would like to punch the huge, fat policeman in the guts, and make him grunt. I would like to shout out, to all the world, that I am a man. But I never did. I put on my best Aboriginal face, and closed my eyes and hung my head and called them sir – just as they wanted me to.

Afterwards, I could sense my girl, Jillianne, was just a little cold towards me. I think she was reminded that I was, after all, a quarter black. But I never cared. I was used to her kind of treatment. Any rate, it didn't last long. It did spoil our evening, though.

But when we went back to tech, it was all right. It made me feel good making out I was a wadgula. I met Jillianne's family, in their double-garage house at Subiaco. They thought I was number one, you know. Her old man got me a job in the Skipper Chrysler workshops.

But you can't keep being false forever. You can never escape from your people, either. They are always watching. Watching.

So my cousin come along and what happened, happened.

You can be what you like on the outside, but inside you are you.

In Fremantle, I met more of my cousins, and an uncle I never even knew I had. Nyoongahs, us South-west people, stick together in Freo, unless they are enemies.

I never had no enemies, so I was right. I tell you, going into Freo is like having a bath. All the bullshit gets washed off you and you learn the truth. You come out clean, you might say.

That is why I do the given-up-don't-care shuffle around the streets and spend my dole money on getting drunk at Beaufort or Guildford Park with my people. I live with my two cousins and my woman in a tent at Lockridge.

Not my wadgula woman, Jillianne. A Nyoongah girl – Phyllis Kennedy – who I knew a little bit. *She* come to see me sweating it out in jail; Jillianne didn't. So what did you expect? She'd welcome me with open arms and a great big hello-I'm-glad-you're-free kiss? Buddy, she was off a month after I got put away – with a wadgula lawyer. How she must of laughed at silly black Tommy, as she showed him around to all the gawking, squawking white crows.

Peck out your eyes. Peck out your life. Leave the bones to bleach, lost and forgotten, in the corner of some paddock.

That's when I started hating the white people.

Phyllis is pregnant to Paddy Needles, who took off when he found out. But I love her. Sometimes, when she's rasping away in her harsh voice, I feel disgusted with her and wish she would speak softer, and better English. I wonder why I can live with her, with her torn, dirty clothes and untidy hair and her smell. But it's not our fault. We got no water here, only a tap, and a creek that runs dry in summer. When Phyllis come out of Niandi she was given all these new clothes by that girls' home. But you can't keep nothing clean in this place. Besides, all her sisters come and take her clothes off her. Then she got this pretty way of throwing her arms about that makes her look like a ballerina. And her hair *is* beautiful and soft. Her eyes, too, look at me with such warmth and happiness and trusting. We are very happy together.

Sometimes, however, she doesn't understand me, because I never belt her around and I share everything with her and worry about her, like an old chook. Even when she gets me wild, all I do is go for a walk, somewhere peaceful, and think.

No-one understands me. They weren't me, brought up in my family.

Mum thought she was really good, marrying a white bloke, you know. She dressed in good clothes and wore shoes when she went to town – and jewels. When we was given all our rights then she may as well have been a wadgula. But before that, even, she could look a white person in the eye with pride.

Her first man, Freddy Jackson, was sitting back in Fremantle. (He was that uncle I never knew about.) What he done was get drunk on metho and paint cleaner (because coloured people wasn't allowed to drink legally then) and run amuck in the reserve by the railway line. He got an axe and killed Mum's brother, who also had got drunk.

He got life for that and had already done twenty years when I went there. He'd sort of grown onto the place, like a piece of fungus. He's not even a human anymore. If they let him out tomorrow he wouldn't know where to go or what to do. They did let him out once, I remember; after he had done eight years, when I was about five years old. He come down to see Mum and his son Jojo, who was nine.

I won't never forget that night. Not that I knew what was going on. I didn't. It was just the violence that was to be with me all my life, bursting in, that I remember.

It started off quiet. Dad, a couple of his mates and Mum was getting drunk, playing poker around the kitchen table. Me and my true sister Geraldine, who was only two, and my half-brother, Jojo, was supposed to be asleep. But we always watched the 'Saturday Night Show'.

We reckoned it was funny to watch Mum laugh and stumble around the kitchen and throw her body around in a dance for the white men. It was the only time Dad got happy.

They would listen to the radio, or Dad would drag out his guitar. Sometimes, one of Dad's mates would try to get a piece of Mum. We would giggle from our corner as the whitefella fumbled Mum's heavy breasts and threw floppy arms around her shoulders, and kissed her – and then dragged her, laughing, into the bedroom. Dad would laugh too: he didn't care. Only once, when Mum was pregnant, he got in one of his sudden violent rages, and tried to kill the unborn baby and Mum. But Jojo – who was fourteen then, but big and strong and sullen – stopped him.

But Mum only went with Dad's mates when she was blue-drunk and didn't know what she was doing. Next morning, when she was sober, she would straighten herself up and forget about it and pretend she was a white lady again. But Dad, over in his chair by the stove, looking like a cockroach, sort of, would cackle and grin, with his yellow teeth, and tease her about it. Then she would be ashamed and go away to cry.

Yeah, we *used* to laugh at the 'Saturday Night Show'. But as we got older we became ashamed, then disgusted, then angry. Nyoongahs lose their laughter young in life, you know.

But this night I am telling you about, we was laughing softly as huge Morry Gascoyne, who was a ringer in the shearing shed, tried it on with Mum. Then there was a soft knock on the door. Skinny Jim (who we called Dad's brother) opens it and there stood … Uncle Freddy. I could see the front door from where I lay. It was raining and the rain run down Uncle Freddy's ragged clothes and formed in a pool around his feet so it looked as if he had risen up out of that dirty puddle. It run down over his face, so it glistened in the light from the kitchen and looked like tears.

Uncle Freddy mumbled something to Skinny Jimmy who snarled back, 'No, you can't. Piss off!'

'Who's that?' Dad shouts.

'It's '*im*. Come back to see his missus.'

Us kids was wide-eyed watching this new twist to the show. We hardly ever had any visitors here, especially not Nyoongahs who Mum discouraged. Any rate, as far as I could see this bloke was a stranger. But Dad and Skinny Jim and big Morry seemed to know who 'im was.

We could see something was up because Dad looked uneasy, and big Morry was going to get up. But then Dad grinned and motioned the giant to stay where he was.

'Bring him in, Jim. We ain't ignorant.'

Mum, she didn't know what was going on because she'd been drinking Vio Port and whisky and straight gin all night, and she may as well have been dead.

Uncle Freddy come shuffling up the hall with his prison gait, hands nervously shoved in his pockets. His hooded eyes flicked glances around the room without seeming to move. He was only about thirty then but in my mind he looked ten years older.

He looked up and seen Mum and Mum seen him. Mum tried to struggle to her feet, but only fell off the chair. Her dress went right up her legs so her old petticoat showed. No-one laughed. Not even us.

'So,' was all Uncle Freddy said. His eyes were bleared, like a fused light-globe. Then he shrugged and turned to go.

That would have been an end of it, except for Morry Gascoyne who thought of us all as boongs and not worth a spit unless they was girls.

'So what!' he bellows, and hauls poor dizzy Mum up by the arm. She leaned against the giant and gagged and hung her head.

'What you think of your woman now, the drunk

little gin? Too good for a crazy boong like you. What did he do, sweetheart? Kill his best mate just to show how friendly he was? But we don't care, do we boys? This lovely piece of black velvet has kept us warm many nights.'

Uncle Freddy's hands sprung out of his pockets – big, knobbly, killing hands. He threw his head back and his eyes cleared. He gave a yell as he come in, swinging and kicking.

Morry let go of Mum, who fell back on the floor. Then there was all buggeries let loose. Morry went down to one of Freddy's rights. Dad smashed a bottle over the black-haired head, before ending up groaning in the corner, his kidneys almost busted on him.

Skinny Jim made a grab for a bottle then, but Freddy picked up a butcher's knife and put it right through him. Then the dark angry man worked over Morry Gascoyne so he wouldn't shear a sheep for a long time.

Mum had crawled over to us kids and hugged us to her.

Uncle Freddy busted every bottle in the house, and smashed the painting of the sorrowful white lady dressed in funny clothes, before he calmed down. Then he looked over at Mum, before dismissing her. He limped over to frightened Jojo, smiling with only his mouth. From out of his pocket he bought a medallion on a chain.

'I'm ya daddy, son. I bet ya forgotten me, unna? Well, any rate, I made this thing for ya to keep to remember me by. I won't never see ya again, Jojo.'

He was right. The monaych picked up Uncle Freddy over at the camp the next day after Mum had rung them up. He came quietly, resigned and given up.

Skinny Jim died.

They never let Uncle Freddy Jackson out again.

When I was in there all his teeth was falling out, and he talked to himself, and pissed himself sometimes. He was the joke of the jail, walking up to every new face – black or white – and promising to get them out on bail. Some people believed him, too.

When Dad recovered from his flogging, he laid into Mum and Jojo – just because Jojo was Freddy's son. Jojo ran away and lived by the reserve with his aunty for the next four years. He grew up rough and tough and dangerous, like his dad. He always had a soft spot for me and Geraldine though. When Jojo was thirteen, he went to work as a rousie on a shearing team. He come back home almost as tall as Dad and as strong as a bull. It was all right after that, because Dad was afraid of big Jojo, so he left Mum and us kids alone. Before, he used to flog us for any little thing. That is why I won't never flog my kids or woman, out at camp.

Yesterday, me and Phyllis went down to the beach. We kept out of the way of all the wadgulas trying to turn black. We found a reef and waded around, looking for shells. Phyllis thought it would make the tent look pretty if we got some good shells. I went out deep and found some beauties; like trumpets, they were, and all orange and green and yellow, you know.

Some surfie blokes went by and whistled at Phyllis. Any Nyoongah girl is easy meat, they reckon. Even one who is six months pregnant. Other wadgulas stare at us with their pale eyes, like they always do. But we don't care.

We sit in the shade of some rocks and talk quietly about what is happening outside in the world and inside Phyllis's stomach. That is our world.

Phyllis sleeps and I watch some little kids build a sandcastle.

The last time I built a sandcastle was when I become fourteen. I had just started tech and it was my birthday. Mum still believed I could be all right, you know. Turn out good.

She took us on a picnic down to the beach, to a place only she knew about. She used to come here, with her brother and sisters when she was little, and maybe she wanted to grab hold of her lost youth, or something.

That was fun. Jojo's Uncle Ronny, who was only a year older than Jojo himself (but that's how it works in Nyoongah families) drove us out there in his newly bought car.

There was just them two, Mum, me, Geraldine and the three young ones – all Nyoongahs together. We run around and played chasey and hidey. We swam and lay around, and ate a big feed out of the picnic basket Mum had made. Ronny caught a huge fish and we seen some dolphins way off shore. No-one come to annoy us with their stares and muttered remarks. That was the best part.

Only one thing spoilt it when Mum brought out a flagon of wine. Jojo just stared at her and took himself off for a long walk.

But he came back to help us build the sandcastle. All us kids – even Ronny, who was twenty and a man, really. And Mum too, sat at our side, running the white sand through her fingers and giggling. It was a beauty of a sandcastle with towers and walls and a moat, all covered in stones and shells and seaweed. Geraldine was Queen and I was King, while Ronny and Jojo was the enemies. The little ones ran everywhere, being nothing.

The King of the Sandcastles, that's me – all the way through.

When the sea come in and the sun went down, our castle was washed away, and we all went home. I cried, and the others laughed. But, you see, for one whole day I had owned something beautiful, for the first time in my life.

Why do kids build sandcastles when they know the sea will come right in and wash them away? Why do we dream, you might say?

All I ever do is dream. I'm always going to do something, or be someone, or go somewhere – but I never move.

That's Tommy Caylun for you, all over.

The Storm

All afternoon the cockies had gathered in the hotel. Outside in the red sand the trucks sagged in the oppressive air. The few trees wilted, and the pink galahs flew, screaming, from tree to tree. They swirled up into the sky, then swooped back to earth again – small pink clouds merging with the huge, full, purple clouds that watched from the hill.

There was no wind. The small town stood as though paralysed, like a mouse transfixed by the stare of a great writhing snake. Noise rebounded off the vulgarly wallpapered walls of the hotel as men became drunk. The impending storm was something menacing and inevitable and filled them with an apprehension they could not understand and did not want to admit to. So they drank and sought each other's companionship.

Over at the wheat silo, Eli Johnson finished loading the last of the freight train trucks. The other three men who worked on the wheat bins had gone on down south two hours ago when the sky first began to darken. Eli preferred the loneliness of working by himself. He was a lonely person. He couldn't stand Joe, known as 'Sad Sack', with his deep religious talk; and he couldn't stand Des Keating with his superficial laughter and two-hundred dollar watch; and he could only just tolerate Morrie, who stared at him with blank brown eyes and read war comics and told everyone (when he talked at all) how he had killed gooks in the Vietnam War. Eli had been in the Vietnam War too. Now he wrapped flowers in his long hair and smoked dope and tried not to remember.

The smoke from the woodstoves in the town's kitchens drifted straight up in the still air. Cars roaring past on the highway, half a mile away, left the memory of their drone hanging, with the clothes on the line, still and expectant. The army of quietly menacing cloud-men crept out from their mountains and crawled across the sky, slowly and invincibly.

The sun went out.

Down in the dusty, noisy camp on the Reserve half-naked children rolled in the dirt and screamed like the pink galahs. The half-caste, Dougie Castles, tinkered with his old Holden's engine. He was only eighteen and full of dreams. He would fix up the engine, somehow, then he and his woman and his baby daughter, the flower of his life, would leave the untidy, hopeless Reserve and find better things. He whistled a tune to accompany the music from the battered, old-fashioned wireless that was *his* family heirloom. He glanced up at the cloud-filled sky that squirmed in its awakening. Low rumbles of thunder squeezed through the gaps and the faintest trace of wind began to move in the trees. The youth sniffed the air and smelt the coming of rain. He ran his fingers through his tangled, brown-red curls and rolled a thoughtful cigarette. He stared again at the twisting, angry clouds that looked like Koodgeeda, the snake.

Up in the hotel, big Barney roared with laughter and thumped old Manny Phillips on the back.

'Garn, Manny, where's yer form? Where's yer form?'

'I'm not goin' out there. Ain't yer seen th' sky?'

'I'm not afraid of a few clouds,' roared Barney, like the thunder.

Everyone knew that Barney Eccles was not afraid of anything. He was the tallest, broadest, straightest, noisiest man in the whole district.

He strode out onto the verandah and gazed at the shapeless dark mass above him. The trees were rustling a little now and little dust flurries fled down the street. Clothes began to flap, heavily, in the moving air, and the former columns of smoke from the kitchen chimneys were shattered and lost among grey sky. The galahs shrieked raucously and a burst of thunder shook the ground. Lightning flashed blue-white in the blackness of the day.

Barney Eccles drove off in his old truck.

★

Eli Johnson climbed up the elevator onto the wheat bin roof. Actually, this was the coarse grain silo, where barley or lupins were stored. He felt so near to the glorious, dark shapes in the sky, and he wasn't lonely any more. The wind whipped through the air and tore at his clothes and hair. It beat a song of war upon the loose sheets of iron on the main silo, and the cloud-men in their purple ochre danced a frenzied dance of death. Eli dropped down into the mountain of pale, smooth lupin seeds, and spreading out a tarp, lay on top of them, just below the hole in the roof where the grain elevator spewed out the seed. He rolled himself a number and prepared himself to enjoy the storm in his own way. He dragged the sweetness back inside his body and relaxed. He smiled. He saw a rooster with a lot of tail feathers being chased by a long-necked dragon, spitting mist. A purple-black snake poked its head through the hole in the roof and flickered at him. A fat, juicy drop of rain, like one of those fabled purple grapes that were always out of the fox's reach, splattered on his cheek.

The drops pattered into the dust and thunder rolled across the sky, growling like puppies becoming dogs. The Reserve children yelled in joy and stood still, letting the drops shrivel up on their brown skins. Dougie Castle's young woman came and stood beside him, grinning up with bright teeth. He smiled down at her.

'Goin' t'be a wet one, unna Dougie?'

'Yeah.'

The child of the sky was suddenly born. Huge winds ripped at the soil and flung it into the atmosphere; red dust, black dust, yellow dust. There was no town. No wheat bins, no cars, no galahs, no trees, no Reserve. Only dust and dust, and fleeting glimpses of what was before.

Then it rained.

Great sheets of water slammed viciously against the tin roofs and walls. Wind hammered against doors and windows shattered, smashed by the wind's violent breath.

Out along the track, the truck shuddered in the gale. Not even big Barney's hands could completely control the vehicle. The wind raced across the paddocks, tossing the trees as it caught them, shaking them like a dog does a rabbit.

Even the wheat bin shook. Eli Johnson suddenly noticed that water was gushing down the inside wall and threatening the lupins. He crawled out the hole onto the roof and began to edge his way along to where the gutter was blocked. The wind flicked him off the roof with an idle finger, and sent him spinning through the air, to thump wetly upon the muddy ground and burst open like a broken rain drop.

The water flooded out the lupins.

In the town the wind shrieked like the galahs had an hour before and swooped down, pecking out sections of roofs or windows and, once, a whole wall. The people in the hotel cowered, drinking still, but talking in subdued fashion or gathering in worried knots to look out at the devastation being wreaked before their eyes. The thunder howled like the corrugated iron being torn off the grocery store, and the trees cowered as limb after limb was torn off by the wind's blood-stained teeth. One tree, the jacaranda by the bank, gave up the struggle and with a despairing crack, split in two, falling on a shaking parked car, crushing it out of existence. All the lights in the town suddenly fused.

Down at the Reserve, children huddled into whatever shelter they could find, no longer playing or laughing. The trees were cracking and crashing all around them. Dougie Castle and his woman huddled inside his car. He rolled them both another smoke and his quiet eyes drank in the awesome fury of the storm. *This* was *his* God.

'Is Annie orright?' he asked, anxious yet almost afraid to break the affinity that had built up between the storm and him.

'Yeah. She with Nanny Roberts.'

'Oh, yeah.'

He drew back a lungful of smoke and expelled it slowly. He watched another branch hurtle away across the sky, and an empty petrol drum roll drunkenly down the road. The car shuddered and shook and he imagined that it was about to fly up into the rolling, black, thick clouds and the whirling, swirling rain, and come to earth again in some distant, exciting place.

'Jesus, some storm, unna?'

'Unna!'

Nanny Roberts's little humpy suddenly disintegrated, pieces of it flying haphazardly through the air or jumping along the ground. The old woman was blown over and along the ground like a bundle of rags. Dougie's little child stood in the deluge, too afraid to move. His woman screamed.

He was out of the car and in his storm. Suddenly, it wasn't his storm any more, but an animal born from the heaving, gross belly of the clouds, threatening to destroy his little daughter with its bloody teeth.

His long legs pushed him through the wind and he reached his baby. He scooped her up, then the crazily spinning sheet of iron sliced him in two, neatly, just above the knees.

Big Barney reached home and scuttled into the house, wrestling the door shut behind him: safe at last. He lighted a fire and settled down to wait. There was no electricity and the phone didn't work. Night was falling, but the wind was not dropping, in fact it seemed to Barney that it had built up more force. He took a pot of stew out of the fridge and put it on the stove, stirring it and enjoying the savoury smell as it started to warm up.

The wall caved in and the stove exploded into flames at the same instant as the roof fell, pinning him down. He screamed in terror, then cursed bitterly as he tried to struggle free. But first his screams and finally his whimpers were lost as the wind chewed them up and the flames consumed him.

By the middle of the night the wind had died down and the storm had lost its teeth; by the early hours of the morning the rain had gone and the storm was without its voice. Far-off thunder could be heard, but it was soft and insignificant now. By the time day broke, the townspeople were wandering around their ravaged town, soul-destroyed as they themselves were.

The sky was a tearful, watery blue and the sun had no warmth, as though it were ashamed of having been banished by the storm which, yesterday, had seemed so powerful but now had crawled out to sea to die – a stumbling, old, used-up creature. Its bones vanished with the stars, into the oily sea, to be resurrected on some future catastrophic day.

The only sounds to be heard on the still morning air was the mournful wailing of the ambulance, as it took legless Dougie Castles away from the Reserve from which he had always longed to escape, and the rumbling of the undertaker's van gathering the broken shell of Eli Johnson, secure in his final place of dreams.

Of Barney, the tallest, broadest, straightest, noisiest man in the district, there was nothing left to gather.

It's Only a Game

Kevin Sheedy O'Shea had grown up in a world of football. On the day he was born it was the Grand Final, and his father was not present at the birth. He was out cheering for the stunning victory by the indomitable Cardinals, as West Perth were then known, over East Perth. A pity it couldn't have been over his arch enemies, South Fremantle, but his regret was fleeting in view of the score: 21.21 to 14.10.

Vic O'Shea had burst into the quiet, white, respectable hospital, resplendent in red and blue, with a number of mates in similar attire. They were all drunk on the glorious taste of victory and the many jugs of ice-cold beer they had consumed – an obligatory act after every game, win or lose.

They had pressed their faces against the glass pane of the nursery and expressed with much jollity their approval of the new little footy player to come among their midst. His father had turned a red face to the harassed sister and roared, 'Look at that! Look at that, ay? The little bugger is the spittin' image of 'im!'

'Errr … 'oo's that, Vic?' one voice slurred.

'Why, only the greatest football player of all time! Kevin bloody Sheedy, that's 'oo!'

No-one argued with big Vic. He was a wharfie at Fremantle, and he had to be tough to survive down there, especially as he was probably the only supporter of West Perth on all the docks, and he often let his point of view about the prancing wog poofters who played for South Fremantle be known in the wharfie pubs around the Port city. Not a safe thing to do, as nearly all the patrons were of Italian descent. But Vic was six foot five and weighed eighteen stone, and had been a good ruckman in his day, so nobody corrected him.

So this was how Kevin Sheedy O'Shea came into the world, red and wrinkled, staring into the frightening mass of red and blue and flushed unshaven faces. Truly they would have seemed a crowd of ruffians in his innocent blue eyes had he been able to register any thought.

After this, Vic remembered to go and see Myrtle, who was lying in a darkened room in a state of shock after the prolonged birth. She greeted her drunken conspirator in this act of pain and horror with a wan smile.

'G'day, Vic. Did ja see 'im? 'e looks just like old Uncle Stanley, don't 'e? What ja reckon we call 'im after Uncle Stan?'

Uncle Stanley had played cricket for Nullanulla, where all Myrtle's family had grown up on the outskirts of the desert. Uncle Stanley, in Vic's opinion, was a no-hoper in his cricket whites with his failing, falling-apart sheep farm and his love for cups of tea – nothing stronger.

'Nah. Kevin O'Shea – that's got a nice ring to it. Kevin Sheedy O'Shea.'

'Oh, yairs. Yairs, that's a nice name, Vic.'

The big man mouthed the name again, already seeing the day when his son ran out onto the sacred green oval and hearing the commentator say '… and now Kevin O'Shea, the youngest man ever to captain a WA side; the only person in the living history of the game to win five Sandover Medals in a row! and equalling the great Mel Whinnen to win four fairest and best awards in a row for his team West Perth, he leads this year's WA team onto the ground playing his two hundredth game.'

That was a song worth singing.

The only songs sung in the first few months, however, were shrieks and cries for more milk from Myrtle's abundant supply, or complaints as his teeth came through. Vic bought a football and put it in his son's cot, and the hard cold bedmate probably brought on a few tears as well.

The little footballer grew up in a world of red and blue. Red and blue curtains flapped at the window like two lovers waving a forlorn goodbye to their friend the wind. Scarlet carpet lay on the floor and the walls were painted a flagrant blue. All around the walls were posted posturing players of great fame such as John Watts, Polly Farmer, Mal Brown, John Todd, Syd Jackson, the great Mel Whinnen, Barry Cable and from Victoria, Kevin Sheedy.

There was even one of John Gerovich, the great high flier from South Fremantle (who wasn't a wog, only some sort of European, Vic said). They were little Kev's guardian angels in the long, lonely, dark nights.

When he was five, Kevin was taken to his first football match. Perched high upon his father's broad shoulders he had a good view of the game. He tried to understand the rules, for even at that young age he understood the importance of understanding. Just as young men of the Masai are not considered men until they venture forth with a spear and kill themselves a lion, Australian boys are not considered men until they have mastered the art of aerial acrobatics.

At quarter time he went with his father to listen to the coach's raucous, ribald comments – it was only a Sunday club game, this one, not a proper match at the WAFL, where only special people could go out onto the field at quarter time. At half time he ran out with all the other boys, chasing a tumbling leather ball and trying his hardest to get a kick. All he got was a scabbed knee when he fell over.

He really enjoyed the pie and chips his father bought him – the first he had ever had.

When he was six, a great upheaval overcame the family. His mother's Uncle Stanley died. He had not seen much of his Great-Uncle Stanley after the stooped old man gave him a cricket set for Christmas one year, early on in life. An alien thing was a cricket set in the O'Shea house, and Vic had had a heated row with the venerable and famous Nullanulla cricket player, telling him to keep his poofter games to himself. Cricket was not only a game for poofters, but it had also been invented – and was played – by the English, a race much hated by the fiery O'Sheas for obvious reasons (almost as much as the Italians, who had sneaked into the country after the war and taken all the best jobs on the wharf, but who were, after all, Catholic like the O'Sheas).

With Uncle Stanley's sad passing, the sheep farm passed into his niece's hands. Perhaps nothing would have come of this, other than a quick sale and an increase in the O'Sheas' fortunes, except that Vic's gang of wharfies acquired a new foreman, the son of an Italian migrant about whose native origins and habits Vic had been particularly cutting. The son was bigger, heavier and younger than Vic, with a volatile temper, a long memory and the shame of his father to avenge.

Vic left. Probably the few fights he lost in the Railway Hotel helped him in his decision. Or – never saying Vic was a cowardly man, more a prudent one – perhaps it was the crate that fell with a resounding crash and missed him by inches when he was on his tea break.

The O'Sheas took up farming in dear old Nullanulla, and a whole new life opened up for Vic and his son Kev. There was sheep work to do and fencing and putting in the crop. Around about February of every year, Vic would round up the local lads and start to pummel the Nullanulla Football Club together. In March they would start playing other unheard of towns, until September, when it got too hot, and the shearing season started in earnest.

With the passing away of old Stanley, the cricket team also rapidly faded away. The trophies Stanley had proudly displayed upon his shelves and walls ended up at the local tip and Vic's meagre collection of football awards (two cups for fairest and best) took their place. The only concession Vic made to the memory of Myrtle's Uncle Stanley was a big picture of the great man in his cricket clothes, holding his bat up in the air and wearing a huge smile. Behind him, the scoreboard showed a dismal effort by the Nullanulla players, none of them getting into double figures except for Stanley T.G. Everingham, who had scored 112 not out.

Whenever Vic looked at the picture he would snort. 'Look at the stupid old coot. He couldn't kick a football to save his life, never mind even scoring a goal.'

Being so far away from the hub of football life, Vic could no longer go to the games he loved with such passion, but he could listen to them on the radio and, sometimes, if he were lucky, he could see a replay on television. He missed his drinks with his mates though, making up for it by going over the game kick by kick, handpass by handpass, with his son, who grew from childhood to adolescence knowing that Saturday and not Sunday was the most important day of the week.

Oh, his father ranted and cursed at the decisions umpires made. Kev learnt early on that umpires were his worst enemies, not the Germans or Japs as his

Grandfather O'Shea had told him. His father would pose him questions on what he would have done in a certain situation and, before Kevin could answer him, would answer himself. So Kevin grew up a quiet lad.

In the early days, his father was a god in Kevin's eyes. A huge, muscled, tanned god in his torn red and blue jumper and scruffy football boots. The book of commandments he held under one arm was old and cracked, made of leather and rubber. You boot it, you mark it, you gather it up as it rolls along the ground on its own journey, you hand pass it – to the chest! to the chest! – you drop kick, torpedo, punt, screw kick it, so that it sails in the air as graceful as a bird to land between the two rickety white middle posts on the Nullanulla Football Oval. When you have mastered all these commandments, you get to sit at God's right hand. Perhaps He will ruffle your hair and buy you a bottle of Coke. Then, there is the tackling to be learnt, and shepherding, and the leading for the ball, and more practice on your marking skills. There is the mateship of the team, being able to stick together through hard times and good. Never let your supporters down, not even in Nullanulla!

And so he grew up as his father wished, steeped in the traditions of football. It was a proud day for Vic when his son put on the Nullanulla football jumper for the first time, even if it was only to be water boy. It was the greatest day in the older man's life when young Kevin Sheedy O'Shea ran onto the dry, cracked oval (Nullanulla and neighbouring districts were in the grip of the worst drought on record) to play in his first game against Lower East Nintalinyup. It did not matter that he was not playing for a city team. Who was to say a football scout was not among the shouting, whooping crowd and honking old trucks and cars? Wasn't that the great Australian dream?

In between teaching his oldest child football and crutching the sheep, Vic had found time – since he could no longer go off each night for a middy or two and a game of darts with his footy mates – to father three more children. But there must have been something wrong with Myrtle's genes, for he never had any more sons. So Kev was his pride and joy and went everywhere with him. The girls were shut away in a corner bedroom, or in the kitchen with their mother, given a doll or two to play with and forgotten until puberty brought prospective football players courting and to have a yarn with their father in his twilight years.

The day came when Vic's pride and joy grew too big for the dubious attractions of Nullanulla, and when the farm his father had built up for him held no attraction at all. He wanted to see the world, and where better a place to go than Victoria? That place of mystery held, like Dante's inferno, all manner of demons and pilfering football clubs that took away the cream of young Western Australian stars never to be seen again until they got too old and came back as football coaches.

So, at the tender age of eighteen, our naive young country hero kissed his mother, embraced his fledgling sisters and solemnly shook his father's great calloused hand.

'Now, Kev, yer keep away from them flash young women. Keep yer boot laces done up tight and don't go nowhere near bloody Sydney, orright?' Vic said.

Then the red Nullanulla dust swallowed Kev and his rattling old ute up as he set off on life's great game.

Kev was not a big talker, and he was even less of a letter writer, so his family heard little about him and his adventures over East. But, on the Western Front, things were changing rapidly in Vic O'Shea's once comfortable little world. The WAFL was falling to pieces, crowds were down, and good players were quickly disappearing to the east to fame and fortune. There was a new VFL team in bold blue and brilliant yellow based in Perth, including a few players who had come home from the lucrative eastern states clubs. The West Coast Eagles! There were the Brisbane Bears with the Wests' own Brownlow Medal winner Brad Hardie and his shock of flaming red hair. And the Sydney Swans, with Warwick Capper dancing around, with his too-blond locks, in tight red shorts and white boots. But still he kicked goal after goal. Vic could scarcely credit it. What was happening to the game he held sacred and loved more even than his Myrtle? Dancing girls, fireworks, marching bands! Players with hair longer than his daughters'. Mark Jackson. His conversation around the kitchen table, or in the cool and quiet Nullanulla pub, left no-one in any doubt about his disapproval of such decadence.

Then came a letter from his son. It was not a very long letter and did not say much. Just that he had been shearing and had travelled to northern New South Wales, and now he and a couple of mates might be going down to Sydney for a bit. The last part went: 'I might be playing a few games of football. Love to Dad and all the family. Your son, Kev.'

Football? They don't play football down in Sydney, do they? Then it dawned on him. His son, Kevin Sheedy O'Shea, was playing for the Sydney Swans!

A football scout had been wandering around the northern sheep stations and must have spotted Kev playing with the old Vic O'Shea magic and skill. Everything he had taught his son – and everything he had dreamed about – had paid off and come true. This was better than playing for the WAFL which, let's face it, had lapsed into ruin; no-one going to the games any more, no interest now. His son would break his teeth in the Sydney Swans, and next year he would be bought up by the West Coast Eagles. After all, if Warwick Capper could be in the team ... well!

Dancing girls, fireworks, marching bands? Well, progress was progress. This was the new breed of football. These things were an integral part of the modern game, as Vic explained to his family and the faithful in the pub. Now, if every boy in America wants to grow up and be the president, then every boy in Australia wants to be a famous football star, and every father shares his son's dreams. What better team to play for than the Sydney Swans – for a start.

So it was that every week Vic pored over the football pages on a Sunday. But not once did he see his son's name. Perhaps he's injured and they're resting him, Vic thought. A doubt crept into his mind that perhaps, after all, his son had not been chosen.

But his anxiety was dispelled when the family got another letter – again short, and not very informative. It told Vic all he wanted to know at the very end.

'By the way, Dad, I'm enjoying football very much. I kicked a record number of field goals in the game last week thanks to your teaching. I'm trying very hard too, ha ha!'

'What's the silly bloody idiot mean, field goals. They're all field goals. You kick a goal on the field, not out of bounds.'

'Per'aps 'e's 'avin a bit of a joke, Vic. That Kev, 'e always was a funny bugger. Always full of laughs, Kev,' Myrtle said.

'Football is not a joke, love, as I've told yer often enough. Still,' he said, calming down, 'it's nice to see 'e's tryin' 'ard, anyway.'

So now he knew, and he was happy in his knowledge. Kev was playing for the reserves. They were saving him up for the Grand Final, in which it seemed certain the Sydney Swans would participate. Vic settled down to wait in great spirits. He never let a chance go by without throwing a few hints Nullanulla's way about his son's whereabouts and rise to fame.

Then, one night, after the work was done, and Vic

and Myrtle had just seen the last of the football-playing prospective sons-in-law off, the phone rang.

'Hey, Mum, Dad. It's Kev. Ringin' all the way from bloody Sydney!' One of the girls shrieked, all thoughts of love in the hay paddock followed by a big wedding and life on an even bigger farm temporarily driven out of her brain by the sound of her now-famous brother's voice.

'I'll take that, Irene,' called the proud father and, scarcely able to contain his excitement, he hobbled inside to hear the news first hand.

What would his son say? Would it be a casual, 'Oh, g'day, Pop, I thought I'd just mention I've been chosen in the Grand Final squad next week?' Would it be an excited, 'I've done it, Dad. Thanks, Dad, for teaching me all I know. I'm on my way now, Dad. Nothing can stop me'?

The sun sank slowly into the harsh red desert, red soil and red sky mingling. If Myrtle had thought about it, she might have said it was beautiful. But she never thought much about anything. The mournful calling of some crows on their flight home and the murmuring of Vic on the phone were the only sounds to be heard in this idyllic scene.

Then there was the clump of heavy boots as Vic came out on the verandah. For a long, long time he stared out over his land. At last he turned confused eyes to Myrtle, who reclined in her chair. The daughters had gone off into the bedroom, whispering and giggling about their various boyfriends.

'Where did I go wrong?' Vic asked. 'My … my son 'as been playin' football, all right. Bloody Rugby League for Parrabloodymatta. Now, 'e's been chosen to play for New South Wales against Queensland.' He shook his head slowly, stunned and unbelieving.

'That's nice, dear,' Myrtle murmured from the darkness of her chair.

'Bloody Rugby League. Poofters play that game. They all get together and wrap their arms around each other and stick their heads up bums. They grab each other in any part of the body. I've seen it on television once or twice.'

He was so unnerved he had to sit down.

'Oh, it's real nice but Vic, ay, that Kev's playin' for New South Wales. Will we see 'im on the telly?'

'You never 'eard a word I said, did you, you silly old cow. There's no 'ope for our son, none at all,' he said under his breath.

Then he looked at her, noticing the simple pleasure that was written all over her face at the thought that her son would be on the television, representing a whole state. What did it matter that it was the wrong state and the wrong game. He put an arm around her shoulders and smiled at her in a way he had not done in years.

'Yairs, it is great, love,' he said, adding silently to himself, 'What the hell. It's only a game.'

Ghosts of a Form Present

When he was a boy his father used to take him fishing to this very spot. At the old brewery site on the far shore, nestling under Mount Eliza, the lights of the ship would blink on at dusk. Some clever publicity man had thought of stringing up lights at the back of the brewery in the shape of a ship. At first it had been one of the ferries; then the *Endeavour* and, last of all, *Australia II*, the famous yacht that all of Australia knew as well as its owner.

When he was a boy his father used to say that it was a magic ship, that ship of lights, come to take him back to the land of the fairies ... he was Irish. But old Grandad Mobaitch said that right there – where the brewery stood – was the sacred nest of Wagyll. Any of the men walking along the time-worn track beside the reed-choked, bird-filled river would check to see that the eggs – round smooth stones – were there and safe. At night, when he went to sleep, it was this he dreamed about.

★

Remember that? We never caught any fish. My dad was a great storyteller but a useless fisherman. A dreamer, mate! It was the dreams that killed him – when they turned into nightmares. It's the dreams that are killing me now. The blue devils, or what?

His mother never dreamt. She was a realist: a Mission gin who had no place in this white society that had swept up like the ocean and taken away her people's land. But everyone knew that now, even if it wasn't taught in schools. It was all right if you stayed in your place and did as you were told. That was called assimilation. But, once you tried to better yourself then you were very soon told what you were: a Mission gin who had no place in her country.

'The old rugged cross' was a favourite of hers. I sang it the other day at the Salvos. 'There's an old rugged cross on a hill far away, the emblem of suffering and pain ...' Yeah. All the way through. Then they gave me a feed of soup and stale bread. They all think I'm mad, or else they feel sorry for me, the bastards! I finished up stealing this coat from them because mine was full of holes and it's bloody freezing now. Yeah, they reckon I'm mental from the drink and sometimes I kid them along. 'I'm Brian Boru, the King of Ireland!' I'll cry out. 'I'm black Irish, mate. Black as Guinness. Speaking of which, how about buying me a pint and I'll spin you a yarn?'

Then I'll challenge them to a game of pool and beat the arse off them for twenty dollars, or ten, or a feed. They're getting to know me now, though, and there aren't many pool halls left and, anyway, the drink's getting to me. Hey, maybe I am mad, must be all those fucking chemicals I've been breathing in for the last forty years, but I was a bloody good pool player once.

His mother had given him her surname, the white name of his grandfather – Wandering. His mother's father was the last full-blood member of his tribe and his true name was Mobaitch. The old man could still remember some of the songs and lots of the language but there was no-one left to talk to. Not even his own daughter who was steeped in the rituals of God (not that God was there when trouble came down like a wild and mighty storm). Old Mobaitch had tried to pass on the words to the boy but what was the use of knowing the names of the trees and the birds, insects and animals in the soft beautiful language of the old man.

There is a wattle tree that grows alongside the river here and in the language it is called willyuwa or sometimes koolyung. This is a secluded part of the river, a backwater. Hidden away right in the middle of this huge flowering city and yet untouched by it. It is where the old dero has his camp. Sometimes there is a gwinnen narak to be had, or in the white man's words a duck egg. Not long ago a beautiful nyimarak or mountain duck came with his yok and together they had their coorlunga down among the reeds. Just as the wind murmurs in the leaves or causes the river to lap gently against the shore, so the memories of the old man's murmuring gentle language linger on here.

There is a little freshwater spring here as well, for his tea – although his tea drinking days are long gone. He has camped here for the last five years. It is a special place to him. When the mist rises off the water on a crisp spring day and ducks or swans call out across the water like lost spirits he can almost believe he is back with old Mobaitch in another time. Almost another world.

These young blokes of today wouldn't have a clue. They listen to their reggae and walk around in their Italian suits and buy Japanese cars. Talk to them about culture and they just laugh at you! White culture is football, getting a beer gut, going to the TAB, getting a sheila up the duff and before you know it you're dead. Or, going to university, getting a career, getting the right partner, getting a car, getting a house. (Can you *get* two kids? I bet those sort of people could. They wouldn't know what a good fuck was!) And before you know it you're dead.

My mother's father's culture was the true culture. I watch these young mob today stealing flash cars, sniffing glue and petrol, stealing and murdering to buy European clothes and ideals ... where's the culture in all that!? I know it all, mate. I *seen* it all. Sometimes I feel I been alive for two hundred years at least, probably thousands.

★

The wattle tree shakes softly in the wind and it seems to talk to him like the old man did years ago. A few of the soft yellow balls float down to settle on the still waters and drift away. Midges skate between them in joyful abandon. Apart from the wattle tree, which because of its stately beauty seems out of place in this swampy backwater, there is a clump of shabby paperbark trees huddled together like a gang of ragged ne'er-do-wells planning their next murder. There are one or two gum trees and a single Christmas tree that in December will light up with orange blossom.

This is one story he remembers. Of how the moodgar tree is the spirit tree. No-one can camp beneath it or touch the blossoms although certain people are allowed to partake of the roots. When someone dies they will travel from tree to tree until they reach the coast where they will fly across the waters to Kuranup, the islands of the dead. The Christmas tree, a parasite, grows alone beside its host. But, wherever there is one, always in the distance can be seen another. So it is the journey tree for departed spirits.

My Uncle Mort died just down from here, around the bend of the river where the old water pipes used to lie. He was drinking with some other boys. Well, blacks weren't allowed to drink then and it never mattered if you had blue eyes and red hair; if you had boong blood you were black. So we had to find out-of-the-way places for our social occasions.

Anyway, an argument started about who was the best racehorse of all things, for chrissakes. But that's what drink does; makes little things into big things and big things so huge you can't comprehend them. So there was poor Mort, skinny as a rake, fighting over some horse he'd probably never even backed in his life. They caved his head in with a flagon. Never found out who it was. Cops don't care about a couple of Abos fighting around unless it is in the middle of town.

Another uncle – I never knew him – he died in the Second World War a hero, mate! A fucking hero, Augustus was. He blew up three Japanese machine-gun nests. Just kept walking until he'd blown the shit out of them with his Bren gun and grenades. Turned around to the others, waved his hand, then dropped dead. He was in the papers and all, we was that proud of him. He's one of the legends of our family.

Him and Mort was brothers.

Mobaitch had told him when *he* had been a boy he could remember coming into Perth and all the Aborigines had to leave their spears on the outskirts. Also, they had to wear blankets in the city centre. That's how old he was, the old man. The boy had thought he was the oldest person in the whole world with his long thick white beard and tangled white curls and deep dark eyes. Despite the sadness of being the last of his clan his wide mouth would still turn up in a slow smile. Only for the boy though.

There were those among his people who feared him because they said he was a mabarn man, magic in his ways. A caster of spells who could sing someone to death and who knew the secrets of everyone. There were those – both black and white – who laughed and ridiculed him in his tattered blue suit and horny bare feet and the old black bowler hat he would wear on special occasions.

The boy loved him though. They would go for walks through the last remnants of the bush that clung to the city and the old man would touch the trees and call them brother and imitate the calls of his sisters, the birds. Once, they found a numbat hidden in a log and the old man really smiled for the first time in ages because the numbat was his totem and he worked out he had never seen one in nearly twenty years. It was a good sign, he told the boy. The spirits had not all deserted their people. They never could, really, since the spirits were the blood that made this land survive.

The only spirits I got are the ones in this bottle. That's what the cops told me the other day, 'Come on, old king. Do us one of your tribal dances.'

I tell them straight: 'My mum and dad might not have been able to live together for five years (it being illegal for a white man to live with a black woman unless they got permission from the Protector – and there was a good case of irony, ay!) but at least they loved each other. You wouldn't know who your fathers were, ya pack of bastards.'

A couple of cheeky young rookies beat me up for that. Wouldn't be too hard to do. Me lungs are shot to shit nowadays.

In the old days he was known as the Pug of Perth and many memorable street fights he had. One, out the back of the Shaftesbury, lasted for two hours and money was flying everywhere as bets were laid. But not even that giant Maori seaman could lay him down. The final knockout punch nearly sent him back to New Zealand.

The Shaftesbury is gone now. So is the Governor Broome and the Imperial, the Royal Hotel as well. All his old drinking holes, full of memories as cool and comforting as shaded water in the blue blaze of summer and mates as quiet and secret as tjilgies. He wanders from street to street like a pale emaciated kangaroo. All the tall, fresh, clean-cut new buildings glare down at him – an unwanted stranger in the city where once he was king.

The other day I seen me daughter. In the distance, wheeling along a pram.

'Christ! I can't be a grandfather,' I says. 'I'm not old enough to be a grandfather, am I? Well,' I says, 'I can't have this. Better go and celebrate, I suppose.'

So I bought a bottle of meths and orange juice and went to sing songs to the ducks in Queens Park.

The spittin' image of her mum, my daughter is. I hope she had a girl. If anything is just in this world it'll let the memory of my missus be a part of it until the world ends.

For he had fallen in love once. When he went down to his grandfather Mobaitch's country to find his soul. And to find work for he had heard they were building a railway through there. He and his three cousins cut down their brothers the trees, and dispersed their sisters the birds, and helped lay down two steel lines as straight as spears jabbing into his mother's heart.

On the gang they were treated as equal but after six o'clock they became, magically, 'boongs'. But, in a strange sense, it was better that way. His cousins were people and they shared the same history. Apart from his father the young man distrusted all whites as thieves, liars and two-timers. Friends in the daytime, enemies at night – unless you were a woman or the brother of a beautiful sister. Why be friends at all, he thought. And became a virtual loner.

His grandfather Mobaitch said that when the white people first came everyone treated them as ghosts of the returned dead and welcomed them as kin. Death held no fear now, for if they died they would return like the ghosts. And, like the ghosts, they would have horses and carts, tobacco, sugar, mutton, beef, watermelon and every kind of luxury these new kinsmen brought from the islands of the dead across the sea. So, death having no fear, there was no great demand to hold onto life. But no-one had told them that these new ghosts were imposters and that their islands had no place for black or brown people. Disease swept the ranks of the old and wise, decimating the ageless laws that kept tribes together; confusion swept through the ranks of the young, leaving them listless and unready in this strange and frightening new time.

It was the beginning of the end.

But he had fallen in love once with a girl whose skin was as brown as the earth and whose eyes were as green as the trees that grew upon it and whose hair was as yellow as the summer grass that flows over rolling hills. Her name was Luwarna which she said meant 'beautiful girl' in the Tasmanian language. For her mother had been from that island, brought across to Western Australia by a whaling boat and then making her escape. Whether it was true or not, to him she was beautiful.

Her eyes would sparkle with yellow lights amidst the dark green. Her soft lips would part slightly in amused disbelief as he spun one of his tall stories. The womanly scents from her body drove him to a place he had never been before. He flew like an eagle through clouds rosy with the sun's kiss as night comes down. But no longer solitary, for the warmth of his sun was on his back and shone golden in his golden eyes.

She was his heart and he was her life. Together they could survive in this cruel land that, yet, kept a piece of them close to its most sacred breast.

For six short years they lived together and had three children – two boys and a girl. Then a cold wind came from somewhere and carried her away. As white and as cold as the metho he now drinks was that wind.

But he cannot hide the pain beneath its numbing blanket. Like a piece of paper that turns black in the fire and curls into itself before taking off into the sky like some hideous bat: that was how his soul flew now.

Welfare come and took away me kids. Just took them away. Fuck knows where they are now. I found out where me oldest boy was and went to see him but his foster parents called the cops and they took me away. I could see him looking out the window as they threw me into the back of the van and I cries out, 'All I wanna do is say hello to my son. Hey, Gussie, I'm ya father here.' But he turned away and I never saw him again.

He cries and it seems the wattle weeps as well, spilling golden tears onto the silent water. Lights from the penthouses and buildings reflect on the river and, as the wind ruffles the water, it seems these lights turn into tears trickling across its back. So, even the city that destroyed him cries for him, weeping for all the ghosts in his mind.

*

Brainwashed! They turned him into a white blackfella so he don't belong to either world. My other son, Johnny, well, I never seen him. But I read about him in the papers all the time, especially come footy season. He's a star player and, just like his dad was known as the Pug of Perth and the terror of the pool halls. He's the king of his own little kingdom, the oval. He dances on this ground like his great-grandfather would have danced once in the sacred corroboree or in the sheer joy of life. He was playing a game of our people's also, stolen and moulded into new rules by the wadgula. Some of his marks are higher than the tallest story I ever told, yeah, you bet. And he kept my name. He found out who his dad was and he kept his name. Johnny Wandering. But I never seen him.

Old Mobaitch had forgotten many of the stories passed down for thousands of years but there was one he told the boy that stuck in his mind. It was of a man who had a beautiful wife and many children. But the youngest was a girl who was born twisted with a lame foot and withered arm. The other children used to make fun of her and some of the older people thought she was useless – a burden on the tribe – because she could not gather food and there was no-one who would marry her. So she had a hard time of it.

But her father loved her very much and felt sad for her so, one day, he took her to the council of elders and asked them to do something to take her away from her pain and humiliation. And, the next day, where she had gone to sleep the night before, there sat a most beautiful bird with crimson chest and royal-blue collar and orange, yellow and blue feathers among the green. So was born the first rosella – the bird that stays around the camps and warns the people of any coming attack. The colourful rosella no-one can ever kill, no matter how hungry, for she is protected for all time.

Me daughter, also called Luwarna, was born with a gammy leg and she only had one arm because her mother was given the drug thalidomide to take away the pain of morning sickness. Then, after the birth, she was given a drug to stop her having any more. No-one told her what these drugs would do. No-one ever told her she was having this white man's poison in her wondrous young brown body. Well, the bastards wanted us to die out, didn't they? Sterilisin' the women is a sure way to stop Abo babies popping out to become men and women with dreams.

They tell me this is a new decade. The last ten years of the last thousand. It is a special time. A time of great wonders and also a time of great turmoil. Well, tell me about it! A mere hundred-odd years ago me old grandad Mobaitch would of felt the same thoughts I feel today. Yeah, I drinks metho and lives in cast-off clothes and spends half me time in the lock-ups of this huge grey carcass of a city. I'm worth as much as a maggot too – in youse fellas' eyes. But the blood of me grandfather flows through me veins and whatever else you can change or take away you can't bloody take that away from me, ya bastards.

Night falls down, like a cat hunting. On padded feet ghosts roam the city. They gather at street corners and share cigarettes or converse in pubs or play pool. They laugh softly at some joke or share a story and a bottle of wine. Stars peep down like cats' eyes and the moon is an extended claw, thin and curved, ready to rip out the heart of some unlucky spiritman.

Just as the first flush of dawn touches the top of the hills, a crown for the kings of this city, a V of ducks takes off from the river, rippling the water under the wattle tree. Just as the river is covered in the blood spilt as this new prince is born, a crow takes off from the wattle tree. As black as a piece of burnt paper it wings its way towards the still dark ocean rumbling tumultuously in the west. Coughing raucously like an old man waking up, it flies over Rottnest Island and away to Kuranup.

They find his body that very day; just a pile of dirty rags and newspaper underneath the moodgar tree. Two Nyoongah youths, looking for a place to hide three guns they stole the night before, find him there, lying as still as a ghost.

Dead Roses

No marks could be seen on the head or hands, but beside the face lay two items, a train ticket from Adelaide and a small silver rose.

Senior Constable Newbry stared down at the body that lay across the sandy track. The cheerful, piping notes of small birds seemed incongruous near this scene of violent death. The man's face was twisted in a caricature of grotesque surprise – even more grotesque now a small band of busy black ants was trailing over his face and into his gaping mouth.

Probably attracted by the blood, Senior Constable Newbry thought. There was enough around. The body lay in a pool of thick congealing blood that not even the grey sand of the bush track had entirely soaked away. He had not died quickly, this man. There were wounds from some sharp instrument in his shoulder, thigh and chest. There were signs of a desperate struggle for survival but no-one except his killer would have heard a thing as he died a lonely and savage death. Finally, his throat had been cut.

This was the Senior Constable's first murder case. He had been transferred to the out-of-the-way township of The Rocks for the very fact that it was a quiet place and he was due to retire soon. He had hoped to leave the force with a clean record of everything tackled, everything done. This seemed to be in jeopardy now.

Constable Millson came back from vomiting behind the old tingle-tingle tree, his thin face white. He wouldn't be much use, Senior Constable Newbry thought. He wished he had one of his old mates with him now because he sensed this would be a hard nut to crack. He remembered an old mate of his from Melbourne telling him about a similar case involving a Macedonian, known among the Melbourne Underworld as 'the Turk', that had never been solved. The reason he thought of this now was because the only clue to that murder had been a small ornament of some kind – he couldn't remember what just now. But he had this dithering youth, fresh out of the Academy, who, so far, had appeared none too bright. He wouldn't be able to find a cow in a dairy, the older man thought. The Rocks – the place where all the no-hopers ended up.

The Rocks – a conglomerate of weatherboard houses, peopled mostly by spiders and rats as the population dwindled – moving family by family up to the city. A store, a hall, a police station, post office and small hospital also, all made of dark stained weatherboard and every building covered by a red tin roof. Only the pub (named the Opera House by some wit) was different in that it was made of river-mud bricks and had a green tin roof. It was just as dilapidated as the rest of the town, though, and the only thing even resembling an opera held there would have been 'The Beggars' Opera'.

'Christ, Don, what do you think would have caused *that*?' Constable Millson croaked.

It was his first case of any sort, never mind murder. He had only arrived from the Academy six months ago. Young, full of ideas, very respectful. In a bit of a hurry to get up in the world, though. Senior Constable Newbry had told him to relax; not be so conscientious. At least he had succeeded in getting the youngster to stop calling him sir or, worse yet, Senior Constable. Protocol was quite uncalled for in a place like The Rocks, which most people had never heard of.

They would now.

No-one likes dead bodies lying around. There would be a team of CIB men over here now, this afternoon, buzzing around everywhere like flies; stepping on everyone's toes like elephants. Ordering everyone around.

'Right! Let's get this area sealed off. There's some cord and markers in the car. Then call through on your mobile to Kalveston Central. I want you to stay here and make sure nothing's touched while I go over and find old Benny Kirup. His eyes might see something we don't.'

'What? Stay here with him?' the young policeman said, aghast.

'Don't worry. He won't annoy you, laddie,' the grey old man called back as he strode away.

The pale leaves of the beautiful red tingle-tingle tree cast soft shadows over the prostrate body and the sickened Constable. Its hollowed-out black interior seemed a cave of mysterious thoughts.

That is just what the Senior Constable's mind was as he drove the three or four miles up the lumpy grey track that meandered through the forest and somehow found its way to town. It was not the main road – that was a thin, potholed strip of bitumen that eventually led out to the South Coast Highway – but it was really the only other road in the district, even though it led nowhere. The population of The Rocks was not overly huge, perhaps three hundred with another hundred itinerants, come down to do fruit-picking or shearing or hay-carting or whatever. But most of them kept to a well run circle and had become familiar faces in their seasonal work. The thing that made old Don Newbry morose was that this man who had got himself murdered on his patch was a total stranger.

What was this stranger doing out there on this road to nowhere in the middle of the night (or sometime last night, anyway). A stranger, what is more, who had come all the way from Adelaide to this – The Rocks – where no-one ever came, not even from Kalveston, the nearest thing the district had to a big city, some seventy miles away on the coast.

He found old Benny sunning himself on the pub verandah along with Doctor Fairchild, so he invited them both along. He would have to put the body in the doc's morgue anyway. It had been built to accommodate any accidents at the mill.

Marrilyn Henry had also been sunning herself on the verandah and looking around with interest in her black eyes at the sprawling town and huge shell of the sawmill that had made this town exist. She had hardly left the city in all her twenty-three years and, besides, her country was the red, barren beauty of up North. Well, her mother's country really. She had been talking to old Benny Kirup, the last of the Nyoongahs from this area, about the significance of the rock formation the town was named after.

Old Benny was about sixty, with long white hair streaked with yellow and a craggy brown face. He was reluctant to talk to a stranger – and a woman – about things *his* father had said were special to his family and tribe, even if she was of the same race.

Marrilyn had been angry when called into the editor's office last week and told, in the editor's high-handed manner, that she must go down South.

Apparently there was a man down there called Micky Sierra, whose father had come out from Italy in the 1930s and started up a sawmill with some of his relatives. But during the Second World War most of them had been interned and sent to camps over East. After the war he had come back and, even though he had owned the mill and some of the land round about, he had never made much money. One son and the two daughters had gone back over East to their uncles, aunts and cousins. Another son was a builder in Perth and only the middle son, Michelangelo, or Mick, had stayed looking after his father's mill. It was one of the last independent mills left operating in the country.

It would make a great feature about a battling Aussie, fighting against prejudice and hard times and still being able to survive and now about to get his reward by selling out to a big company. The editor said he had some leaked information that the whole area was to be developed into a woodchip industry. (Surprise, surprise, guess who owned the greater part of the shares in the process terminal that turned wood into chips?? None other than the ... but best to let that slide. No need to worry your pretty little head about politics ... someone more competent could do a follow-up story on that aspect.)

But there was some possibility that a pile of old rocks down there might be of tribal significance. Not that there *was* any tribe there now, they were all long dead. So could she go down and check out the authenticity of this claim, as well as get a story on Micky Sierra?

He didn't exactly say it but the impression was 'because you're an Aborigine and understand about this *Spirits and the land business*'.

She had never been anywhere near the land in her life. She had been fostered out to a white family when young and gone to an exclusive girls' school, then straight to university and a career in journalism. She had no interest in Spirits whatsoever. But the editor thought it was just the story for their Aboriginal cadet reporter to work on, so here she sat, half-asleep on the verandah, listening to an old man's mumbled half answers and irrelevancies.

Until the arrival of Senior Constable Newbry and his exciting news.

When she asked if she could come too, Don looked at her in some surprise. Nice neat clothes, new shoes, a city hairstyle. Was she some sort of relation to old Benny? He didn't know he had any. Don looked inquiringly at the old man.

'I'm a reporter from Perth. I was doing another story here, you see, and it would certainly do my career no harm to get a scoop like this.' She smiled.

'Well, plenty of room in the back, Miss. But it's not a real nice sight. My young Constable himself was sick when he saw the remains,' Don replied, his grey eyes studying her.

Her smile faded but she set her jaw resolutely and followed the three men to the van. There was only room for three in the front, so she had to ride in the back where the prisoners were put. The garrulous old doctor, seeing her plight and embarrassment, sat in with her to keep her company.

She saw the amusing side to this, though, as she was tossed to and fro by the lurching van. Her first – and she knew without a doubt – her last ride in a vehicle which had incarcerated so many of her people. Going to see a dead white man who could make her famous for a while, and another Aborigine was needed to find this white man's killer – who more likely than not would turn out to be white also. There was irony in all that.

So that is how Marrilyn Henry came to The Rocks. The black oily houses stared back at her forebodingly, like black patches in the heavy pressing bush round about, full of their own secrets and unwilling to share them with strangers. The huge rambling old sawmill stood lopsided upon the hill just on the edge of town, empty now except for clattering bits of tin, chattering rats, swooping silent bats and cautious feral cats. The huge old pile of sawdust lay like a red festering sore and the wind howled dismally through the blackened rafters.

When she arrived at the murder site she got quite a shock. The murdered man she had seen alive only last night in the pub. Indeed, he had spoken to her briefly about a few shots she had made during a pool game. Even she, who didn't believe in Spirits, shivered slightly.

Don asked her who else had been there and she mentioned the shearers, especially one called Danny Lacy, and an Italian she thought was called Pedro and a woman who briefly came into the pub: blonde hair, blue eyes, about thirty-five. Very flashy.

'Aah, yes. That'd be Marjorie Perrit. She was a barmaid there once,' Don said.

The investigation into the murdered man began routinely and she was enough of a reporter to know to keep in the investigating officer's good books so she could glean any titbits. Although it didn't seem as big a scoop as she had hoped. No other reporters came down and the piece she sent to the papers was badly hacked around and stuck on page twenty-six, at the bottom. Then she got a midnight phone call from her boss:

'Forget this bloody ponyarse who got himself stiffed.' (He liked to talk like editors in second-rate American movies.) 'It's getting really hot on this woodchip business and I want to be the first to break it. Now pull out your finger and get some juicy bits about Sierra being overpaid to clear out, or the government's lack of concern over Indigenous people's religious and cultural rights, or *anything!*'

At the same time as the editor's gravelly voice was spiralling over the airwaves, punctuated by much crackling and hissing of the ancient line, Don was having a meeting with the three CIB officers from Kalveston.

Benny's sharp eyes had found a few clues, as Don had known they would. The old man was a quiet and somewhat shy – some would have said sullen – man but when it came to tracking he was one of the best. Many a time old Benny had been called out to find some child or city picnicker lost in the huge surrounds of the jarrah and eucalypt forest, or the frightening eeriness of the karri forest with its huge white ghostly trunks and mass of wattle trees below. It could get very cold in this semi-rainforest environment, going down to minus two or three degrees sometimes, and many a child owed its life to this mumbling old brown man with the sharp black eyes.

He had found a much-used tube of vivid crimson lipstick, but what this had to do with the murdered man no-one knew. Still, it was carefully packed away and sent to the lab for further analysis. A path through the bush led from the dead body back to town, coming out just behind The Opera House, and Benny said the way some of the branches were bent showed the person had come and gone the same way. He had also found a set of footprints on the sheltered side of the track that indicated the dead stranger had come up the road. A piece of tweed coat caught on the scraggly hands of a prickle bush and the half-obscured footprint of what appeared to be a heavy industrial boot gave some clue as to the attacker. Also, perhaps not really a clue but included because it was found alongside the tweed coat fragment, was a strand of greasy sheep's wool.

So, Don reasoned, the attacker and the attacked had presumably arranged a meeting at the old tingle-tingle tree. And why not? It was a landmark almost as well known as the rock formation. Once there had been many of these strange giants growing in the bush here, both red and yellow tingle-tingle. They were strange because when they reached a certain height and age the bottom part of them hollowed out, forming living caves. The biggest and most famous one you could drive a car through but, even so, every one of them had been awesome trees.

Senior Constable Newbry pondered over what they had discovered so far. The attacker wore heavy boots and a tweed coat so was probably a man. But that description of footwear applied to just about every man in the district. So a local man kills a total stranger. Why? He couldn't think where the strand of wool or the lipstick fitted in. The former was probably just some wandering sheep and the lipstick some girl's dropped belonging.

The dead man had quite possibly come from Adelaide and they were waiting for reports from the CIB there. He had a penchant for flashy jewellery, two expensive rings on his fingers and an eighteen-carat gold necklace around his neck. In his pockets were found a wallet containing about five hundred dollars in big bills, a series of costly TAB tickets, each one running into units of hundreds, and a pocket box of matches with the logo of a well-known Perth brothel. Also a packet of very expensive cigars, of which only one had been smoked.

Why would a person of obvious means come down here in the first place? A tourist, perhaps? The only people here were unemployed sawyers, out-of-work farmers and ne'er-do-well larrikins with no fruit-picking and very little shearing and plenty of time and trouble on their hands. Yet this was no simple attempted robbery gone wrong. He could sense it was something bigger.

Despite his well filled wallet, expensive tastes and, if *he* had bought the ticket, his willingness to outlay a large amount of money to come over here, the clothes he wore were seedy and crumpled as though he had lived in them for some time. A brown coat, thin brown trousers, a stained yellow shirt, threadbare yellow socks and a pair of well-worn Hush Puppies. Not the sort of attire to go traipsing about the bush in at two o'clock in the morning (the time the doctor had determined death to be) when it had been about minus one degree. Very misty and cold. He would have known it would be cold when he saw the mist rising off the river as he came into town. He must have really desperately wanted to see this person whom he had met beside the tree. Why? old Don Newbry asked himself again.

Marrilyn Henry set out the next morning to go and do her master's bidding. She found out from the publican where Michelangelo Sierra lived – just out of town in the original old sawmill of his father's. There was only one phone in town now for public use and that was at the Opera House. The other phone was at the police station so she couldn't ring to organise a meeting. She just hoped she could surprise him and trick him into saying something of interest by pretending she knew more than she did. She doubted it though. There was nothing in this town of the slightest interest to the rest of Australia.

Various members of the Sierra clan had cannibalised parts of the old mill to make houses of their own, so the skeleton of a former empire lay haphazardly around the sucker-populated clearing. It appeared Mick's house was the back part of the old mill and where the sawdust heap had lain there now was a wonderful garden tended by the loving hands of Mick's tough little Northern Italian wife, Anna.

Mick himself was a large, easy-going Southern Italian, with a huge gap-toothed grin and work-roughened hands.

Marrilyn saw him and two younger men fussing about with an old car so she drove up to them and put on her best reporter's smile. A smile guaranteed to soften the heart of a rock; a smile that said 'I'm your friend and I sympathise with you. Tell me all your problems so I can alert the world and we will sort them out.'

The smile worked for Mick who gave a cheery wave and stood up, stretching his back. Probably he wasn't too interested in car engines anyway, she thought, noticing how abruptly he moved over towards her in his ambling lurch.

The other two scowled at her and she noticed with a slight shock that one was a man she had had a run-in with at the pub last night. She hoped there would be no more trouble. She noticed several youngsters peering around doors in suspicion or wonder. Apparently visitors were a novelty to the Sierra clan. But Mick himself was a shining ray of friendliness.

'Gudday. I 'eard youse was comin'. So, ya wanna do a story ona ole Mick, ay? No worries!'

He helped her out of the car, bowing slightly. The smile on his face was huge, yet his eyes were shrewd. He would be a hard fish to catch, she reasoned and looked forward to the battle. The migrant and the Original Owner both sparring about land the white Australians had an interest in.

Mick spoke with his hands a fair bit.

'Me nephew Pedro and me baby son, Giovanni!' He waved a huge paw in their direction.

Just then three other youths came out of the trees, talking and laughing between themselves until they spotted Marrilyn, when they froze – just like a mob of kangaroos she had once observed at the zoo as a child. Bodies still and black eyes fastened on her as though they had never seen an Aboriginal before. She felt flustered under their gaze but a burst of Italian from the youths at the car caused them to carry on laughing towards the house. Although one faded away back into the bush with an idle wave to his companions. She wondered if they had been out planting trees, for one carried a shovel and another several green plastic bags.

'I've met Pedro, last night. I suppose you might say he was The Rocks' welcoming committee. As you say, he is your nephew and they say this is your town,' she said coolly.

'Aah, sure,' Mick laughed. 'He tell me about this Abo girl. I 'ear ya give 'im one good talkin' to, better than his mama, my sister never give him. Good job! 'E's too cheeky for 'is own good.'

For a moment her eyes flashed then she let it rest. How was he to know that 'Abo' was as hurtful to her as 'wog' or 'dago' or 'refo' might be to him? Besides, it was not as bad as the snide remarks Pedro had made to her last night, nearly driving her from the room.

'Aah, ya just a boong! Give youse fancy clothes, like, and powder yersel' up an' put on all youse 'igh-falutin' ways, youse still just a gin. Garn, I got no time for ya! Black greenie, white greenie, youse all the bloody same.

93

Youse fuck up the work for us and then go back to youse 'omes, clappin' yersel' ona back and say what a good job ya done savin' the fuckin' trees!'

Then Pedro had waved a grubby finger near her face, causing her to step backwards in a hurry, spilling her red wine all over her dress.

'Another thing too! Don't come at that "rock bein' a sacred site" bullshit. My uncle was born 'ere and grew up with the Abos. 'E's got a lot of time for them 'oo got some claim to the place, youse can ask ole Benny Kirup. But don't youse come in 'ere and start takin' away every bit of the country 'cos youse a boong. It don't work that way down 'ere!'

There had been a commotion at the door then and four or five heavy-shouldered shearers had clumped in, bringing the scent of rain and the smell of lanoline and sheep shit on their clothes. Their rowdy voices had cut into the Italian youth's tirade that had begun when she innocently inquired did he work at the mill and did he know why the town was named The Rocks? She had tried to be cunning and had ended up the focus of attention of the whole pub, humiliated because of the volatile Italian. She noticed the publican glance at her then look away and heard the suppressed laughter of the only other customer in the pub (a man half-hidden in the shadows) when she spilt her drink. She blushed in shame and embarrassment. The noisy shearers in their heavy boots and with their loud voices had come just in time to cause a diversion.

Marrilyn noticed two of the shearers were Nyoongahs – one a big-gutted, heavy-set man in his early thirties and the other a slender youth of perhaps nineteen. It was this youth who sidled over to her. His eyes were black and piercing and proud – as black as hers. He flashed her a showy, snowy grin and she smelt the wine on him so she was afraid again. Growing up as she had with white people, most of their prejudices had rubbed off on her, so whenever she came across a drunken member of her own race, she was as embarrassed and disgusted or patronisingly sorry as her white counterparts. She'd had no taste of the very social life Aboriginal families lead and the humour which a close family life nurtures, the humour helped along by social drinking. All she ever felt when she saw a drunk Aboriginal was curiosity as to whether they might be a relative. This uncertainty and unwillingness to face up to her Aboriginality made her wary in Nyoongah company.

She flashed him a shy smile.

'What ya talkin' about, Pedro, ya stupid dago? Ya can't even talk English proper, anyways! Don't ya know "boong" means bum in the Koori language? I read it in a book one time, and what ya see 'ere sure ain't no bum, coodah!' the youth called out, then rubbed his wool-greasy hand on the back of his jeans and stuck it out to her. 'Danny Lacy, that's me, and this is me Uncle Fraser.' He introduced the other Nyoongah who nodded slightly then looked away, shy of this flash city stranger. 'We call 'im Fraze the Daze cos 'e dazes ya with 'is shearin'.

And me mates, 'oward, 'orace and Pete. We shearers!' he cried out proudly.

They had been lucky to get work. Most of the farmers were shearing their own sheep now, the ones they hadn't yet shot. It was almost a pointless exercise since the price of wool was at an all-time low and there were huge stockpiles in every capital city. This job was a solid one though and the pay cheque, lower than in past years, was still better than a dole cheque, so the five shearers were happy and ready to make a party of it.

The three white men among them looked Marrilyn up and down and then at each other, and nodded, winked and nudged among themselves like a flock of blue and white or red galahs. They grinned at her through broken yellow teeth.

'Lost, are ya, darlin'? Only people 'oo get lost wind up in this dump, ay Harry?' one asked the publican. 'Come and 'ave a bit of a sing-song at the old Opera House.'

'Course, then ya never git found again, ay!' another cackled.

'Unless, like, ya know, we could always go out of our way to help ya find yaself,' the first one said.

'Coooorr! Nice legs,' the third one added to the conversation and giggled to himself as he nearly fell over.

'Ah, come on. These three couldn't organise a game of two-up in the Perth Mint. What ya say to a game of pool? You look like ya hung around a few pubs in ya time,' Danny said, touching her on the arm.

He had such a friendly smile and warm eyes and she

felt so cold in this place that she accepted his invitation. Besides, his easy-going banter engulfed her in a spirit of camaraderie she had not felt in a long time. He was not after her body in any form. Rather, he had a pocketful of pay and who better to share it with than a nice woman. If she had told him to leave her alone he would have cheerfully gone over to his uncle and mates and this was the sort of companionship she sought now.

He fancied himself as a hybrid between John Travolta, James Dean and Vince from *The Colour of Money*, a film he had seen three times when it made its long-awaited debut at the Kalveston drive-in. However, the only coat he had to wear was not the leather of James Dean but threadbare cloth hunched around his slender body and the only music 'John Travolta' had to dance to was Slim Dusty or the Everley Brothers or Gene Pitney.

> If I didn't have a dime
> and I didn't take the time
> to play the Juke Box
> OOOH! Saturday night
> would have been a lonely night
> for me!

That was one of his favourites and he played it over and over again.

And he could certainly play pool! He beat her time and again, much to the amusement of the three shearers and the scorn of the Italian. Uncle Fraser had gone home long ago, for he wasn't much of a one for parties. The man in the corner came out of the shadows to give paternalistic advice to the poor female who couldn't play tiddlywinks. When she was just playing with Danny Lacy her mistakes had not mattered. It had been a fun way to spend an evening. Now the stranger's drawling commentary and the audience of the other shearers, chipping in with unwanted hints, spoiled it all for her and she began making more and worse mistakes.

Once, during the uneven contest, a woman had walked in the door and the stranger had flashed her the smile he saved for women, apparently. Obviously she didn't feel like staying in a room full of drunk males so she left pretty quickly afterwards.

As the night wore on Danny became more drunk and his smile slipped, while his bright black eyes, the best part about him, blurred. He looked a miserable sight with his Jackie Howe singlet hanging out. Marrilyn decided to leave. He wasn't too happy about that. She knew he would have liked to have been her boyfriend for the night. She knew with a woman's intuition that he desired her. All his body language the whole night long had told her that. He certainly was handsome enough and he was not unintelligent either, having an appealing rough philosophy on life. And he had been over East, shearing, so had some interesting stories to tell. But she had two or three boyfriends in Perth with whom she travelled the nightclub circuit and she wasn't really interested in a one-night stand with a young shearer.

'Hey, hey, listen,' he stumbled, 'd'ya wanna smoke a nyaandi?' He pulled a bag out of his pocket and waved it. Rather incongruously now that the whole pub, almost empty though it was, had seen what he had, he learned forward and whispered, 'I got some, ya know. It makes ya real 'appy.' He clung to the side of the pool table in despair.

'I know,' she smiled at him. 'But I think you're happy enough. You should go home now. It's getting near closing time.' She patted him maternally on the shoulder. 'Thanks for a great night. I had fun.'

'Home?' he mumbled and ran his fingers through his hair, held down by liberal doses of hair oil like all his heroes of fantasy. 'Yeah, thanks,' he murmured and staggered off over to his three mates, who grinned at each other and put arms around his shoulder to cheer him up. As she went to her room one was suggesting a flagon of red would warm him up.

So that had been her little adventure in this small town. Someone else had had an even greater adventure, though – the stranger who had leered at her last night and spoken to her in a drawling cynical voice. That was part of her adventure too, of course, but that was for the police to work out. She was in charge of getting a great story.

If there was anything Mick loved more than cutting down trees it was talking, especially about his beloved father and much loved family. So he filled her in on the story of how his father struggled and suffered and yet still survived, just as Mick and his sons were doing today. She was the professional, sniffing around for exciting bylines in half-said sentences and blurry word pictures. She would come down again with a photographer and take some photos of the Sierra clan, she said, and this prompted him to bring out the old photo albums. There they all were, his brothers, Guiseppe and Luigi, who had been in Perth but now lived at Kalveston with his building business; his nephew Pedro over from the Eastern states for a visit and his nieces Angeline, Juanita and Rosa. And all the other little Sierras.

'Buono. It is good.' Mick beamed.

He told of his own interests, his three racehorses and seven greyhounds. Then the proposed purchase of the sawmill by the woodchip enterprise came into conversation, gently coaxed on by Marrilyn's innocent questions.

'What do you think about the fact that this proposed woodchip industry is going to interfere with what many archaeologists consider to be one of the most important Aboriginal sites in the South-west?' she lied.

In truth no-one knew or cared at all, except the editor, who wanted only to stir up excitement and expose possible government corruption for a good story.

'Say, I tell youse what I think all right!' Mick waved his hands in the air. 'You an Abo, and I'm a ding, all right? If youse come over and started diggin' up the Pope's house

I sure be pretty damn mad. Hey,' he waved his hands even harder, 'I don't like this bloody woodchip all right? What youse think? Money from that woodchip goin' a go to Japan straightaway! Youse seen the unemployment in this town? They employ bloody Japan no worries. No boys 'ere get work! I don't want that woodchip business 'ere and I tell 'im too. Fuck off! 'E come back again and again, offer me much more and more money, I still tell 'im fuck off. In the end 'e say all right stick your mill, we go ahead without you, pretty soon you go bung anyhow, we cut down all the trees, no more left for you. If I got just my mill, cut down few trees 'ere, few trees there, enough for business but no bloody kill the whole forest. All right! OK! Ever'body 'appy. I give them boys job an' look after tree. No worries. That woodchip come along,' he threw out his hands expressively, 'pfffft! Nothin' left. All gone bloody Japan.'

She was surprised and secretly elated. Here was a much better story than the editor had supposed. His story was to have been about how the government was paying off a small sawmill, a home-grown business that had been earning the State money for thirty years or so, so that some people in high places could make a killing. That still applied of course, but *her* version would have a lot more guts to it. She was disappointed that the murdered man seemed to have nothing to do with the sawmill business. *That* would have been an interesting slant indeed.

★

Meanwhile, on the cold, grey and chilling day, Don and the young Constable Millson were going about their interviews. Heeding the words of Marrilyn Henry from yesterday and knowing that possibly the clue to all this lay in the confines of the Opera House, they proceeded there early in the morning.

The rain fell in slanting icy curtains across the wildly buffeting trees, almost as though it was trying to hide from the rest of the world the unpleasantness this town had experienced. A few brave birds tried to fly into the heaving winds and scurrying clouds but they were cartwheeled across the gloomy black sky like so many leaves. Most of the people of The Rocks were snuffling and shuffling about inside their damp dark houses, probably thinking of the time some five years ago when the river burst its banks. It looked as though it would do it again, but right now that was the least of Don's worries.

He saw Marjorie Perrit hurrying through the swirling squalls on her way back to her new husband. She was one of the success stories of this town and God knows there weren't many of them. But she had met her husband a year ago when he bought up the old Matthews place as a hobby farm. He was quite a well-known film producer, looking for a rural retreat. She was working as a barmaid in the Opera House at the time. Suddenly Marjorie had found herself catapulted into the social pages of the Australian press. But she, like him, was a shy and introverted person and they kept very much to themselves. Well, it took all sorts to make a town, even one as small and dull as The Rocks.

Don glanced beside him at Constable Millson as they pulled up alongside the hotel. He still seemed a bit pale. Hadn't recovered from the shock of yesterday, it appeared. Really, he'd have to do better than this if he was to ever rise in the force.

The first person to be seen when they entered the gloomy interior was a very sick looking Danny, nursing a beer and a bruised cheekbone. Don walked across to him.

'How are you, Danny, mate? Still skinning the sheep?'

He knew all the Lacy family well and had a high regard for them. If, sometimes, they were a little wild, they were never really bad, just impetuous.

'Tryin' to, boss. Not much shearin' round though this year. Not much sheep round neither,' he said gloomily, then gave a faint smile. 'Got a job, but. Out on Rabinovitz's place. 'E's got a big shed and can cover about five 'undred so this rain won't 'old us up much 'less it keeps goin'. Shearin' five thousand, Mr Newbry. That's better than a poke in the arse with a brandin' iron, ay. No rams this time either.'

'Was that a ram got you with his horns there, Danny? I'd of thought you'd be more careful.'

'Aah!' his usually sharp eyes looked shifty and he shuffled his big boots. 'Goes with the trade,' he muttered.

'Did you see any strangers here, last night? Brown coat, brown trousers, yellow shirt. Age about thirty-five, forty.

Black hair, blue eyes. About one eighty centimetres?' Don pressed.

'Nuh. Rob the town bank, did 'e?' Danny murmured and gave a feeble laugh at his joke.

'You were here, weren't you? What time did you leave?'

Curiously the youth flicked a glance at Constable Millson before looking at Don then lowering his gaze to his beer.

'Oh, you know, boss. Closin' time, like always. Me and the boys got paid up, ya see, so we 'ad a bit of a party.'

Don gazed at the youth for a long moment until Danny became noticeably edgy, then the old policeman put aside his notebook and nodded imperceptibly. 'I see.'

They set off back to the police station to see if any information had come from the lab in Kalveston. It was still too early.

'What do you reckon about Danny Lacy, Don?' Constable Millson said timidly. 'A bit of a roughie, ay ... but not too bad.'

'I reckon I want to know why Danny's lying.'

'The bloke could of snuck out. If he didn't want anyone ...'

'No, no, no! There's only one door to that brothel of a place. Danny *had* to see him. As well ... why is he lying about that bruise on his face? That was no bloody ram's hoof or horn did that. I'd say it was some sort of sharp instrument.'

Don shuffled through a mass of papers on his desk.

'What do we know about Danny Lacy?' Then he

answered his own question. 'Well, he's pretty clean. Once, when he was younger, he was up for break and enter in the Perrits's house, I think. Then, last year he was caught with a gram or two of marijuana.'

He leant back in his chair and closed his eyes, thinking.

The news came through at midday. The victim's name was William Abraham Clarendon alias William Abrahams, Abraham Lowenstein and Bill Clare. He had done time in Adelaide, Sydney and Queensland for various petty crimes involving fraud, forgery and simple cons or shams. In fact he was wanted in Adelaide on a charge of forging and uttering right now. He was, after all was said and done, a small-time con merchant and sometime blackmailer. Better off dead, really, thought Don unkindly. He had no time for these spiders who hunched in their nests of deceit and poisoned any they came across. But why did he have to die in this part of Australia? Possibly because he was on the run from the South Australian law and here was as good a place as any to lie low. What else was here to interest a meagre crook like him?

There was some other information that Don had actually already known. The TAB tickets had all been winners. All in all William Abraham Clarendon – or whoever he last called himself – had been an extremely wealthy man for perhaps the first time in his miserable life. And finally the report mentioned that, caught in one of the expensive rings, were several hairs, black, belonging to a young male and anointed with some kind of hair oil.

Aaaah, Don sighed, the wonders of modern science.

When they got back to the pub they were told by Harry that the shearers had gone back to Rabinovitz's farm. He also contributed the information that the stranger had not only talked to Danny but had finished the evening playing pool with him after Marrilyn's departure.

The shearers were having a break when the police car nosed up to the shed. The rain fell with a whispering roar on the tin roof and now the machines were off there could be heard the nervous clattering of sheep's hooves and throaty baas. The five men were gathered around on the greasy floor, holding big mugs of steaming tea in their sweaty hands.

Don smiled his fatherly smile at them then shouted through the noise of the rain.

'Listen, Danny, can I have a word with you about last night? Harry reckons you *did* see that bloke and I just want to get everything sorted out.'

Body language is an important factor in Aboriginal affairs, Don knew. A whole conversation can be held without one word being spoken. Why, then, did Danny look first to his uncle and why did his uncle give the faintest, almost imperceptible nod.

Danny moved warily forward, away from his circle of mates, still clutching his cup of tea like a shield in front of him.

'Aren't you cold, mate?' Don asked amiably. 'Go and get your coat while we sit in the car and get warm.'

'Nah, Don. I'm all right!' Danny said.

'Go and get his coat, Simon. He's making me cold just looking at him.'

Before Danny could object the constable walked over and took Danny's old green coat from where it hung beside his name and tally for the day. When he brought it back Don realised that it was in fact a tweed material. It was just so old and worn the pattern had all but faded away. It was so greasy with sweat and lanoline from the sheep that bits of wool were stuck all over it.

He searched the pockets while Danny looked on in sudden resignation. All life seemed to go from his sparkling black eyes. The Senior Constable brought out a large plastic bag full of green vegetation and sniffed it. He looked first at the other shearers, who all looked elsewhere, and then at Danny with a triumphant, yet sad smile. He had liked this bubbly, friendly youth. Now it seemed he was in real trouble.

'A bit of the old ha ha weed, ay, Danny? Did our mate William get a bit nasty last night and threaten to dob you in? Is that it? So you said you'd meet him up the track by the big tree and you'd pay him your shearer's cheque to keep quiet. Except he wanted more, so you hit him a bit too hard? Was that how it happened?'

'I dunno what ya on about! I never 'it no-one!' cried a fearful Danny.

'Well, can you tell me why your hairs are found

in a dead man's hand?' Don said calmly, his grey eyes watching every little sign on Danny's face.

'Look! Ya got me for the drugs, fair enough. But I never killed 'im.'

'It's open and shut, matey,' Don said sadly and put his hand upon the thin brown arm. 'Come on along with us.'

'Ya can't lock me up! I only 'ad a fight with 'im. I couldn't stand gettin' locked up,' the youth cried wildly and looked around for a mate.

But there were none in this shed. The three white men looked away, ignoring the problem and Uncle Fraser, seemingly about to say something, bit his lip and stared at his nephew with dark smouldering eyes. The sheep stood impassively.

Danny threw the cup of tea at Constable Millson and made to run out the door but he was caught in the grip of Senior Constable Newbry. The young constable recovered and rushed forward to manhandle the struggling youth into the back of the van. Don turned to face the uncle who had now stood up.

'Yes, Fraser? Do you have something to say?' Don asked.

'He can't stand to get locked up.'

'Well, he shouldn't go around committing crimes.'

'He never killed no-one.'

'Now, Fraze, you want to be careful. I seem to remember you're not long out of jail yourself. If you've been involved in this it'll go bad for your parole, don't you reckon?'

The man gazed at the policeman for a long instance. Then he tossed the dregs of his tea upon the floor and turned towards the stands. Tea break was over and work must go on.

Back in her hotel room Marrilyn heard the latest news from Harry. Constable Millson had come in and told him how the youth had reacted to getting locked up. He had had to be restrained somewhat, so upset had he become. But they can't handle closed spaces, these bush abos, the young constable said (with half a year's experience in the bush). They were going to transfer him to Kalveston Central tomorrow to the main jail, there to await trial, Constable Millson said with some importance. Charlie was secretly pleased about the huge tea stain all over the youngster's shirt. That must have hurt, he thought. It might have woken the dozy bastard up at last, he chuckled.

Marrilyn was by now convinced that here was a story she could build her name on. The wicked government (or members of it) first trying to pay Mick off then threatening to close his business down was the background. Maybe, if there *was* corruption on a government level, she could draw a conclusion by emphasising what happened to one who corrupted at a local level. He had his throat cut by an irate Nyoongah youth whose money he had undoubtedly stolen and whose pride he had shattered. What would happen if a government stole and shattered an emblem like the sacred rock formation out of town? But she was too tired to work on it tonight. She would write it up tomorrow. For now, she wanted a long hot shower, a hot bowl of home-made soup and a cuddle-up with her dreams in her bed. Fuck the story, and fuck the editor too, she thought with uncharacteristic venom as she let the steaming water wash all her worries away. To think she had played pool with a killer last night and spoken with a dead man. Even though the murder was, most probably, an accident, it made her shiver just to think of it.

Don sat in the office at the police station and listened to the soothing song of the rain. But his thoughts were turbulent. He had known the Lacys for years and, rough though they may be, he could not think of any of them as murderers. Still, there was a first time for everything. It made him sad though.

When the phone call came through about midnight he was dozing in his chair. The rain had become harder now and he wondered again if the river would rise and flood the town like it had a few years ago. Everyone had helped that night with sandbags and brackets and he could not forget Marjorie Perrit (who had just begun work in the pub) even in all that gloom and mud, with her nail polish, eye shadow and bright lipstick. She was never without them, and it was the source of many a good joke. That was the sort of woman she was, however.

There was even speculation she put makeup on instead of taking it off before she went to bed.

'Gee, it's good to see some people are industrious, Don,' came the Senior CIB Detective's jovial tones. 'I'm only ringing up to say that there are further developments on the Clarendon case. In fact we have it all wrapped up this end.'

'Didn't Simon get in touch with you today?' Don queried.

'No! What? Well, never mind, we've come up with this: the silver rose found by Clarendon's body yesterday – or one similar to it – was not owned by him but by his wife, whose maiden name was Roberts. Marjorie Roberts.'

Roberts. Marjorie Roberts. Now Don remembered what had seemed so strange to him when he had seen her yesterday. She had been wearing her lurid blue eye shadow and her revolting pink nail polish but, for a woman so vain, her lips were dry and bare. Indeed, now he thought about it her whole face had seemed older and haggard. Had she been without lipstick because she had lost it at the scene of the murder?

'She calls herself Marjorie Perrit now, I understand,' the CIB man carried on. 'She had a colourful life of her own. She was a high-class prostitute and he was her pimp before they married. She ran a call-girl service in Adelaide about five years before they caught up with her for tax evasion. Whereupon she disappeared into thin air. Well, it seems that Clarendon saw her in the Adelaide papers with her new "husband" and, even though she has cleverly disguised herself he knew who she was all right and decided to try a little blackmail. Only it never worked. The irony is, of course, that he had just entered gamblers' heaven and had won about two hundred thousand dollars on the TAB! But, once a greedy thief always a greedy thief.'

'Can we prove this? That she was the killer?'

'The silver rose was never his. It was always hers. She must have dropped it in the fight. Ask her what happened to her rose and see if she can answer you that!' the CIB officer said. It was always good to wrap up a case quickly and this one had looked like being a humdinger of a dandy with mysterious strangers and few real clues. 'Remember that lipstick? I'll bet you'll find it's hers. In any case she's wanted for tax evasion back in Adelaide so I'd grab her first thing tomorrow. Now, what was Constable Millson supposed to tell me and didn't?'

The Senior Officer had little time for the young constable, Don knew. He considered the lad too vague and with no stomach for police work and, quite frankly, too lazy and stupid to make a truly good lawman. He decided to take some pressure off the young policeman.

'Nothing. It's OK. I can handle this.'

'Good. Well, don't forget to pick her up tomorrow and hit her with the facts, then we can close this case. And good riddance to bad rubbish, I say!'

After he put the phone down Don decided to go and tell Danny the good news. Why, he thought, I might even let the poor bugger go. We're after bigger fish than him and what would a charge of possession of cannabis get him? Six months' jail? It wasn't worth it to ruin a basically decent youth's life. Why not let him go? He's had a good scare now.

The two lock-up cells were in a separate section of the yard to the office and he had to walk through a thundering passage, as rain hurled icy javelins at the structures of law and order in this small town. He could hardly hear himself think as he made his way to the far cell. It was as though all the demons from the very pits of hell, and the watery bowels of all the rivers and oceans had gathered in the sky to shriek over the injustice of mankind. He flung open the door as he snapped the light on, smiling to himself at the surprise he would give Danny.

The youth swung slowly in the middle of the room, a torn grey blanket around his neck and through the bars of the cell window. His face was a ghastly yellow and his eyes and tongue protruded like some terrible clown.

Don was really in trouble now. He could see the impeccable record he had built up painstakingly over the years being torn asunder. Right when he was due to retire too. To make matters worse, when he went out to detain Marjorie Perrit he found she had gone. 'Disappeared into thin air,' he said angrily to young Constable Millson.

He still didn't look too good and Don felt it was time for a permanent rest for Simon Millson. He just wasn't cut out to be a cop, shaking and white-faced two days after a murder. It just wasn't good enough and he was in too much trouble himself now to worry about watching his partner's most unreliable back. He didn't have much time either to listen to the woes of Marjorie's 'husband' who bewailed the fact the shame and scandal would surely ruin him but could give him no idea as to where she may have fled.

When Marrilyn heard about the fate that had befallen poor young Danny Lacy she could not help but think about the night they had been together. If she had let him come upstairs with her as he wished, he would have spent the night in a warm and exuberant dream and would have had a tight alibi and never gone to jail and thus been so frightened ... so scared ... that he hung himself. It wasn't only that. She remembered what old Benny Kirup had said to her in his gloomy cracked voice. 'Why ya think there isn't any Nyoongahs live around 'ere? Only me, cos I don't care no more!'

For a while she lay on her bed and cried. After all, he was only a young boy, really, hardly out of his teens. Perhaps he had thought of himself as a tough, rugged man about town. But when you got right down to it, he was just a child.

Most of all, though, she felt for the first time that he was of her blood. She felt ashamed of the way she had led her life up to now. Living the European dream of power and prestige and riches gotten in any manner conceivable. Did anyone really appreciate the stories she wrote – or even read them? What of her friends in the discos around town? When it came down to the raw truth they only associated with her because of her colour, so they could say they were liberal minded. When she had been alone in a strange, cold, atmosphere it had been a total stranger who had come to her defence and offered her protection, simply because she was of the same race.

Harry had told her that after she left that night Danny had murdered the black ball with a resounding crack of the white and a flourish of his cue cum guitar, then whirled around and challenged the stranger to a game.

Then it was on. Oh, the stranger drew Danny Lacy out like a spider does an iridescent beetle, with cunning and patience and infinite trickery. He lost a few games, then brought in the subject of money – an item Danny had little of. So they began playing for twenty dollars and the stranger lost forty and he won twenty, then a hundred, and he cleaned Danny Lacy out. It was pure magic to watch the ease with which this shark wiped out this tiny fish in a little pond.

She lay on her bed most of the afternoon and then her mind was made up. She would go back to the roots of her being. She would, tonight, visit the rock formation and try to find the mystic magic of this land. She would try to find some of the simple joy of the youth Danny Lacy, who was so proud of his little life – so full of life! For so short a time.

And the night came down, purple and black and grey, with drifting rain and swirling mists. Whispering trees shook softly in the gentle wind and a constant pattering deluge drenched the town. The river rose slowly and surely, a rumbling brown snake with whitish yellow foam in patches on its back like a snake's peeling skin.

She set off about eleven o'clock, wanting desperately to be alone, so waiting until the pub closed and the loud arrogant Pedro had been ushered down the stairs. Then she set off on her journey of atonement.

It was further than she thought to the rocks, perhaps a half-hour walk going by her watch. By the time she arrived she was wet through. Yet, it seemed to her, the rain was kind on her skin and the trees seemed to chant out a long forgotten chorus. A tune of welcome for the lost Spirit returning home.

The rock formation appeared at last through the haze of misty drizzle bathed in bright moonlight, and what a wonder it really was. Once, to her, it would have only been a clump of rather untidy boulders, grey and misshapen, splotched with pale green or yellow lichen and miniature forests of luxuriant green moss. But now it stood, solemn and majestic, a tower of some ancient civilisation. It stood strong and powerful – forever – and she knew that this was a part of her. A part no foreign race could truly comprehend.

She moved up to the rocks and touched them with

her hand. Scaly cold surface or soft moss surface. Spirits abounded here by the plenty and she was surrounded by an aura of such an ancient past it was almost tangible. The very boulders seemed to move and take shape: here a brave warrior, there a crouching woman, there an old wise man. Voices seemed to drift out of the mist and encircle her, feeling her out with cold tendrils tainted with stories from ages gone. Then, as she moved further into the tumbled towers to be away from the rain and closer to her new Gods, she came across something of an entirely different age from the one she travelled in so esoterically at the present.

She was pulled back to reality at once.

For there, in the many caves in the centre of the formation, were bags and bags – all green plastic and all very bulky. She opened one and needed to look no further. Here was perhaps three million dollars worth of cannabis, all ready processed and set to go. She was possessed of a surge of elation and fierce ambition which totally dispelled her recent feelings of affinity, compassion and spirituality.

Here was her story, she thought. This would constitute one of the state's biggest drug busts. She would bring in the slant of how a sacred site was being abused for gain and greed and how a youth (who admitted to her, on his last night alive, to smoking this weed) had died because of the oppressive laws of another race whose very existence was based on greed. His death gave the whole story just the right dramatic touch to make it front-page stuff, she thought.

She closed up the bag and hurried back to the Opera House. The river had reached the bottom steps now but it seemed the old building would last another day and many more, for the heavy rain had abated and there was just the merest of drizzle. But she did not care for the river or the rain. Even the beauty of the rocks had faded. She had a story to write.

'I am sorry you had to find out about that,' came the soft voice from the shadows. 'Clarendon found out about my operations because of his scummy mates in jail and a lack of security among my people. But he is no loss really. Just a fool who thought he could blackmail me. Me? Didn't he realise how big my operations are over East? So I brushed him off like the fly he was. But you? I could have liked you, Marrilyn Henry. I am sorry for the boy too, but he had to die. He knew too much of my operations, he was one of my drivers, you see. Young Millson will have to have an accident too, only because his usefulness has been outlived and he is becoming a nuisance. Anyhow, he is too much of a threat, having executed Danny. A policeman's lot is not a happy one … if you get my drift. Greed is a terrible curse and it comes in many guises, does it not? If you had not wanted your story so badly you would be leaving this town but now … Don't be so surprised. You were seen leaving, you see, and home is where the heart is, isn't that what they say? And this old Opera House is the only home you had in this town.'

A small silver rose arched out of the shadows and landed near her drenched new shoes.

'Just so those greedy ones over East will know who I am and who killed you, even if no-one else does. It only remains now for me to say, Arrivederci, signorina.'

A body lay on the steps. One hand rested just above the water and a narrow watchband was visible below the cuff of a light coloured coat. Dark hair curled damply to the nape of the neck. The legs were a little apart; the new sole of a woven brown leather shoe faced upwards.

The Island

It rose out of the misty blue sea like ancient Avalon and, like that mystic isle, magic and romance abounded. Across the heaving waters of the bay lay the city. Tall grey buildings creeping out of the smog, shimmered like the beckoning fingers of witches and bad fairies full of evil and cruel curses. But, this weekend, it was their island and the city with all its vile ways could wait until Monday to take their lives into its mocking hands again.

The sun was a red ball, hurtful to the eyes in its intensity as it hung in the purple smog that drifted over the city under the clear blue summer sky. The main tourist island was to the north of this island. In fact, this was actually a wildlife reserve and a home for the deadly tiger snake – and the ever-welcome serum their poison provided. It was a nesting place for a number of sea birds as well. On the far side of the island, that was only some nine hundred metres across, a cliff face rose raggedly from the blue–green sea and it was here a number of orange crabs scuttled in their foam-washed kingdom. On the bay side there was a long streak of white beach in a small semi-protected cove where a large, lumbering. scarred old sea lion had been their welcoming committee. These were the only inhabitants of the island.

Even though humans weren't supposed to go there, Davy had insisted. He was of larrikin and convict stock and the British laws were made to be broken by every good Irishman, he joked. Even one who had never seen Ireland – nor ever would. Part of the reason Gracie loved him was because he never seemed to take anything seriously. Yet, there were times when his impassive face hid every emotion so you couldn't tell what he was thinking. Now, here they were, via his mate's boat, on this island they could call their own for two whole days ... on a holiday. He had taken her on a holiday!

When had they first met? Down at Kovalski's farm when he was shearing there with his two brothers just before Lyle raped that girl and all the trouble started for the Higgins clan. She had been cooking for the Kovalskis and trying to keep Mr Kovalski's hands off her. The look in his little blue eyes, every time she dodged or thwarted his fumbling, said that she should be glad of this kind of attention from a gentleman of his standing. After all, she was only a half-caste gin and fit only for the low-life whites or her own shiftless kind. This is what the eyes of the foreigner told her, but she needed the money if not the amorous attentions of the old man.

Every time she brought the Higgins brothers their tea and scones she sensed Davy's strange hazel eyes upon her; strange because, depending on his mood they appeared light green or a deep smouldering brown. But the really strange thing was the light way back in them that frightened her with its intensity, yet aroused her curiosity as well and drew her to him like a moth to a flickering destructive flame. A deep sadness had encircled his heart and, just as the moon's light will shine from a waterhole, seemingly at the bottom, beautiful, melancholy yet unreachable, so too did the light shine from Davy Higgins's sombre eyes.

'Davy don't take no milk. 'e 'ates anythin' white!' Marcus grinned.

'Yeah, 'e likes things 'ot, black and sweet,' cackled Lyle with typical lack of originality.

'Course, 'e don't mind a little bit of cream mixed in,' carried on Marcus, referring to her coffee-brown skin.

Lyle was dark-haired and swarthy with royal blue eyes while Marcus was red-headed with squinting, cloudy grey eyes. Not one of the sons looked like the father, who was a hulking black-eyed monster and it led to speculation among the townsfolk about the fidelity of Mrs Higgins, now long since departed for a happier land.

Like his brothers, Davy was short though stocky and his sunburnt arms were covered in tattoos: old girlfriends' initials; one for his mother, whom he had loved with all his heart, that read simply and predictably 'I love my mother' in scroll writing; a spider web on his elbow; a rose on his shoulder and a tiger on his forearm. All done in jail with Indian ink. A naked woman with wings coming out of her back and a snake twisted around her body on his upper arm, done in intricate colour and design by a tattoo artist in Perth where he stayed for a while after being released. He looked like a walking picture show, joked Marcus.

Like the other boys he was sparse of word but, unlike the other boys this was not because he was sparse of intelligence. He was like his mother in that respect, as well as looking like her. He would say the most unusual things sometimes and was always reading whenever he could. Admittedly he was not a fast reader and often lost interest in a book he had picked up, but at least he gave it a go, unlike his brothers who could scarcely read a comic.

He thanked Gracie softly for his scones and, as usual, ignored his brothers' crude remarks. He ignored her too, even though after a while she took to combing her hair – even putting a ribbon in it every now and then – and dabbing on a little of Mrs Kovalski's perfume while cleaning out her bedroom.

Gracie Fields had been named just as her mother and grandmother before her. The famous singer who had so impressed her great-grandmother that she named her baby after her was all but forgotten by the Fields clan, but tired old jokes still emanated from the withered old men who leant against the pub verandah.

'That's Gracie Fields, she's off to entertain the troops!'

'Give us a song there, Gracie.'

'Is your dad W.C. Fields? W.C.? Stands for Wily Coon, of course!'

But she endured all the jokes just as her mother and grandmother had. The Fields were a proud and happy family. Their ancestors had fought and died for this land and this valley watched over by two big hills – and not only in the two big white man's wars that the world had suffered this century. Before that her ancestors had been involved in guerrilla warfare, terrifying the settlers and spearing their livestock. The old ones had cast spells and the young ones spears but the European tide had swept over them.

Then the remnants of the fourteen tribes of Bibbulmun lived on handouts and were herded like the stock they had killed into Missions or onto Reserves. A new order came over the land and they were pushed aside as unwanted and unloved.

The old ones drank to forget the sadness and pain and the young ones died in stolen cars, heads full of white man's drugs, pursuing the white man's dream while the songs of their Dreaming faded in their ears. But they were a proud and independent people and kept closely to their hearts all the secrets of their land. That was one thing the Europeans could never take from them.

Davy's ancestors had been a part of that destructive tide of humanity that crept as soft and illusive as mist over the shores. His people had been dragged away from their small grey-stoned cottage among the rolling green hills of Sligo where there was verdant vegetation all the year around and startlingly blue lakes full of trout. Here was the source of the great and stately Shannon.

Here were leprechauns and magic and legends told in the soft forbidden Celtic tongue.

The British soldiers had torn down the door in their little house not far from Achrony in the middle of County Sligo. They had rounded up the men while grey clouds raced like dogs across the sky and a bitter wind howled around them. They separated the women then, having found three guns to be used in the fight for the freedom of Eire, they burnt the house, turned the women and younger children out into the cold, and hauled the four older males off to jail.

Two were hanged. The two youngest, boys of thirteen and fifteen, were sent to the waiting shores of sunny Australia for seven years each. Taken from one island to another huge, dry, mysterious island where the lakes were salt and the grass was a dry yellow. A land where, it seemed to the boy who had come from a fair green isle of fairies and history, heroes and song, all magic had been obliterated by the all-powerful sun.

They were sent here because they wanted their land to be free, only to take land from another race, already free, but now enslaved by white man's laws. Davy and Gracie, of course, could not see the ironic twist in all that. Davy had left school at fifteen and Gracie had never gone at all much so history and race relations meant nothing to them.

Perhaps they fell in love because their people had a similar history. Out at the old Mission, when Gracie had the weekend off, she and her cousins would share a bottle or two and then she would let her imagination roam — and she had a vivid imagination – idly dreaming of the boy with the handsome face and fine, curly, honey-blonde hair and curious hazel eyes. Of living a life together.

Whenever she was with someone else – a boy from another town or one of the flash ones from Perth, come to impress with their fast cars, fast money and stories of dangerous times – she would imagine it was Davy Higgins she held in her thin brown arms.

But she never really thought this love would grow. It was just one of her dreams. In the same way as she dreamed of becoming a famous Country and Western singer one day. The unspoken code of the country town would never have allowed it. Everyone knew their place so life could go by fairly pleasantly. The Fields boys played in the football team and worked the farms but they were not welcome in the pub or inside certain homes – just as the Higgins boys knew where not to go.

The shearing shed with its aroma of sheep and lanoline, tar and oily wood, with its buzz of shears, throaty coughs of nervous sheep and the clanking tin of the roof in the wind, was where their love was spawned, but it was in the bush that their love was consummated. The soft green bush that was as silent as the boy and as wildly beautiful and secret as the girl. Oh, yes, it held so many secrets to its wild tangled heart!

One tea break, while his two brothers engaged in their crazy horseplay that so easily turned to violence, Davy cornered her beside the sheep pen as she gazed in at some early lambs not long born.

'Doin' anythin', Sat'd'y? It's our afternoon off, see, and I thought you might like to go on a picnic, like. If ya not doin' nothing', he murmured.

A thrill went up her spine so she shivered in delight.

'Yeah? Where'd we go then, Davy?' she answered back, happy that he noticed her at last.

'Oh, I thought up past Wallaby Road, turn off along to the Red 'ill. Get a good view from there, what ya reckon?'

She sensed a silence in the shed then and turned to see the other two brothers staring at her with bold cynical eyes so she ducked her head in shy embarrassment and scurried off down the hill towards the main homestead. But not before she gave him a demure smile of assent, her black eyes sparkling.

Gracie Fields had been assigned to an old tin shed that had once been a garage. In it was a stove, a fridge, some broken old armchairs and a sofa that had all been destined for the dump. She had her own TV – the Kovalskis' old black and white one – and a squeaky old bed with a lumpy kapok mattress. But it was her home and her very first job. She had stepped out into the white man's world with her dreams clutched closely to her breast. Now she was fulfilling some of them. She was proud of the money she earned each week and took home to her mother and two younger brothers.

On Saturday afternoon she made sure she finished work early. Instead of catching the old Bedford mail truck into town though, she dressed herself carefully in clean jeans that hugged her narrow hips, her new red shirt, previously unworn, and her best walking shoes. She packed a small picnic basket with a cake she had baked, some sausages, and bread and butter.

The Kovalskis had come out from Hungary after the war and bought-up one of the many soldier settlement farms from a disillusioned cocky. These blocks were three thousand acres each with a small asbestos house. Everything else – the sheds, the superphosphate for the crops, the fencing – came from the farmer's pocket (with some help from government subsidies). So it was a hard life in an unrelenting land and any bad season would bring the smallholders down. This was what was happening now with the price of wheat and wool dropping. It was only Mr Kovalski's pigs and his knowledge of smallgoods manufacturing that kept them going right now. Gracie had borrowed some of his excellent homemade sausages and they nestled in the basket with other goodies for her special day.

As she passed the kitchen she sensed Mrs Kovalski watching her like a bird of prey, with eyes as black as a bird's as she pruned the grape vines around the back door. She would not let it spoil her day. Likewise when she passed the pig pens and the old man glanced at her, with the look of one of his pigs. She walked on by, head held high. She was going to see her man.

Up in the old shearers' quarters, which consisted of two small bunk houses, a bathroom and a kitchen-dining room all in a row, the three brothers lounged outside on the narrow kitchen verandah. A mob of woolly sheep rested placidly in the holding paddock, ready for Monday, if it didn't rain before then. This was the last of the flock. Another week and, like the smothering dust kicked up by the sheep's restless feet, the restless Higgins brothers would be gone to the next shed.

Grey and dark black-blue eyes stared at her slim body. Grins were plastered over two lean faces like the occasional silent flashes of faraway lightning – and just as dangerous. They had had a great time teasing their dour youngest brother all week.

'Looks like a bit of a grey day for a picnic. I'd rather be tucked up in bed,' Marcus grinned.

'Depends on what ya pickin', Nick!' Lyle chuckled with a rare flash of original wit.

As usual, Davy said not a word to his brothers but merely ambled off the verandah. He scooped up an esky that sat at his feet.

'Ya left some beer for us, I hope. I'm not givin' me beer away to every girl ya fancy, you know!' Marcus cried.

'Ya owe me a carton from last week, ya know very well,' Davy growled over his shoulder. Then he and Gracie set off for the heavily wooded hills.

Marcus let out a wolf whistle and their cackles echoed off the cobwebby old verandah like the cries of the wheeling cockatoos that settled in the gnarled pine tree by the shearing shed.

Even though Davy didn't look at her, seething as he was at some inner turmoil, he laid his big scarred hand in her frail slender one and his warmth went right up her spine to her heart. The chilly wind that blew across Mount Kudjalkurlongerup and carried with it the salty breath of the cold currents that swirled around distant Albany did not affect her. She was with her man at last.

It was a wonderful day. A quiet day, as quiet as this curly-headed youth who kept everything to himself. But he let the affection he was beginning to feel for her be known in little ways: a touch here, a smile, a look in his hazel eyes that melted the loneliness there and made the girl feel powerful ... magic ... that she had been the one to do that.

What also made it such a wonderful day was that he took her to a special place and she wondered if he knew of its significance. Red Hill was so called because of the purple and crimson rocks on its crest that often turned deep red in the dying sunlight. After the distant blue peak of Mount Kudjalkurlongerup it was the highest point in the district. There was a spring there and a small jumble of moss-covered orange boulders. It was set in a forest of thin she-oak which continued sparsely up its slopes to the peak – those gentle trees with the long thin leaves, like hair hanging down, that made a crooning sound from the wind or, sometimes, a high keening. In days gone by her people had come hunting here for emus who came to eat the nuts from the trees. Emu meat was very sweet and the oil from an emu was supposed to be good to rub on babies and warriors and the old people's joints to aid their stiffness. So the killing of an emu was a big event and a joy to the clan who caught it.

But this place had also been the meeting and ceremonial place of the women of the valley so she always felt at peace here. The Spirits of her ancestors gathered around her like the crooked dark old trees and made her feel whole. They spoke to her in the voice of the leaves and made her believe in herself again. And on this day the women of her valley seemed to say that here was a good man for their descendant.

'Ya know, on a clear day you c'n almost see Maitelup from 'ere. You c'n see the railway line anyways,' Davy said as he made a fire.

''Oo wants to see that poxy town! It's the end of the bloody world!' she retorted.

'Well … it's 'ome, ay!' he murmured placatingly.

'I'm goin' up ta Perth, soon, and becomin' a nurse,' she stated proudly.

'Oh, yeah? I dunno what I'll be doin'. The arse 'as dropped out of shearin'. I might give it a burl up North there. On a cattle station.'

But they both knew theirs were only words to be blown away in the cold wind. This town would never let them go and this town would never let them forget who they were. They both knew they had no real home anywhere. Even though the Higgins clan had been in Australia for three generations and the Fields clan had trodden this valley floor and the surrounding hills for forty thousand years or so, this new Australia had no place for either of them.

They had each other, though. And, having each other, they found a home for themselves.

This first meeting of the two was a time of serene smiles and tranquil words. It was the songs of the magpies and parrots foretelling the coming of the storm, with sharp cries and hurried flight, filtering through the moaning leaves. It was the far-off call of a lonely crow. It was the tinkling of water as it fell in endless motion from the crack in the rock into the small, cool pool formed by the ageless boulders. The angry sky was reflected in the water's peaceful eye.

How eerie it is, the stillness before a storm breaks! There is the distant roll of thunder and the flashing of jagged lightning upon the horizon while the air becomes oppressive and yet there is the sweet heady scent of rain on the breath of the wind. All this was part of their day too.

She told him some of her words and stories passed down from old Uncle Clyde Kickup and Uncle 'Djungie' Baker: Koorlbardie and Wardong – Magpie and Crow – two brothers who could never get along. (A bit like us 'iggenses, ay! Lyle's an old Crow, anyrate, Davy grinned.) Tjitty-tjitty, the messenger bird, otherwise known as Willy Wagtail. He could bring news, or trouble for children because some said he was an old moorook who used his magic to turn into a huge red dingo that would eat children after luring them away from camp in the guise of cheeky tjitty-tjitty.

She told him of the weerloo with their weird human eyes who always brought bad luck and news of a death with their haunting undulating cry. Her voice softened now and the brightness faded from her eyes, turning them dark and dim. Her subdued eyes glanced around nervously.

'There's things out there, Davy,' she whispered and crept closer to him. And he, who had a Celtic belief in all things faerie, did not mock her but put an arm around her, comforting her.

She told of cheeky Koomal the possum who had no respect for any laws but just wanted everyone's woman. And why not? He was such a good dancer. They laughed together at the adventures she told of him.

'You might be possum too, unna, Davy. You a good dancer, bud?'

'I'd trip over meself if I tried to dance. It's called trippin' the light fantastic!' he smiled into her face.

She told how Kudjalkurlongerup meant the place of two children so the two hills in the valley must have been important once. Their shadows crept out towards each other every day and covered the valley floor.

Yes! It truly was a wonderful day, that first day of the courtship of Davy Higgins and Gracie Fields. She made certain he saw her in a new light. The light that shone for her people from the land and made them glow with an inner being, no matter how poor or drunk they appeared. She made sure he shared some of that light as well.

This became their meeting place, just to come and talk. They talked of their ambitions and told stories of their families. Her uncles, like his dad, had fought in the

Second World War and Marcus had fought in the Vietnam War along with her third cousin Murphy Baker. They had grown up together in the district and were interested in the gossip of their contemporaries. Sometimes they just lay or sat together in silence, at peace, and calm in each other's company. But she would not tell Davy the secret significance of the Red Hill for her. He was a man and if it had been two hundred years ago and if he had been a darker brown they both would have been killed for coming here. Even now, it was always Davy who was cutting or hurting himself. As though the land was telling him to keep away.

If anyone knew of their love they kept it to themselves. It seemed they had found a friendship that belonged only to them. This was an old farming district, set and conservative in its ways. But because the two of them were shy about their feelings and only saw each other occasionally no-one really knew and they preferred it that way.

She was not an outstandingly beautiful girl – being short and plumpish with legs and arms a little too thin some might say; with an unruly mop of bushy tangled brown hair. Her eyes were black opals though and her smile a jewel more precious than any and her heart was full of affection for him. For his part he, too, in his silent – some might say sullen – way began to love her. And in his eyes she was pretty enough, with an infectious laugh and sense of humour. The sometimes crazy light in his hazel eyes began to grow dingy and shorn of its beams.

At last, one day, the inevitable happened and the cushion of she-oak leaves upon the ground became their bed while the spring sang them a special lullaby and all the trees closed around them, keeping their act of passion shrouded from the outside world. Neither of them were new in the game of love and yet, with the meeting of their bodies, they did seem to find something new upon the sacred earth that had been her tribeswomen's secret place for centuries. The trees and the rocks and the birds shimmered in the stillness and it seemed to her as if the whole hill let out an audible sigh along with herself.

Now he began taking her to his sacred place – The Royal Hotel in Maitelup. For she was his lady now and they had found their place in this district. He was as proud as could be.

But the people in the district, with small town bigotry, tore his pride and lady to pieces. Like a pack of African hunting dogs, those fierce predators of the green savannahs, around a lone defiant creature, they ripped into him gleefully. He was not only a despised Higgins but he was living with an Abo.

'What ya wanna live with an Abo for?' roared his drunken old dad. 'What's th' flamin' matter with ya, goin' steady with a boong? 'Ow ya goin' to work if no-one in the district'll employ ya! A man oughta belt some sense inta ya!'

He didn't though. Davy might have been only five foot six but two years in jail with nothing to do except exercise had hardened his compact body into iron. There would be no more beltings from his father or older brothers. If the truth was to be told they were all a little frightened of him since his run-in with big Jerry Horgan. They were a violent family and solved their differences with fists but that fight had been cold and calm and calculated.

However, it didn't stop Lyle's cheeky mouth from putting forth his two bob's worth.

'Mate, mate,' he grinned, putting an arm around Davy's shoulder. 'Root 'em, yeah. I 'ad a few meself when I was scratchin' for some boom–boom, ya know? But, matey, ya gotta 'ave kangaroos loose in ya top paddock to live with 'em. Just give 'em a good time then goodbye.' He made an obscene gesture with his fingers. 'Know what I mean?'

Gracie saw and heard it as she was over by the juke box, choosing a song for her and Davy. She turned her head and glanced at Davy to see if that's how he really thought about her, like her cousins had warned her he might.

'Those wadgulas are all the same. Baandji men the lot!'

There was a longing in her eyes, asking him to disagree, to say that all the last three months of happiness and joy had not been a huge lie. But she couldn't say anything. Her trees and birds were far away. This was the white man's Dreaming place.

It was her look more than anything that made Davy slam his brother back against the pool table. There was a moment of startled surprise then Lyle came back swinging, only to crash to the floor. Then Marcus ran across from the bar to put in a few good punches before he too hit the floor, and that was the biggest shock of all. For Marcus had never been quite right after he returned from overseas service. He had been one of the unlucky ones to become affected by Agent Orange, those who knew these things said. His unstable temper and vicious fists had the whole town terrified – or concerned, anyway.

They remembered then Davy's wicked temper that had almost killed a man in this very pub. Bloodied and bruised he put a hand in the hand of his lady and staggered from the pub, leaving a collection of startled drinkers to gape after him.

After the fight Lyle, in a foul temper, had driven his ute over to Katanning, where he drowned his woes in the company of relative strangers who had not seen his defeat. He met a nurse from the hospital there and in the course of the night he finished up raping her and subsequently going to jail.

The rest of the Higgins clan blamed Davy and he was driven from the family home amidst accusations and hatred. After all, it had only been a joke on Lyle's part. Davy didn't have to take things so seriously. Besides, what Lyle had said was true and Davy had turned against his own family, his own flesh and blood, for the sake of a boong.

He couldn't get a job anywhere either, as his father had predicted, but that was also partly because he was one of the infamous Higgins. Mr Kovalski, now he knew the girl he secretly and fruitlessly lusted over had a real boyfriend – a maniac like Davy Higgins – was only too glad to find an excuse to get rid of her. So Gracie lost her precious job as well.

She and her man set up house with her mother and two younger brothers – and any cousins or friends that dropped in for a visit. They were friendly people, a sharing people from a communal background and he was part of their family now. The only way to survive was to share what little they had. Where before they shared the sweet meat of the emu or gamey meat of the kangaroo and the stories of their country's creation, now they shared their welfare money and bottles of beer and troubles, so the worries were spread thin and diffused with good family humour.

Gracie Fields the senior was not all that pleased her daughter had taken up with a Higgins.

'Those wadgulas are kartwarrah, girl, and Davy 'iggins is the worst of a bad lot. Ya couldn't find no-one better, or what? 'e'll finish up killin' you,' she warned. ''e's got the eyes of the devil, true!'

Some of her old boyfriends, who came around to meet her, were annoyed as well. But, after a few arguments and when they saw that this was the man she wanted they left him alone. The main thing in Davy's favour though was when word got around that he had defended their cousin Lewis 'Bulbul' Baker when the other wadgulas had mobbed him in jail. That truly made him one of them now. He helped them with any problems that they had and he could help them with. He was kind and courteous to those who deserved it and deadly with any of their enemies.

So they lived like this for another three months and Christmas was coming. The football season was over and everyone was gearing up for the cricket. This was what Davy lived for because he was an excellent cricketer and he began practising with the Nyoongah youths out on the flat behind the old Mission. He was able to gather up his dreams again that had scattered with his settling down with his lady. It was all very well to sit around and drink and talk about what they would do one day, but he was a person who tired of inertia. Since no-one would give him a job there was little for him to do, except listen to Gracie's many plans for the two of them. They could go to Albany, where her cousins lived and he could get a job on the wharf. They could go to Beverley and get work on the farms there – or stay with her aunt at least. He fell into a pattern of married life, where she would cook him meals and they would sleep in a crowded lumpy bed, the household sounds of the Fields family taking the place of the birds and wind from Red Hill. But he was happy in a way. She, like a dark little mouse, had crept into his heart and made him feel wanted and whole again. She didn't care who he was or what he had done, she just loved him.

He even told her his most inner secret: that he blamed himself for his mother's death, for she had not been a well woman when he was born and she had died not many years later. She had been a strong-willed woman of Danish stock, with all the tenacity and fighting spirit of the Danes. She had been far more intelligent than the hulking Joseph Higgins. She had whispered to him stories, when he was young, of Ogier the Dane and his love affair with the fairy sister of King Arthur, Morgan Le Fey. This had been a happier, more tranquil moment in the whirlpool of his life and he held onto it. It gave him comfort when all the chips were down and all the world seemed against him, those whispered gentle words from his mother.

Now he had another woman to give him comfort. He would not lose her in a hurry.

Gracie held him in her warm arms and muttered endearments to him. It was not his fault. It was just the way things went. Like her dad drowning in the river on a peaceful sunny day. He just let out a cry and disappeared and his body was never recovered, no matter how much they dragged the bottom. That is why none of the Nyoongahs swam in that part of the wandering brown waterway. Thus they talked of intensely personal things and their hearts truly became as one.

Things came to a head at the annual Cricket Cabaret held in the old tin shed the town rather dubiously called a hall. It was also the meeting place of the RSL and the CWA and the place where any movies that made their way to this forgotten part of Australia were shown. So it was an important structure and the social centre of the town.

'Ya 'ave ta go. You're the vice-captain,' Marcus told him in the pub. 'You'd look a bit of a dill if ya never showed up. Besides, don't let 'em put it over ya. We're as good as them, matey.'

Because, despite their differences, they had a common enemy – the attitude of the district's wealthier settlers. They were constantly reminded, in small and nasty ways, that they were of convict stock. Not many convicts had come to Western Australia so the older established families were contemptuous still of their descendants.

So Davy dressed in his best clothes, shined his shoes and combed his hair and walked into the hall like a king. They had a band over from Katanning and all the local lads gathered for some fun, for there was little enough of that in Maitelup. Darts, pool comps, drinking, talk of football or cricket, drinking, organising gymkhanas, finding a girlfriend, drinking. So a good time was had by all and even Davy was accepted, if somewhat warily and only because he was the best cricket player the team had. He could pretend he belonged in this town that so often shunned him and his brothers.

He stepped out of the hall for a moment. The blue darkness fell over him like a mantle. He watched the pale watermelon slice of the moon grin down at him from where it sat among the whispering branches of the gumtrees. The clack of cicadas and the burping croaks and calls of numerous frogs from the river's side sang a song of a summer almost here. Spirits came down to enter anyone alone in the magic bush.

As he turned he bumped into Gracie who had crept up behind him as quiet as a spirit, and now leant against the verandah post watching him. But, for the first time, he didn't feel comfortable in her company. None of the Aborigines ever came to the annual Cricket Cabaret, even if any were playing in the team. It was an unspoken rule in the town that this was a purely European do.

For a second he was annoyed. Then he was annoyed with himself. See what this town is doing to you, he thought. If not for your prowess with the bat and ball neither you nor Marcus would be within cooee of this party.

He gave his lady a smile. She smiled back at him – a smile that wasn't a smile. Her eyes fluttered like trapped butterflies about to be pinned to a board forever. The hazy light of the moon had not hidden the look on his face when he had first turned around.

'Surprised ya, unna, Davy, doll! I thought I'd check out if you was runnin' around be'ind me back. Knockin' all them Katanning wadgula yorgas for six, unna!' she said in the soft nasal voice he had grown to like.

She had combed her hair and put on her best shoes and a nice flowery-patterned print dress.

'Ya wanna 'ave a dance with old Dave the dancer,' he grinned. 'They call me Davy Astaire!'

'They'd stare at you all right if they seen ya dancin', cob! Trip over ya own feet, ya do,' she giggled.

'You c'n be Ginger Rogers, if ya like.'

'What? In there?' she inclined her head towards the

lighted noisy hall. 'More likely I'd be Black Mary, unna?' she smiled faintly.

'Look, this is the 1970s not the 1870s an' if I feel like dancin' with me missus then I bloody well will, see!' he said. And gently taking hold of her hand, he led her into the hall.

In the old days a man would paint himself in yellow and red wilgie and dance for the women. If any liked him enough then they let it be known through the elders. If a man rubbed up against a woman and she left on her body the wilgie that had rubbed off, that meant she liked the man. Possum was a good dancer but he always had red on his face because the wilgie had no meaning for him since he was always chasing other men's wives. But dance was an important part of the intricate courtship ritual of her people. This was the first time she had gone to a dance with her man, even though they had been going together for over six months now.

'Yeah, Davy,' she murmured, slowly losing her shyness. 'Good to dance with you, mate.'

So they danced, happy together. She was a good dancer and he was all right. They ignored the muted conversations around the room that drifted like mist around their swaying bodies. They ignored the stares that quivered over them like the bright light from a thousand suns and danced like snakes with the shadows on the walls.

Towards the end of the evening when he was getting some food for her at the supper table, big Jerry Horgan and his two mates ambled over, made brave by alcohol and numbers.

'What's she doin' here? This is a cricketers only night,' Jerry spat out.

'Oh yeah, Jerry? Your old lady thinkin' of becomin' the team's fast bowler, is she?' Davy countered, looking in the direction of a small cluster of women over in the corner.

'Your brother's Lyle Higgins, ay mate?' asked one of Jerry's pals, a heavy-set, stubble-chinned man in a check shirt and dirty black jeans.

'What of it?' Davy asked, suspicious.

'He raped my sister,' the monolith stated while his eyes burned hatred.

So this was Jerry's plan, was it, Davy thought, staring with contempt at the big shaggy man. He had been waiting four years to get back at Davy Higgins and now he thought he had him.

'Youse Higginses are all the same. Youse can't get a woman fair and square. Ya gotta rape 'em or else get a boong a dog wouldn't root,' the third man sneered. And then all hell burst loose.

Gracie's supper ended up in the third man's face while a boot in the stomach sent Jerry reeling.

'Come on, you little combo prick, I want you!' shouted the Katanning man.

Then they were bouncing all over the floor while women screamed and plates crashed as the pair fell into the supper table. Jerry came back into the fray and things

144

were going bad for Davy until his brother burst through the door and took on the Katanning man with a cry of 'Come on, big fella! I'm one of the 'iggins as well. The maddest one!'

As soon as things were evened up the fight was over in a few minutes since there was no-one could fight the Higgins boys once their considerable temper got going. While Davy stood over the fallen body of Jerry Horgan, shaking in the residue of rage and dripping blood, old Alf McNamara, President of the Maitelup RSL and coach of the cricket team stormed over to him. Gracie had come up beside him and put a skinny arm around his waist but he felt nothing, reliving an event four years ago when his boots had put Jerry in hospital and himself in jail.

'Right, you young hooligan! You can get out now and forget any idea of playing cricket this year. Clear off out of this. And take that black slut with you!'

Davy had looked up then and the old man recoiled at the depths of coldness – emptiness – in those hazel eyes. He had been in Changi POW camp and seen that look a hundred times a day.

'Fuck off, Alf, ya old cunt,' Davy had answered, as soft as a snake sliding across the floor.

The old man had walked away then and the town had watched Davy wobble out the door, supported by the brown arm of Gracie Fields, his last dream shattered into a million fragments too small for him to piece together.

★

He decided he had to go. This dusty dying town had no place or use for him. His new dream was to go to Perth, get a job and bring Gracie up later. It would be so much better in Perth, he reasoned to Gracie, on their last night. He might even score a job on one of the mining camps up North and then they would be able to afford a house.

Down by the stagnant brown river, murky in the shadows, her murky black eyes looked up at him. The paperbark trees that grew here huddled together and their small white flowers sent out their scent. A duck quacked from the shadows, as dismal as they were, and the pungent smell of the thick black mud assailed their nostrils. A flock of black cockatoos screeched raucously overhead, their weird screams a cacophony of wild sound.

'Red-tail cockatoos, Davy. Very rare, they are. That means rain comin' if ya 'ear them call. I'll tell ya the story of them, one day – if ya want. Uncle Clyde tole me one time, yeah, an' it's a deadly love story, babe!'

'Soon, darlin'. As soon as we settle in Perth.'

Frogs croaked, a hiccupping sound, and something slithered in the bushes. A grey heron waded through the yellow-green shallows of the river, searching for choice titbits. Every now and then the silent bird, the colour of a ghost, would emit an eerie, high-pitched cry.

All of this they knew. It was part of their lives. But she understood it better than he – it was her people's past as well as their future.

'This place 'ere. Just along the bank a bit. Well, that's

where me Dad was drowned,' she whispered. 'We don't go there now.'

A look she could not fathom crept into his eyes then. But he took her into his arms to comfort her and the look passed away into one of her dreams.

'Oh, baby,' he murmured. 'You got special places all over this valley, ay.'

For a year he had sought his dream and he had found it in the old rowdy Port of Fremantle. He got a job on an Italian fishing boat, as a deckhand. It was an entirely different place to Maitelup and the best part of all, no-one knew who he was or what he had been. The old men held a wisdom, kindness and spirit of family that Davy had never felt since his mother died. The young men who, to many, appeared aloof, keeping to their own kind, could be friendly to a kindred spirit who worked on their boats. Soon he had people calling out to him from the street cafés for a cup of cappuccino or a chat or a game of cards. He really felt he belonged in this bustling busy port. As for the Italian girls with their bold black eyes, clear olive skin and shining black hair ...

He began forgetting about the bad times in Maitelup. But he also began to forget about Gracie as well – her midnight eyes, her infectious laugh, her gentle smile that had cheered up his grey world: her soul that had wrapped itself around his own naked spirit like a soft brown blanket.

His new friends admired his skill and perseverance on the boat. He wanted to learn and so they taught him. There was great camaraderie among them. Some of his new friends also read books and had strange thoughts like him on the world and its future. Being Italian – and being from the city with plenty of money always in their pocket – his new companions had a love of the good life which they showed to Davy. He grew more sophisticated and put his old life and rough ways behind him. Now he could go to the movies every night if he wanted and eat out in restaurants or go to flash hotels and listen to good bands. He bought himself expensive designer clothes and Italian or Spanish leather shoes. He joined the Fremantle Cricket Club and soon became a shining star in the Division team competition. So he made more friends and expanded his horizons.

Gracie Fields's face and body faded away like one of her dreams. Soon she was only a beautiful memory to the busy boy.

Then, one day, during the off-season, she came to visit him. There was a knock on the door of the house he shared with other sailors and there she stood, a new floral dress, a little lipstick, some perfume, a shy smile – all for her man. He did not question how she knew where he lived. He knew her people relied on word of mouth for most of their news. A cousin here, an auntie there, someone in a pub somewhere and word got around.

'Ya know Gracie's hungry man, Davy 'Iggins? Well 'e's workin' on the boats with the dings in Freo and, brooootherrr, 'e's loaded wicked!'

'Ya said ya'd call me, Davy,' she mildly accused, as she stared up at him.

'When I got enough money together, I said,' he whispered.

The other men he shared the house with had stared at her curiously when she appeared. They were a gossipy, friendly lot so they were surprised Davy had never mentioned his girlfriend before. He had not been one for bringing girls home, although he could have, plenty of times. This girl must have been the reason why. They stared at her, then at Davy, shrugged and smiled. He could have got a prettier girl, they thought. But they could also see the affection in the way he held her, and appreciated love in its many disguises.

'Well, I 'ad nothin' better to do so I thought I'd just drop in to surprise ya, like,' she lied and snuggled up close to him. 'Knowin' 'ow you like surprises.'

In truth she had missed him desperately when he went. After he left some of her old boyfriends came visiting but she had no interest in them. She knew then that she truly was in love with Davy and waited for a call from him.

'Ya shouldn't of come. See, I wanted to rock into Maitelup an' pick ya up. In a flash car an' all. Show them bastards down there what I become, ay! I don't 'ave to shear their bloody sheep to be someone. I'm me own boss now!' he grinned at her. But it was a bright and white and noisy grin, like the city all around them. It frightened her somehow.

'I 'ear ya in the cricket team, now!' she tried again.

149

'Yeah, I might even play for the State soon. I 'it four centuries this season and me best bowlin' average isn't too bad either. That's gotta count for somethin',' he said proudly and loudly.

'Knockin' all the girls for six, I'll bet,' she smiled her soft smile.

But this was a new Davy. The city had changed him. A year apart had changed them both. He was fitter than he had ever been and he was more sure of himself. He was more of a conversationalist now than a pugilist. No-one here cared if he was a Higgins. They just took him on his merits and they liked what they saw. He was quiet and a good worker and he was free and easy with his money, yet still saved up enough to have a nest egg. So men knew him as a hard-working companion and women knew him as a fun-loving yet prudent man. He had made a lot of friends among the tight-knit Italian community and Maitelup with all its pettiness and problems seemed far away.

For Gracie's part, the stagnant mood of the country town had rubbed off on her as all her dreams turned to dust. All her plans were only words to her now – feeding the dream of becoming the somebody she could be. She had never lost sight of the magic in her valley, though. And she never forgot the love of Davy Higgins.

So she was here now, among the old sandstone buildings that stood like hills beside the hot bitumen roads running like black smelly rivers between them. People, more people than she had ever seen in one place, called out like angry birds, their voices reverberating in the blue sky. But the trees and birds and animals of her valley were not here and the Red Hill was far, far away.

He took her down to the pub on Friday night to try to recapture the old camaraderie. She was excited at first, this big city life of bright lights and crowds of people being all new to her. But in the pub some of Davy's Italian female friends flirted with him, as they did every Friday night. She, being tipsy and happy at last in her man's company, gave them a belligerent flash of her black eyes.

'This is my mardong 'ere! Me and 'im known each other down 'ome, unna Davy,' she said and wrapped a possessive arm around him, glaring at all his new friends.

'They grow a wild bunch down Davy's neck of the woods,' he heard someone whisper, and then muffled laughter.

When she turned, smiling up at her man she caught the look in his eyes. It was the same look the other townsfolk had given her and Davy all the time down in Maitelup. Now he reserved it for her. Then his face softened.

'T'morrow I'll borrow Giovanni's boat and we'll go to the island. Just the two of us, ay?'

She could not forget his previous look and was saddened somehow. Things weren't working out the way she had planned. Nothing ever did, it seemed, in her life.

In the old days when someone went to the islands it was their spirit leaving the dead body and travelling

151

from orange-flamed Christmas trees to Kurranup, the island of the dead, across the seas, that was the home of the Spirits. It was why when the Europeans arrived they were welcomed as long-lost family bringing remarkable gifts of the Spirits like cattle, sheep, steel knives and axes, guns ... all from the islands lost upon the hazy horizon.

As she lay in bed that night with Davy on top of her, murmuring soft endearments and nibbling her ear gently, she clung tightly to her dream, clasping him hungrily with her arms and legs and biting into his neck.

Tomorrow, she too would go to the islands.

The sun beat down with a shimmering though fierce heat and clothed the small island in a hot white glare. Sounds became amplified in the atmosphere and distances became distorted, seeming to make things further away than they were. The only sounds were the screeching gulls and the booming surf and these, too, seemed to emphasise the loneliness of this place. In the evenings a cool wind would blow in from the ocean. It reminded her of the she-oak grove on top of the Red Hill and all the joy they had known there.

Davy lit a fire from driftwood when they arrived to cook any fish they might catch that day. As well as her first time in the city it was her first time by the sea – never mind being completely surrounded by it. Perhaps some of her ancestors, on their way to Rottnest prison, confused, angry or miserable, would have spotted this very island as the last free piece of land some of them would ever see again. But she did not let such sad thoughts enter her head.

She let the salty breath of the wind and all the little marvels the island had to offer wash away her fears, so she was relaxed and happy. Davy, too, appeared happy and more his laconic self. With just the two of them, alone, it was like the times up on the Red Hill or down by the river that meandered through her people's valley.

He wore a pair of torn-off jeans, but soon stripped off, so the loving sun caressed his sturdy tattooed body. At first she had giggled at his nakedness and been too modest to follow suit but the island weaved a magic of its own and soon she too was as naked as her ancestors of old.

They swam across to the other small island that was really only a jagged rock jutting up out of the reef. They had gone gidji-ing among the cruelly sharp grey rocks and he had caught a crayfish while she found some pretty shells.

'I could make these into some nice earrings, ay, Davy?' she smiled, but he sensed they would end their days in some dusty box or forgotten drawer and never adorn her ears.

She was curious about the big wriggling orange crayfish, too.

'True, ay! Bigger than them tjilgis down 'ome, unna? I never seen a crayfish before,' she said in awestruck wonder. She touched it with gentle fingers and giggled at its raspy feel. She turned her big dark eyes up to Davy.

'Let 'im go, Davy. Let 'im go back to 'is countrymen down there in the reef, ay.'

'Let 'im go, Gracie? Nah, bugger that. This'll do us for our tea. You never tried cray before, 'ave ya! Well, it costs about twenty bucks for a half in a good restaurant. Sometimes as much as sixty bucks, yeah!'

The thought of all that wealth, wasted just for something to eat, still bothered him, even though he was becoming used to that sort of life.

They swam back to their island and he speared a big silver fish that darted through the azure depths. In the water she noticed how he became whiter in the distortion of the currents and this made her uneasy somehow. Back on shore she had one last try to save the life of her friend.

'Ya could of let 'im go, Davy. 'E weren't causin' no fuss to no-one and ya got a deadly big fish now.'

'Baby, this is a beautiful feed. Not often ya lucky enough to get one of these fellas so close to Perth. Now, I'll leave 'im in the bag in the sea until teatime and then cook 'im up.' He smiled down at her, but it was a superior smile; a smile of one who was comfortable in this new world. 'Trust me, you'll really enjoy it.'

He looked at her small brown breasts and thin brown thighs as she squatted on the blindingly white sand. Crayfish was no stranger to Davy because his boat hauled in hundreds in a good season. The friends he hung around with enjoyed good food and, since they caught most of it, they made sure they got their share. This ocean was his friend now – not the slow brown river with its green tjilgis, black mud and memories drifting upon its lazy currents as it idled between the hills in the valley of his birth. He looked at her with worried eyes that went a deep brown, darkening in sorrow and confusion.

That night, beside the flickering fire with the cold white stars above, she tried to bring him back into her life. She reminded him of mutual acquaintances, in the Nyoongah way when old friends meet, after a time apart: who was dead, who was in jail, who was having babies – and by whom. The little adventures that made life big for her people.

He listened to the crying of the gulls and the faintly lapping water and the moaning wind. And he thought about the Italian girls in the pub across the bay.

But that night he made passionate, sensual love to her, not once but three times. As his sweating pale body pounded her into the pale sand, her dark hands gently encircled him, like shadows. The whites of her eyes caught the moonlight and cold starlight as she gazed up at him and saw the wildness there. It was not the usual way he made love to her. There seemed to be a desperate edge to his ardour, almost uncaring as he thrust into her. In her mind the odd gull who sang out became the warning call of a curlew and her heart was as quiet as the drifting sand tossed by the wind's unruly hands.

The next day they went for a walk around their island. This is what Davy had called it the first day when they had arrived and she had laughed then. Now they walked, hand in hand, wordless because of the emotions that churned inside their breasts with a turmoil akin to the waves that charged and frothed over the crabs' slippery kingdom. Every now and then he would glance at her with his hazel eyes and, it seemed to her, try to say something. But he was a man of few words and he could not bring himself to express this catastrophe he sensed was welling up between them. For her part she uttered banalities and squeezed his hand desperately to let him know she was by his side.

On the far side of the island was a blowhole in the cliff some twenty metres in diameter. The great rolling tides from the turquoise ocean would smash into this with a resounding whoosh and the roar of the huge waves dashing themselves against the smooth wet sides into fine sprays of mist. It was a place of great fascination to Davy – perhaps mirroring his own turbulent soul, perhaps because the element of danger excited him. On a previous visit, when he had come by himself, he spent hours there, staring into the boiling, pale-blue, white-foamed water. He took her there the second day.

'Hey! Gracie! Come 'ere and check out these beauties,' he cried.

She had been cheerfully watching the antics of some seagulls buffeted in the wind. When she came to his side he pointed into the maelstrom, his eyes alight with savage joy.

'See?'

Three sharks, their slim grey bodies two to three metres long, darted around their prison, sometimes just shady images under the water, trying to find a way out. They must have been sucked in by the rips and now were being pounded by the incoming waves. She could see their black pig-eyes and ugly gaping jaws. She shivered in the hot sunlight.

'Proper mean fellas, unna Davy doll,' she whispered, drawing back in fear. 'Was they with us all the time we was in the water, Davy?' she whispered again.

'Well ... there's always sharks. This is an ocean, after all,' he joked and laughed.

But there was nothing nice about the laughter, she thought. It was as though he were laughing at her. The sharks did not scare him. They were part of the new world he had made for himself.

Gracie would not go back in the water with him after that. Half the fun of the island was taken away from her.

'Come on,' he murmured gently. 'Come and see these baby seagulls I found.' He took hold of her hand again and smiled down at her. 'You should come with me and explore a bit. I dunno why ya lie around on the beach all day. I'm the one 'oo needs a suntan, ay.'

But even with his smile the warmth appeared to be missing.

All weekend Davy's mind had been in angry debate. He told himself that nothing mattered and everything would be like it had once been. He told himself he loved this girl. But he knew he was telling himself lies. He had seen the looks on his friends' faces and heard their muttered remarks when she showed up. He had made it in this city. He had realised his dreams. He did not want anything to spoil that.

Wasn't she one of his dreams also?

Red lips brushed against black as he breathed, 'I love you, Gracie Fields.'

But it was more to reassure himself than to express a true adoration. How strange it was. This island with its circling flocks of seagulls so free against the summer sky and its hordes of deadly tiger snakes so hated upon the mainland, yet free and safe here in the sand dunes of the island. Davy Higgins and Gracie Fields were free here too. Yet, really, they were more like the fluffy brown chicks that came cheeping out of the broken green eggshells only to be eaten by a swift sure snake.

And when Ogier the Dane was born, so the story of his mother went, all the fairies had gathered at his bed. For was he not the son of a King? Among the fairies was Morgan Le Fey, the half-sister of another King – King Arthur – and a famous figure in the ethereal world of Fairyland. She was the mother of Oberon, the King of the Fairies who, when he died, had been transported by a band of Angels to Paradise. But it was Morgan Le Fey who fell in love with the brave and fierce warrior Dane and she brought him to Avalon, her home, when he was over a hundred years old, restored him to his youth, and they lived in love for over two hundred years on their magic island.

They walked around the island on the small path made by feet from long ago. The only vegetation was small tough bushes and long thin grass through which the wind whistled like a larrikin as it tousled their hair cheekily. The ever-angry voice of the ocean wafted up into the air a hundred feet to where the two crawled around the edge of the cliffs. They came to the seagull colony and laughed at the brown fluffy chicks squawking among the broken green shells, and hugged each other in simple joy, laughing at the baby seagulls' first impressions of life. Then they made their way back towards the beach.

They came to a cave and Davy told Gracie to go on while he answered a call of Nature. When he came out he stood in the shade awhile and watched Gracie's dark form, distorted by the heat. Against the white of the sand she stood out sharply black as she talked to the sea lion. Her tinkling laughter drifted up to him faintly. She, of course, had never seen a sea lion before and the fat old creature both amused and amazed her.

The island was all at once menacing in its silence. The heat was suddenly oppressive and the girl seemed far, far away. Davy suddenly wished she was; he knew now he couldn't keep this affair up. There were no fairies and magnificent kings and misty places of magic. Not for him and Gracie. There was only a black girl who really didn't want much from life and a white boy who was ambitious and eager for new adventures.

Davy rolled a smoke while he collected his thoughts. He told himself it wasn't so much him that he was worried about but sensitive shy Gracie who would be torn apart by his newfound friends. The catty remarks and curious looks and unintentional snubs would upset her too much. And, even though she was a fighter, a person can't fight forever without becoming worn down. Most of all, she would miss the Valley and her family and the small town that waited with open, dusty arms. For this was the only place where her magic lay and all her kings, spirits and brave heroes drifted like fog to cloud out the reality of life to her.

He told himself all this but he couldn't entirely tell himself it was true. He had an image of Gracie at one of the Club Cricket matches and the sly remarks that could be made in the changing room after the match. He had an image of Gracie in his favourite restaurant and saw the glances of other patrons and the maitre d'. It would go right over her head, he knew. But he would see and hear and feel it and it would drag him back into the life he had left behind with all its violence and pettiness and shattered dreams.

He set off down the length of the beach and finally came up to where she and the sea lion cavorted in the shallows. She thought, quite correctly, that sharks would keep away from her with her big, scarred brown friend nearby.

He gazed out over the glassy blue water of the protected bay to the rougher sea beyond the teeth of the reef. The only sounds were incessant gulls and the little black radio they had brought with them. Gracie noticed he was quiet and called out to him, to bring him into the fun of things, at the wriggling clumsy movements of the sea lion.

'Hey Davy! Look at this fella. 'E's funny, orright, unna?'

'Yeah,' he murmured.

His voice was as far away as the mainland and devoid of the humour he usually reserved just for her. It was flat and as dead as his soul for he realised he must tell Gracie their time together must end. How did you tell a bird she must no longer fly?

'Gracie,' he muttered and turned his head away.

She came out of the water and ran up the sand toward him, laughing. She towelled herself off as she hummed along to the song on the radio then lay down beside him. She touched him softly with one of her kind hands that had never hurt a living thing. His nostrils drew in the earthy scent of her. It was as though she were a wild thing and smelt of the trees, the earth, the very history of this beautiful though dangerous land.

'Gracie?' he said, almost as though she wasn't there and he was making sure.

She turned her smiling eyes to him but they faded a little when they saw his troubled, taut face.

'Wassa matter, Davy doll? That crayfish give ya the shits or what?'

The boy paused as though he were about to jump into that boiling cauldron he loved so much, with the three thin sharks as his companions. Then his hazel eyes stared straight into her black ones.

'We won't be seein' each other after this, Gracie. I'm leavin' ya. I want to work in the city and I'll never go back to that town, see! We wasn't made for each other, Gracie, an' we'd only be miserable, I reckon. So it's best if we split, ay!'

The girl's fluttering butterflies of eyes became still and a deep pained expression came into them. Davy was reminded of Lyle's horses back home when Lyle was sometimes cruel to them for no reason, when they trusted him. He tried to avoid Gracie's eyes but they bored right into his soul. Then her sad bewildered voice broke through the barriers he had set up.

'Davy? What ya sayin', Davy? We was made for lovers. I don't want no-one but you.'

'It would be easier if you just believed what I said. It wouldn't work. We can't stay together,' he said abruptly.

He went to stand up but then he noticed her unshed tears in her shy unhappy eyes.

'Hey,' he crooned. 'Don't cry, honey. You'll find someone else.'

He stretched out a hand to comfort her but she broke away, pushing him from her. She was ugly in her anger as her eyes flashed and her hands balled into knobbly fists.

'That's it! Ya got another yorga up 'ere, in Perth, ya fuckin' ole baandji man! I'll scratch 'er fuckin eyes out, the white bitch! Or is she one of the dings we seen at the pub, ay? You took me to see ya latest girlfriend, ay?' She screeched like one of the gulls and her eyes shone like a snake's, hard and black.

162

'No, there's no-one like that. I just –' he began, concerned at her uncharacteristic anger.

She hit him hard in the face so he fell over with a muffled cry. Then she was on him, punching and scratching. It took all his strength to hold her off. Even so, she bloodied his nose and blackened his eye as she swept over him in a fury.

Then she rolled off him and ran away up the beach to fall down in the sand, a black dejected heap.

It was no use talking to her now, he thought ruefully as he felt his bruises. She was too upset. But, he sensed sadly, they would not even remain friends now. She would drift out of his life as she had drifted into it, like a piece of wood carried by the ocean's whim or a swirling current in the old brown river down home. Over the radio came a low droning voice:

You have taken the best of me
So come take the rest of me
Look back, finish what … you begun

The orange sun sank lower beneath the sea and grey shadows crept out from the dunes to lie upon the ruffled sand. The sea turned a deep orange itself while the sky became purple. The rocks took on an orange hue and the island was red – like the giant dingo Gracie had told him about once. The crash of the waves became the dingo's muffled roar as the island turned from a safe place of friendship and love into a hateful, horrible place devouring hearts and the sweet essence of love.

It had started out a free and happy weekend but now it must end in bitterness and loneliness. They must leave their Avalon and go back to the mainland of reality. Back to that smouldering city, hiding behind the dark clouds of pollution and peopled by prejudice. There was no angel with flaming sword to drive them out. There were no fairies to see them off. Only circling seagulls ... shadows in the dying sun's rays. No, there were only the dying embers of the sun, and the dying embers of their own emotions had overpowered and blackened the contentment of these past few days. For these two young lovers, naked and vulnerable in their Garden of Eden, the world's attitudes seemed as hard and fresh as apples.

Davy moved towards the huddled heap. He knelt down beside her and put an arm around her naked shoulder. This time Gracie didn't shake it off but she would not look at him.

'Better get the boat out before it gets too dark, Gracie. Don't want to crash on the reefs. Giovanni'd 'ave a fit, I bet.' He paused for a moment, staring at her. The shadows of the island covered her protectively. 'I'm sorry things turned out this way, baby. It's just the way of the world – the spin of the pennies, ya know.' He patted her unresponsive shoulder. 'Don't think I'm not 'urtin' too, girl,' he said softly, surrendering his heart.

She would not answer him, so after a moment he took his hand away and moved off to their campsite. He loaded their few possessions into the gently bobbing boat then took Gracie's dress over to her. He himself had pulled on a pair of tattered blue Levis – city clothes.

'Bought you an apple, Gracie – for the return journey, like. And ya dress.'

She accepted them with mute agony and put the dress over her naked body.

'We'll, be off, what ya reckon?'

She stayed silent and walked away from him across the sand on her splayed feet – Aboriginal feet.

He stared down at the tracks in the wet sand and then followed her dark wraith-like figure.

The engine of the small launch chugged and coughed to life. It nudged its way out to sea, past the reefs and onwards to the mainland.

They were two spirits returning home, bearing with them gifts both wished they had not been given. They stayed as wordless as ghosts while the spray of misery from the sea of lost love wet them through and chilled them. It swept around them like fairies taunting and mocking those who believed only in the good of their kind. There were bad fairies too who enjoyed malicious jokes and cruel tricks.

Behind them the island sank lower into the blackness until, for them, it disappeared – their brief life of joy, contentment, happiness faded, and they were alone on the buffeting sea.

The Lilies of the Valley

There was no use denying it. He was in love with her. Every part of her. Her long straight black hair falling down past her perfect, rounded bottom, catching flashes of purple in its twisting tresses whenever she went out in the sun. Her hands, small and delicate. Her long, supple fingers. Her olive arms covered with fine hairs that were golden in the light, making her glow even more than she did in his eyes. Her copper-skinned face, heart-shaped, and her large sultry reddish mouth and her liquid eyes that were black and green shining behind the black. Liquorice. And there was something behind the green as well, some demon lurking, maybe, with all its miseries. They were disturbing eyes but they swam in the most perfect white.

And she craved him. She put her whole soul into making him happy, and her. When she lay there afterwards, naked and gentle on the crumpled bed, he could look at her smooth brownness and her small wonderful breasts and her thighs, all tangled in sleepiness, and he'd know without a lie that he was in love with her. And she was in love with him.

Sometimes, she'd sing to him too, a song she'd learned from when she was a kid, that she'd never forgotten: 'Let him kiss me with the kisses of his mouth,' she'd sing, 'for thy love is better than wine', or, 'thy name is an ointment poured forth, therefore do the virgins love thee ...'

Have you ever loved a woman? I love a woman whose skin is as rare as old ivory, all yellow-brown and smooth. Her teeth are as white as the beaches of my home.

'I am black,' she'd sing, 'but comely ...' And she'd tease him, 'look not upon me, because I am black.'

Love came hard for the young man. He was a semi-orphan, from the bush, and he would not easily allow anyone close to him. His beloved brother had got into his heart. But then he died. He would not allow that to happen again.

My brother! Did you know my brother? I loved my brother as much as I love this woman. Sometimes he'd disappear for weeks at a time, but he was always in my mind and in my heart. He had golden-brown eyes, like the tops of barren hills when the sun kisses them and turns them into life in the early morning. And brown ringlets falling about his lean smiling brown face. A brown man, my brother was.

The young man, whose name was Lyndall Stones, was as dark as the girl, with secretive eyes and curly black hair that went blue in the sun. He was not without charm himself, average height, more skinny than slim, thin wiry arms, long legs and no bum whatsoever.

'Great legs Lyndall's got, ya know girls, until they get up and turn into his body which is really bad news,' his mate Sharkey used to joke.

'To say nothin' about 'is face,' and that would be Sharkey's brother Rags, whose humour could be cynical, to say the least, and cruel at worst.

The last remnants of his grandmother's race were there in Lyndall's face. His nose was broad and flat and his lips full, and it was there in his dreamy eyes, all dark and mysterious behind long lashes. They spoke of his ancestors who had walked this land forever. Now his uncertain feet were treading the same forgotten paths. They'd watched the first white men sail into the huge natural harbour and raise the foreign flag upon their wild soil, off Albany, Frederickstown then. They learned to survive the white man's new world. Well, Lyndall was surviving too, as best he could, here in the city where he'd come to find his older brother, the last one left for him.

She was one of the Hot and Steamy Raunchy Girls, that came and danced in the pub he frequented every Thursday, and that's how he met her. But goddesses are carved from rock or wood and even they can become cracked in the making.

She has costumes that mostly consist of nothing at all. I watch her from the back of the room, the lights shining on her sweating

body and her limbs twisting and wriggling in a dance just for
me. Oh, yes, she's watching me too and I know that one day
she'll talk to me and then what will I do? I know nothing about
womanly things and am shy of all things womanly. There
only ever was my much loved brother and me. No mother, no
sisters ... and if my brother had a girlfriend, I never saw her.

Sometimes she was a High Priestess. The pool table was her altar where she spun for all the shouting, jostling, drunken blokes. Sometimes she was a leopard, and her eyes would shine with a leopard's fierce pride as she performed her set for the men who stood around and smirked and chuckled into their beer or made comments as she moved in front of them. But they never touched her as they did the other girls. Her eyes warned them to leave her alone.

It's true, he was an incurable romantic, and he'd become embarrassed at the lewd display. Among his mates he was even considered to be a virgin at the old age of twenty-four. And there were jokes about that and his time in jail and what he'd learned there. Some of the dancers would exploit his awkwardness and get a good laugh from the crowd. They'd dance around him, all erotic, and he'd become flustered. Sober, he'd try to merge with the shadows of the filthy old wall behind him or want to sink through the cracked green-tile floor. But a little drunk, he'd get into the sport of it and put on a little show with them. He was a gentle youth and anyway, it was all just acting – the meaningful looks, the languid eyes, the pouting mouths, the bumping grind of pelvis and hip against a customer. And his people had been actors for generations. It was how families had kept each other entertained, before the white man came.

Yveline saw his shyness and it seemed she was taken by it, older than him as she was. Perhaps it was just that she was dark of skin too, in this rowdy pub of white people. Although her skin came from the island of Malta where she'd been born. By and by, she made his acquaintance. For he was there every Thursday with his pals, and almost every other day. The Newbury Hotel stood on the corner of the street, like a beacon for the people living in the crowded Homeswest flats or in the old houses around. People were at ease there; it was their hotel. If there was nothing on the telly, or the missus was kicking up, or the boyfriend was too drunk and obnoxious at home, there would always be that big, friendly room with the pool tables, the jukebox and your mates. He needed this place. He could fade away in here if he was in a quiet mood, or he could talk to one of his pals. A lot of people would be lost without the shadow of the Newbury Hotel to nestle into.

I kissed her tonight, as we were leaving and the pub was as empty and lonely as could be. The laughter of my mates echoed down the corridors of time and swirled around me, dragging me out the front with them and away from her. But her arms, as slender as reeds by a river, pulled me to her and her mouth was as cool and refreshing as that river, yet as hot as the sandbank upon which

the reeds lie. I heard a sound of wind among the paperbark trees.
But it was her murmurs. I smelled the fragrance of the paperbark
trees. But it was her perfume. Her eyes devoured me like the
night and all the dreams of the night came true. I was only a
star, small and pale, cold and infinitely alone in the magnitude
of her gaze.

Later she sang and he understood. 'I am the rose of
Sharon,' she sang, 'and the lily of the valley ...' He kissed
her, and she assured him with her song '... as the lily
among thorns, so is my love among the daughters,' and
he knew he'd found a rare flower, the most gorgeous one
that grew upon his nation's land.

Lyndall was a cat burglar, the best, and even his short
criminal record spoke of this. He loved it, the thrill and
adventure, his wits against the alarms and the police. At
night, when the moon would be hidden behind unruly
clouds, he'd don soft sandshoes and dress himself black,
he'd pack his bag with tools and he'd head off to work.
He'd spend days studying the building he was claiming.
He'd check out alarms, he'd watch the security, if any,
coming and going. Then he'd know, in some way or
other, when he was ready and he'd sneak out, sliding into
the world he wished to own with his agile, silent fingers.

This was his only profession, and he'd practised it
since he was twelve, when he'd come to town. With his
brother, at first, and now on his own. His brother had

taught him well. So he'd been caught only three times: three months, six months and the last one, two years ago, fifteen months because he had a name now and the judge reckoned he was in with the big time. Besides, he hadn't turned in any mates. Rocky and Lyndall never would, though many policemen had tried to make them. So he was known around as a good sort, even a hero to many less daring than he. It did hurt him, that last sentence, but he had had some money hidden away for just such a time.

Then Yveline came into his life. He was reticent about his lifestyle at first, but as her strange liquorice eyes ate into him and her voice too, he opened up to her and let out secrets like rare and wonderful floating butterflies, all for her. He was emptied then. She knew everything about him, even the loss of his brother. Her whispered words wakened a sadness inside Lyndall Stones. She might have been Pandora but he had given her the key. Besides, she loved him and kept him from the harm of this world that had killed so many ancestors and kin with promises that turned to lies. The whole pub could tell she loved him just by her warmth, the way she looked at him. So, because he was special and because everyone felt that there was something special about her, even if they couldn't put a finger on it, she was welcomed into Lyndall's company, every one of them a ship passing in the night, some soon to die or soon to go to jail, others just drifting, but every one of them carrying some precious cargo and for all of them, the pub was like a harbour for their souls.

Yveline gave up her job as a dancer with the Girls and became a barmaid at her lover's hotel and a very popular one too, good humoured as she was, however set apart from them all. It was this that fascinated them, and Lyndall too. He gave up his career and spent what money he had to set them up in a flat nearby with a small garden, a dartboard, a full fridge and a video. Their friends were always welcome there.

He had never had a woman before and he had a lot to learn. But his real mates were there to look after him. Like Sharkey who almost had a fight with Rags, about Rags's joking. 'He might as well learn from a beauty, more than one 'oo looks like a camel's arse. Though, come to think of it, that would make 'im more comfortable. He could stick 'is black dick in 'er mouth and think 'e was back in the desert again.'

The Collins boys, Sharkey and Rags, were as much a part of the pub as Lyndall. They had long Irish noses and blue Irish eyes and red in their shaggy hair. There was an older brother, Big Steve. Not Little Steve or Paddington Steve who drank at The Paddington Arms and only came over looking for a fight or to muscle into the drug scene. Big Steve was in jail for armed robbery for fifteen years. Rocky had known him, way back. He was a hero in the Newbury too, the only armed robber the hotel had, so his two brothers basked in his glory. Sharkey, as in 'Pool-shark', was himself a gun pool player, a gangly, amiable sort of chap and his slow ways and the huge grin plastered all over his face often fooled newcomers who ended up

173

parting with fifty or a hundred dollars at the end of the night. He never lost, no matter how drunk he was. He had some type of magic and nine times out of ten he'd sink the black for a win. He was Lyndall's age. If either of them had a best mate the other was it, and they'd spend hours drinking a slow jug of beer or two, or sharing a joint and spinning yarns about pool feats or tricky burglaries. They looked out for each other, always had, since the early days. Rags didn't do anything much except maybe supply a few illicit pills now and then to the hungry. That was what brought him into strife with Paddington Steve, but there was nothing Rags liked more than a fight.

'Bloody Rags is a psychopath,' Sharkey would warn Lyndall. 'I reckon Mum must of dropped 'im on 'is head when 'e was a baby and scrambled what brains he ever 'ad. Wouldn't of been hard to do. The number of gins she had, she could of started up 'er own tribe,' he'd joke, and then he'd remember Lyndall's lineage and apologise.

One dark and gloomy day in winter, when Lyndall was wrapped up with olive-skinned Yveline, with the rain drumming, and they were whispering to each about their future, Yveline breathed gently into his ear and ran light fingers up his jaw.

'Honey?' she murmured. 'Do you remember that dress we saw the other day in town, with all the sequins and all?'

'It cost a bit if I remember.'

'But you could get it for me, ay? You could go on a bit of a trip and get the money. It's Maureen's wedding

174

next month, see, and I know I'd look just gorgeous in it. Purple's my colour, ay!'

'I dunno,' he grinned, teasing her as she liked to tease him, 'what with the recession and all, and all the businesses goin' bust and all the millionaires goin' to jail, an honest thief could starve to death.'

These are the times I love best. The rain in torrents with a wild song from the skies and the trees buffeted by a cold wind. When all the buildings in this great city stand drenched and glum and pouring tears onto oily pavements. I feel like a true king of my country. I can identify with this rain, I adore it. I'll be dead and my son's sons will hear its wrath. It was here for my grandmother's people sheltering in their bark and grass tree mia-mias and it told them the same stories it tells me. And they must have held onto a warm woman or man and told dreams like I tell mine.

He knew that he could lie in this bed the richest man in the whole city. Compared to the warm woman beside him, her apple-like breasts rising and falling, pressed into his shoulder, they could keep their millions and their objets d'art and famous paintings, racehorses and luxury cars. He lay there savouring the faint perfumes of her body that left just the hint of the adventures they had had that day.

'I know a place might accommodate your desires,' he grinned at her again. He loved using big words. It was another splash of ochre painted onto his man's body, for his initiation into this strange new world the Europeans had caused to be born. 'I'll need someone to help me, but.'

And there is a story among my people that tells of a giant warrior who ran off with a beautiful woman called Kay-tan. When members of her family caught up with them, they slew him in a great fight, then scattered his body all over the area. That is why all around Katanning, Kart *meaning head in the old language, there are names describing feet, intestines, eyes, ears and the nose. That's how close the land is to us. Ewlyamart Lake, Martinup, Martling,* Mart *being a leg, Twonkwillingup Pond from* Twonk, *an ear, Moulyerup from* Mouly, *a nose,* Miel, *an eye, becoming Mielyup, Chanchanup from* Jenna, *feet. The Coblinine River was his entrails. This is the language of the first people and I could say in my language,* Yveline mardong yorga. *I could sing to her the songs of my land, the cries of parrots and smokebirds flitting through the trees that shelter my land, the rumble of the sea on the lonely white beaches that fringe my land, and how no man could ever be alone as long as he had the earth to sleep on. To lie upon her warm breast and hear the breathing of centuries like the sighing of mountains. Have you ever heard a mountain sigh? That is something no history book could ever teach you. I love my woman like I love my land. Both are real to me and indestructible. The legends of my land are shadows in her eyes.*

On the wall, his brother's eyes stared down at him from out of a photo. Once the two of them would have gone off to get the money for this dress, over a thousand dollars. Rocky would have loved this girl just as much as he did and they would have gone off and done this house that he had been keeping for a special occasion, even though it was out of his territory. Lyndall and Yveline rolled together in a relaxed, rocking love dance. 'Behold thou art fair, my love ...' she hummed.

The following afternoon, Elvis Presley was warbling from the jukebox about being lonesome, over the mind-lulling clack of pool balls. As Sharkey and Lyndall watched the games and listened to their favourite music, Rags wandered in and plonked himself down at the rickety, beer-stained table.

'So I hear ya goin' out on a break soon, Lyndall,' he said. 'Bring any stuff ya get to me and I'll give you a good price, 'specially videos and silver,' he sniffed.

'Who told ya that?' Lyndall wanted to know.

'Ya missus, of course. Don't worry, cock. It's all in the family, ay? Take young Sharkey along as ya offsider.'

'I work alone, Rags, you know that.' Lyndall growled because there was no love lost between these two.

'But not on this job. Ya need a mate. Ya missus told me.'

'What else did she tell ya, Rags?'

'She told me 'ow beautiful I was and 'ow we'd piss off to Bali just as soon as you get us all the money.'

Lyndall should have laughed. Rags in Bali would have been like a penguin in the Sahara. But the thin red-head had a lot of slyness. Perhaps he was trying to win over Yveline. He did spend a lot of time talking to her.

'Yeah, Rags? Funny that. 'Cos the other day she told me you was a brain-dead fuckwit!' Lyndall smiled up at him.

Rags's grin was sly and crooked and sparks shone in his blue eyes.

'You walk around in a dreamworld, Lyndall, you know that? You really do think you're better than us, ya big-shot, big-time crim. Not up to ya standards, ay?' He blew a raspberry. 'I'll bet you get caught again, ya useless black bastard. Me, I never been near to bein' caught, ever!'

He would have gone on and there would have been a fight which is what Rags wanted, to show him up in front of his woman. But Sharkey spoke up.

'What are ya, Rags, my manager? I can ask 'im myself if I wanna go. Bugger off.'

'Sorry I breathed. I'll just go away and die somewhere, then,' Rags snarled and he staggered to his feet. 'Ya little wuss!' he said to Lyndall who ignored him, a dreamy smile on his lips. 'My brother's doin' time for armed robbery, not your little pissy breaks.' He pointed a finger at Lyndall's chest. 'And what about your brother, ay?'

Lyndall's smile slipped from his face and his dark eyes went as cold as a river, full of hidden, dangerous currents.

'What do you know about my brother, Rags?'

Even Rags could tell when he'd said too much so he turned away without a word and zigzagged his way over to the other corner.

'Hey, bud, let it rest. Rags is only stoned out of 'is

cakehole,' came Sharkey's voice, from afar it seemed to Lyndall.

If I was the sun, then my brother, he was the moon and together we made day and night. Days and nights make weeks and weeks years and life, life, life. Except he's dead and he did not have to die. He would sail through life like the moon through the sky and that's how long life is, he'd say. Just one night long. Then a new day and the next night, another moon, and the old one just forgotten. A moon, that's what my brother was.

And Sharkey droned on, dragging his mate back from the bad thoughts. 'Hey listen, ya hear about all the Catholics at Mass, now. And this was a day when Naomi Campbell, Elle Macpherson and all these models was in town. Well, old Father Pat was goin' on about how if you was good you'd go to 'eaven when this lad up and starts out the door. Well, the Father calls out, where ya going? Don't you want to go to 'eaven, and the lad says, you stay here and be good and go to 'eaven if ya like, I'm going to be real bad and go to Elle.'

The freckled face was already brightening into a famous Sharkey laugh. And then the pair of them burst out laughing, cracking open the thin layer of memories Lyndall had been wrapping around himself like a pauper will wrap a thin, holey, old blanket around him to keep out the cold. They threw arms around each other's shoulders and laughed and laughed. Afterwards, as they sat gasping for breath and rubbing tears away, Lyndall

179

leaned across and muttered out of the side of his mouth, 'You can come on this job with me if ya want,' and then he put on his Jimmy Cagney accent: 'This could be the start of a beautiful thing, Dutch.'

'You killed my brother, ya doity rat. I'll get you yet,' Sharkey answered and his impersonation was so bad it started the two off laughing again.

The next night found them a long way from home. This suburb was full of large, gloomy old houses set in shadowy gardens of leafy trees and foreign bushes. The descendants of the people who had killed or dispersed Lyndall's people with guns and disease lived here. They'd shackled Sharkey's great-grandfather like a mad dog and sent him over for fifteen years for stealing a sheep to feed his family. There were no friends here. They sailed a rough sea, these two pirates, and the wind in the leaves of the English trees was like the sound of angry waves. The stars shone down, too small and hidden to remind Lyndall of the stories of his heroes and heroines, the creators of the old world. The moon skulked from cloud to wispy cloud, yellow like old ivory, and clouds as purple as the dress he'd soon be buying his woman. And the moon shone down with the face of his brother.

Lyndall's eyes grew sharper and his hearing too, but to Sharkey it was all new so he shook like a captured young colt, though he was grinning with excitement. Lyndall caught it too as they slid down the street, black as the night, their place of concealment, their comrade. It was quiet at three o'clock in the morning.

'This place is as dead as old Lang 'ancock,' whispered Sharkey.

'Let's 'ope we find some of 'is millions he's salted away, then.'

With a quick glance left and right, sturdier Lyndall hoisted Sharkey over the high sandstone wall. A soft clink and a muffled thud and his bag of tricks followed. A car drifted by and he pretended he was lighting a cigarette. Then, quick as a thought, he vaulted over the wall. Now there was only them and all the house had to offer. It didn't matter to Lyndall that the people of the house might still be home. These were arrogant people, softened by their wealth and their power and their belief in their invulnerability. It only made it more exciting that he and Sharkey would be flitting from room to room as the owner, an old man, slept in a warm, soft bed. Often his cunning fingers had lifted trinkets while the owner snored right next to him.

He had been checking up on this house for two years now, working as a gardener for the yacht club, weeding out information. He knew about a wall safe behind the picture of the owner's yacht and he knew that the little window in the ornate tower, so high up and smaller than average, wasn't covered with bars or alarms. The plan was simple. They'd scale the drainpipe and slip in through the window. If things worked out, Lyndall would tear out the golden heart of the house. Sharkey would descend, by rope this time, and hold it while Lyndall lowered the loot. With one on each end of the rope there was little chance of creating any noise. They'd take the loot to the side of the wall, one would get the car, already hidden, and they'd be off like rotten pork. Lyndall was proud that his mate was there to observe his skill.

'Up we go. Make sure your fingers have always got something to grip on before ya pull yaself up,' he warned.

'As the prostitute said to the bishop,' muttered Sharkey, giggling as he started up the drainpipe. Up and up they went, up two storeys, and then the tower.

'Hot work, ay,' wheezed Sharkey.

'As the bishop said to the prostitute,' puffed Lyndall.

'Shit, Mum, you can see our castle from 'ere,' Sharkey gasped a little later, near the top, and he turned a grinning face to Lyndall as he reached up to grab the guttering. 'Where's bloody Tarzan when you need 'im, ay?' he said.

And then there was a horrible, ripping tear and he was gone. But he was no falling star, him and half the rotten, rusted guttering spiralling out into the dark. There was no beauty, only a cry from Lyndall and a wet thump as his mate hit the ground. Not a sound from that doomed throat. Even in death Sharkey looked after his best mate.

Lyndall shimmied down the drainpipe, flashing down in careless haste, not caring about the blood on his hands. He took a few tentative steps towards the huddle on the ground. He thought he heard a low moan but it was only the wind in the trees on the lawn. At once the night was no longer his friend and he ran.

He ran and he thought about his brother then, his

brother dead not so many years ago in an accident like this, some god's game, a twisting Commodore straight into a lightpole, cut almost in half and Rocky tossed through a windscreen and flung into a tree, hanging there and swinging slowly like a man hanged. Who was the Judas who'd turned his brother in so the police were waiting for him, to chase him to his death? And now his only other best mate lay mangled behind him and he really was alone in the world and so he ran.

No-one saw Lyndall for a week after that. He stayed at home in bed, heartbroken. Yveline tried comforting him but even his love for her had dimmed. Still she was there. When he did come into the pub he wasn't the same; everyone had heard and kept away from him. They'd all had a week of Rags drunk and dangerous and they didn't want to upset Lyndall too. So he sat in a corner by himself, playing pool and the Elvis songs over and over. He bought a middy for Sharkey, the way he always had, and it sat there as alone as he was, going flat. About eight o'clock that night, with him well on the way to mindlessness, Rags fell through the door, his own eyes red-rimmed from drink and dope and unaccustomed tears. He went straight up to Lyndall's table and stood there swaying and glaring down at him.

'How come ya never even came to Sharkey's funeral, ya fuckin' murderer!' cried Rags. 'Some mate, ya nigger's arsehole!'

'Leave him alone, Rags!' Yveline called out from across the bar, where she'd been watching her boyfriend all afternoon with worried eyes. But Rags just bent down and picked up the glass of flat beer.

'So, ya bought old Sharkey a goodbye drink, did ya?' he shouted. 'Well, he don't wanna drink with you!' He threw the contents into Lyndall's face. 'Get up and fight, ya murderin' bastard!'

He picked up a chair and swung it at Lyndall's head. The thin, dark youth ducked, so it only caught him a glancing blow and he dived at Rags.

'You never loved 'im, anyways. Ya own brother,' snarled Lyndall, and Yveline screamed and the manager ran for the phone. The two rolled on the floor, kicking and punching.

The two hands that tore them apart were very strong. Detective-Sergeant Crosslie, one of the sharks that glided around their pirate harbour.

'My, oh, my,' he rumbled, 'it's entertaining to watch thieves fall out. So, tell me some news. Done any breaks lately, Lyndall? Been snorting some of your own shit, have ya, Rags?' He'd been waiting for some sort of blow-up, a test of his suspicions. But he wanted proof as well.

'Bad luck about old Sharkey, ay, Lyndall?' and then he stared at Rags, ''Course he might of lived, if he'd been found sooner ...'

Rags's face went white. Crosslie was gratified. 'Take him away and charge him with drunk and disorderly,' he ordered the two policemen behind him.

'Ya didn't 'ave to tell Rags that,' Lyndall whispered, when they were alone.

'Why don't you tell me, Lyndall, why a job with all your hallmarks on it should end up with your best mate's body at the scene?'

'I wouldn't 'ave a clue. I was with my woman that night.'

The huge man leaned closer and breathed into Lyndall's ear. 'I hope you were, old son, because I'm on to you. Your race is done, me old mate. You and your brother both got on my pip. Now there's one less of you bastards around to give me a hard time,' he hissed and then he turned and walked out the door.

Lyndall's path to the bar was shaky. He propped there and looked up at Yveline behind it. She wasn't any Goddess or Queen from Exotic Isles. She was just an ordinary woman and she was caught up in a life that no-one would want to be in now.

Things became miserable for the two of them. Detective-Sergeant Crosslie was going to break Lyndall's silence. Lyndall couldn't even go down the street for a loaf of bread without being stopped and questioned or taken away for a session at the police station that stood like a castle on the corner of the busy highway. Any breaks that happened and the police would be right around to his flat. And every time they made some mention of Sharkey's death.

'It's just as well the silly bugger did die. He'd only of ended up getting his bum burgled in jail. Still, you can accommodate all the nice men when we get you there instead. Some of those blokes like a bit of dark meat with their gravy.'

The Detective-Sergeant and Lyndall were old sparring partners, had been since the boy first got into trouble, and Lyndall could have survived if they'd left Yveline alone. They'd come straight into the flat and throw the furniture around and they'd break small things that she treasured. They strip-searched her, twice, for drugs, and they'd raid the flat when they knew the two of them would be in bed. So even the love that was left was battered in the hurricane stirred up by Detective-Sergeant Crosslie, and all their affection was sent spiralling away. There was nothing he could do for her; he was a boat that had slipped its anchor. He was drifting onto rocks, even in the harbour he knew, and she began to close even more of her soul.

But it was Yveline who suggested the way out. They'd just been raided again. It was four in the morning, and they lay on their upheaved bed with their things scattered all around them. He held her hand tightly, because she had been shaken by the menace of these men and women who blew in like the wind. She was staring up at the cracked old ceiling, her black eyes dull, no green gleam.

'It's time we got out, honey,' she whispered. 'Go to Sydney, where none of this shit's goin' down.'

'Leave here? Me mates?'

'Mates! Everyone's too scared of gettin' busted to visit

here any more. And the pub … you know you aren't welcome there, with Rags and all. You got no mates!'

She rolls onto her side and looks into my eyes. Her eyes … something in them tells men to keep away.

And Yveline hummed, perhaps only to herself this time though maybe to him, if he'd been listening, 'I sought him but I could not find him, I called him but he gave no answer …' For one moment only, Lyndall was frightened by her eyes, and then she spoke.

'I know a place just made for you, baby. Down by the wharfs. It's a shipping agent and you could get enough moolah to keep us in high society for a year and still leave plenty of change.'

'What do you know about shipping agents? It's way down in Fremantle, anyway, isn't it?' Lyndall was almost scornful that a woman, even one he loved, should know anything about his trade.

Yveline stroked his face with a finger. 'I was a dancer, remember, babes. I know all the pubs all over Perth. Thursday nights they bring in all the pay for Friday, see. They still pay cash. You go in on a Thursday you could end up with five, ten thousand dollars. Maybe more.'

Lyndall had never had that much cash in his life. Over ten thousand dollars? He'd be a millionaire!

'Down in Freo, Crosslie won't be there to annoy you. You've only ever done breaks up here, ay? He can't follow you everywhere, can he?'

'Last time I went out of my territory, look what happened,' he breathed, staring into her eyes.

'Honey, I can't take this any longer. Just look at this room. Do you want this to go on until they break you … or me, more likely. Or do you want to fuck off out of it, richer than all our dreams?' Yveline was very persuasive. 'I love you, baby.'

I smile at her. I am one of the best cat burglars in Perth. My brother has taught me all I know. After tomorrow night, I could be free of Perth and all the ghosts. I will take my beautiful woman to a new life in Sydney.

'I'll be busy tomorrow night. Better make up tonight for what I'll miss, ay.' In a burst of muffled giggles they buried themselves under the blankets and her scent buried Crosslie, Rags, Sharkey, even the quiet photo of his brother touched by one ray of the dying moon.

There was no moon at all next night, and it was cold, well into winter now. He would rather have been home in bed with Yveline but what was the point. They would just get raided. But tonight would put an end to all that. So, he hunched into a corner of the train that rocketed him to Fremantle, some fifteen kilometres away. He felt good about getting out of his neighbourhood, no, out of the whole of Perth.

He hadn't seen the ocean in a long time and he

peered through the windows at the white lines rolling in the inky black water. Then they shuddered across the old bridge and they were in the port city. Huge cargo ships lay at bay; rusting, creaking hulks. Sailors were everywhere, from all over the world. Seagulls wheeled, eerie and grey. The smell of the salt sea drowned the place and the wind that chilled the streets was an old wind from Africa.

He whiled away a bit of time in a noisy, renovated pub catering for a trendier set. The only sailors here were in photos on the wall. Beer cost twice as much as in the Newbury but, so what, he thought with a smirk. What was money after tonight? He'd come back and buy the pub. And so he dreamed while he sat in a corner, jostled by laughing career men and women who would have forgotten the thin, dark boy by tomorrow morning. The final bell went and the tail-end of a rowdy crowd staggered into the drizzling streets. They breathed wreaths of iced breath, pulled their jackets around them and went home to a fine house or a fashionable flat. Lyndall wandered, found a late feed of fish and chips, then made his way towards the cracked street where the shipping office waited, lit feebly by an occasional street light, smoothed by a fog creeping in from the sea on feet as quiet as Lyndall's. Better and better, he thought.

A cat ran squalling from one lane to another and he jumped over its path because it was black and he wanted no bad luck. Another lane gaped open like a drunk's mouth and garbage dribbled into the street. He sheltered there and he took in the situation. No-one ever came here at night, it seemed. Only the murmuring rain and the creak of corrugated iron flapping in the wind. Perfect, he thought.

And it was true, what Yveline said! The top storey window on the right was ajar. She'd said, no alarms on the top floor and the old Chubb's safe was a truly old safe. He'd be out of here in half an hour and on the last train home to Perth. He came to the back of the building. Now the hard part, the exciting one. He began scaling the side of the building – half-bat, half-cat himself, rising like an ancestral spirit. Sharkey he put out of his mind. He made it, up to the top of the steep, slippery roof and, as sure as a possum, he scrabbled over to the front of the building.

He hadn't brought his usual bag of tricks. Too risky carrying them around an unknown part of the city. But the screwdriver in his pocket was all he'd need, said Yveline. The safe was that decrepit, if it was locked at all. There'd never been a robbery here, after all. He used the screwdriver on the window that was complaining, stuck down only with the dirt of years. 'Open Sesame,' he whispered, squeezing through, just like Ali Baba, and this was the moment when he was as vulnerable as he was triumphant, teetering there, half-in, half-out the window. And just then it was that a spotlight down in the street burst into life from nowhere and caught his wriggling, black body in its white glare. And before he could move, lights flared in rooms down the hall and footsteps thudded towards him.

'He's in the last room!' someone shouted and then his mind came wide awake. In he went, grazing his back, and up against the cold, grey side of a filing cabinet, heart beating. It's not over till the fat copper farts, is what his brother used to say, and then he'd chuckle. The door was flung open and someone crowded in and the light snapped on. The certainty of the trap was what made them careless.

'Where'd the little boong bastard go?' the same voice cried, and Lyndall leapt from his unsafe place and, quick as a rat, was past the two coppers and into the long, empty hall.

Run, run, get to the bottom floor! Down on the ground and break a window at the back and get away as fast as I can! Let 'em prove I was in here, let 'em bash me if they want, I won't tell them a thing.

He ran and far outpaced the two heavy-set men. Spinning around a corner he flung a look behind him and slammed straight into Detective-Sergeant Crosslie.

'Hello, sweetheart,' the policeman boomed, 'would you care to have this dance with me?' and he laughed. Lyndall knew now he was doomed.

'Lost, Lyndall?' and Crosslie hustled Lyndall up the hall towards two panting policemen. 'Think this is your flat and you just forgot your key?'

'Holy Toledo, Robin. Is that Batman?'

'Looks like a bit of a Joker to me,' and the three of them laughed. It was always good to be in on a big arrest.

Crosslie searched Lyndall's pockets and raised a knowing eyebrow. 'Is this a screwdriver I see before me?' And then he smiled. 'Alas, poor Lyndall. I knew him well.'

Detective-Sergeant Crosslie was true to nothing if not his threats. A few sessions down the Station and even Lyndall had to slip up. It was a game they both played well, but Lyndall just didn't care any more.

Someone had dobbed him in. But not just someone, and he did not know why.

So he told Detective-Sergeant Crosslie everything and in the strange way of these things, the abrupt, gruff policeman became his confidant and only friend. After all, they'd known each other since one had been a mere constable and the other just a small, shy wraith of a child, knowing things about each other that no-one else would ever know.

But the judge and the jury weren't close to him at all and they gave him a total of eight years' jail on two counts of burglary with intent and on a manslaughter charge that was perhaps unfair.

The first visit he got was from Yveline. He wasn't angry to see her, just resigned, and she did bring memories, though memories in that dry hard place can be dangerous or send you mad. She spent a long time just watching him, just like when she was a dancer and they first met a long year ago.

'It was Rags, Lyndall. You have to believe me. He told me about the office and all, and I just so much wanted to get out of Perth.' And in a broken whisper, 'I love you.'

He started suddenly in surprise to see an unexpected tear squeezed from the green-black depths of her eyes, and he murmured, 'Don't cry, honey. Don't cry, beautiful woman.'

He was still not allowed contact visits so he couldn't reach out and touch her. He could only sit and watch and lace his fingers through the heavy wire netting. In the light of the visiting room her tear appeared as green as her eyes, as if her soul was melting and trickling down her olive cheek.

'I just wanted us to get away and start a new life. That's all,' she whispered, drying her eyes. 'We can still do that, Lyndall: you'll get parole and you can learn a proper trade and I'll wait for you, baby, I promise. I'm just so sorry all this happened.'

She put her hands against the wire netting and they tried to touch but not even their souls could get through.

Out in the yard, the pale sun warmed Lyndall. And, oh, he was hot enough inside! Hadn't she just said that she'd wait forever, that she hadn't turned him in? He would get a good job in here, possibly the wood shop, he'd learn cabinet-making. He'd learn reading and writing, and if he behaved, was a model prisoner, he'd get remissions. Even if he did do his eight years, he'd only be thirty-two. Just the right age to start a family. His eyes slid away into the dreamworld he needed so.

He was in love with a beautiful woman. And she was in love with him.

He was still dreaming when a hand tapped him on the shoulder. A grinning, gap-toothed face with merry eyes and a broken nose gazed down at him. The man had massive, prison-exercised shoulders.

'You Rocky Stones's brother? 'Cause you're alike as two peas and I picked ya out when ya come in lars week. But it only just twigged when I see ya with her. So you're 'ot for 'er dot now, are ya?'

'Do you know 'er, mate?' Lyndall's surprise showed.

'Know 'er, mate?' The big man gave a rusty cackle. 'Well, not as good as ya brother, I suppose. She was mad for 'im, and I can see why she likes you, you're the bloody same. Like seein' a ghost, it is. She was real cut up, but, when 'e took orf like that. She swore she'd fix 'is hoot, ya know.' Lyndall was rising to his feet but the other man seemed oblivious. 'But she never meant to kill him, I don't reckon. Only scare 'im, like. She didn't know 'e'd be flyin' from the cops next time he used the car.'

He babbled on. And then the tattooed man stopped and looked down at Lyndall, who had sunk to the bench again. He was a huge, friendly man.

Death didn't have such a special meaning in prison. Half the people here had killed someone and the other half lived a lingering death, confined behind these walls.

But Rocky had been his brother and to find all this out so … Lyndall groaned and went yellow from the pain.

'Hey listen, you don't worry about a thing while you're in 'ere, orright? I'm her step-brother, see. Yveline, isn't she? So we could of been step-brothers-in-law, ay?' and he roared with laughter as he rolled away on bandy legs. 'You and me got all the time we want in 'ere, bro-in-law,' he called over his shoulder, laughing again.

Lyndall couldn't move from the bench. The fire within was out, and his eyes burned into dead black coals. He was alone now, a small leaking boat. Once his ancestors had watched just such a boat limp into their harbour, the sun a spirit woman in the sky, and they'd wondered at the white ghosts and treated them like brothers. But it was the signal for the killing to begin.

She'd killed Rocky, then. True murder. Was that the story? Her own step-brother had just said. Was that it, to wipe out the entire Stones family, to soothe her broken heart. Or what? Was that the story? Why would she? What was the tattooed man saying? It was the only explanation. Sure.

Lyndall was as destroyed as though it were the last battle on earth and there was no earth left any more. No more of his people's land. Gone. She'd killed his brother, ay, and now she'd killed him. That's what the grinning, tattooed man told him, whether he knew it or not. That's all it could mean. Don't trust her, Sharkey would have said. Trust us. Family. A brotherhood of mates. And now he was destroyed as though he was that ancestor who had first seen the beautiful ship come in. Forget 'er, Rocky might have warned him, never trust them, and it was like the old, old story. When Eve was driven from the Garden by Gabriel and his flaming sword, she'd wept tears of repentance and as each one touched the earth, a lily grew whose flower was as pale and beautiful as the crying woman whom he once loved, a lily as white as death, it seemed to Lyndall.

And all this time, over in a corner of the yard where the walls join and shadows whisper in conversation, a silent shadow moved. The tattooed man, the big prisoner. He'd been biding his time for a week and here, especially, friendship was the easiest thing to pretend. He'd weakened his enemy, he was alone now in the presence of his enemy and he made a quick animal decision. As huge as a bear, his eyes as angry as a hungry lion's, as soft as a leopard in his approach, he crept forward. Big Steve Collins moved towards Lyndall whom he'd destroyed with a story that the boy could just as well have invented in his own mind. Big Steve, who loved his brother Sharkey like no other, crept towards the grief-numbed Lyndall with murder on his mind and a shiv in one hairy paw.

Chains around My Heart

They call her Froggy. No-one knows why except perhaps it's because of her grandfather, old Bullfrog Jinnall, and the name was passed down from grandfather to grand-daughter.

She looks a bit like old Bullfrog too, with her bright black eyes and wide mouth, with her long skinny black legs and her ears that stick way out from the side of her head. But unlike her grandfather – who was a tall, stolid, quiet man – she is small and yappy, always talking about something or other. Always cheerful and full of fun she is.

Froggy is not terribly bright and left school at fourteen to go and work in a fast food chain. Even when she was at school she had always been the one up the back, giggling over one of her girlfriends' stories and dreaming of the time someone would kiss her and take her away on *that* adventure. Her whole body would thrill as she thought about it and she listened with shining eyes as her girlfriends told in awed whispers of wonderment about what happened to them on the beach or at the drive-ins and cinemas or up in Kings Park late on a Friday or Saturday night.

But the boys think Froggy is too small, too thin, too talkative – and not very intelligent. As if most of them were! But no-one seems to want her as a girlfriend at all.

She sits like a frog in the middle of a pond, watching all the gnats go by. The sun shines down on her dappled skin and makes her black eyes appear sleepy. But, hungry for information, she snaps the droning insects up one by one on the end of her talkative inquisitive tongue. She believes everything everyone tells her.

That is how Roger meets her. It is the trick he uses upon her, once the other boys tell him she is a virgin, her love and belief of the stories he tells her about himself.

At twenty-one he is four years older than Froggy's seventeen, but still only as tall as she is. He has a terrible sway back that causes him to waddle everywhere like a duck. He has dull black eyes like a duck as well and his hair is as brown as a wild duck's down.

Even though his parents are richer than most – and this could be a lever into society for one as ugly as him – no-one seems to like him much. He has pompous ways and his father works high up in an office so he is always assured of a job. This makes him different from the other boys who gather like ragged crows in their black t-shirts with Heavy Metal motifs on them and checked shirts hanging around their sparse frames like forlorn wings. He doesn't smoke or drink or play their wild games. He does own a flash, silver-grey Commodore though, so several of the boys pretend to be his friend just so they can ride around in his car. And that is the worst sort of friendship of all.

There is one boy who is honest enough to tell Roger what he thinks of him. But he tells everyone what he thinks of them and everyone listens because they are all frightened by him. In fact he is a bit of a loner. A boy who is proud to say he enjoys his own company over the twittering, tottering girls who come every Friday and Saturday night heavily (and inexpertly) made up with their big sisters' or mothers' accessories and perfume. With their young, unformed bodies squeezed tight into jeans, or the more daring into short dresses. He enjoys his own company over the loud brash boys who gather in groups at the corner of the fast food shop that is their courtship place and guarded just as jealously as any bower bird's dancing pad.

They are frightened of him because he once was like them but now he is there to remind them of what they could become. So they shun his company and it is the way he wants it.

He has a thin troubled face, russetty-red, untidy hair and sharp yellow eyes that glint in the light of the shop windows. He looks no different from a dozen other thin, gangling youths who talk about girls and fast cars. Except from the knee down Charlie's left leg is a contraption of plastic. This is why he walks with a limp and why he never again will ride his beloved Harley Davidson that carried him, like an insignificant gnat, to smash into a warehouse door that glittered as grey and wide as a mouth one night when he was mad and wild and racing for a bet out in the industrial area where such bets took place.

He won the bet. But lost his leg, his bike, his reason for living. Now he huddles to the shadows and hears the crowing of roosters and the cackling of hens while he misses nothing with his aloof, cold yellow eyes.

Roger begins his capture of Froggy in the normal way. By asking her for one of her special hamburgers.

'They say you make them just right, girl!' he says, flattering her. 'I'll give you an extra two bucks,' he adds magnanimously.

She looks around to see if the boss is here for she is supposed to be serving in front this night. But it is quiet, so she slides over to the popping, hissing grill.

'You could give me an extra piece of meat, couldn't you? No-one would ever know,' he whispers and smiles a fat smile.

Joining in his conspiracy makes her feel wicked and part of the crowd she is only on the edges of. She is doing something illegal for her man, just like the women in the gangster and war videos she loves so much. She even gives him a piece of pineapple and hopes at least one of her girlfriends sees she is speaking to Roger of the flash silver-grey Commodore and lots of money.

'On the 'ouse,' she smiles shyly.

He smirks and goes outside without another word. 'Treat them mean to keep them keen' is his motto as well. He disdainfully throws away the pineapple, hating the fruit and, although he hardly ever eats junk food, he eats that hamburger – because he is greedy for the flesh of Froggy and he has to do something while he waits for his gang. The way to a man's heart is through his stomach, isn't that so? An army marches on its stomach. That was true as well. He had to have time to work out his campaign for the capture of Froggy Jinnall's unknown delights.

Back inside Froggy hugs herself and shivers in anticipation. All her girlfriends at this age have at least been kissed. Some even have babies – miniature Heavy Metal heads just like their dads. But she has nothing but the love of her family and her job that she is so proud of. Now she has her eyes upon the richest fella of all those who mooch around her shop.

At night, before she goes to work, she pats on a little perfume that she got her cousin, who is experienced in such things, to buy her. She shyly and clumsily puts a bit of lipstick on her wide mouth and some eyeshadow around her big eyes. With the wonder of a woman's magic even this transforms her into a beautiful looking girl. Just as an ugly frog hiding in the damp shadows can suddenly dazzle with the glory of its golden eyes, so too did Froggy seem to blossom just for the eyes of Roger.

Charlie noticed as well.

It probably helped that Roger was Nyoongah like Froggy. But that is where any similarity stopped. Old Bullfrog Jinnall had fought in boxing tents and in the Second World War. But the biggest fight of his life had been for his people's rights. Roger's family, on the other hand, had been 'Greek' until not so long ago. Now they were

Nyoongahs, accepting token handouts for token jobs, some said bitterly. The older Jinnalls would contemptuously – or in a cruel humour – call them 'coconuts' and grumble into their Saturday morning beers about how it was people like them who were ripping the Jinnalls off.

With such a background Roger knows one thing. Everything has a price and he knows he can afford it.

Froggy's price is cheap into the bargain. All she wants is to be romanced and recognised as a woman – and loved as one. All her dreams come to this; all the gnats buzzing dully around her head tell her this. She is bloated with sweet complacency and dreams of her beloved Roger and his flash, silver-grey car.

It is in his Commodore that Roger finally takes Froggy Jinnall for her ride – down to the bucking, rollicking waves of Cottesloe one dark autumn night. It has taken a long time, for Froggy is naturally shy and Roger must play her like a fish on a line or he will lose her. Their courtship takes place among the rowdy noisy boys and girls. It's a quiet, somewhat gentle thing, with her smile flashing on as though a light has suddenly come on in a deserted house. She talks non-stop of her little adventures and Roger pretends to laugh and listen while he eats his free hamburgers.

But this night they drive in silence down to the Surf Lifesaving Club and listen to the wind roar around the car.

'Feel like going for a walk?' Roger says at last.

'Bit cold, don't ya reckon?' Froggy murmurs back.

'I've got a blanket here. We could go and find some shelter in the dunes and drink this bottle of whisky I brought us. That'll warm you up.'

'I don't drink alcohol,' she says, a little frightened.

'You've got to start sometime, ay?' he says and puts an unobtrusive arm upon her slight shoulder.

That night, in the sand dunes, while the wind batters them and the sand and salt spray sting Froggy's naked, skinny body, Roger has his way with her. She thinks, none of the other girls ever talked about the things he is doing to her. I must be special and he must really love me, she thinks, as she does everything her girlfriends say *they* do to make their boyfriends feel great.

But, when all is said and done, the act of love and the adventure of losing your virginity is all a bit of a let-down. Froggy doesn't feel a bit how she thought she might although Roger seems to have enjoyed himself. She huddles to herself as the cold closes around her and Roger dresses in the dark, an oily smirk on his face and his eyes two black holes swallowing all her pride and soul.

He drops her off at home where old Bullfrog snores on the verandah and Auntie Vera and Uncle Coco sing cowboy songs in the kitchen, cackling gently at their jokes and reminiscences as brother and sister. For the first time in her life Froggy doesn't feel at home. She has left something on the rumpled sand of Cottesloe Beach and she will never be the same again.

But if Froggy thinks Roger shares this new feeling with her she is sadly mistaken. He shares it in another, crueller, way. And why not? He has devoured her and now he flies away to other fat conquests sitting in a dream on a sunny bank.

The first Froggy knows about the real Roger is when her best girlfriend shuns her. She's left with her mouth open, about to tell of her adventure, when the girl flounces away. Then she notices other girls staring at her as though she was the most vile toad to be found. Boys nudge each other and giggle into their cans of cool drink. The more bold come up to her and ask her for one of her special burgers and everyone knows they aren't talking about any food in the shop.

Then, one day, her girlfriend confronts her as she trudges dejectedly home.

'Did you really do all those things to Roger like he says?' she asks bluntly. 'You know, nice girls don't do those sorts of things. I always thought you were a slut!' She storms off, leaving Froggy wide-eyed and pale.

Cars idle past and boys throw casual comments that spear her heart.

'Comin' to the dunes, Froggy?'

'I could show ya some tricks Roger don't know. You could show me some too, I'll bet.'

'Has Roger rogered you today?'

'They always reckon the quiet ones are the ones that really go for it. Like a nun, ay?'

'Boom-boom cha-cha hoo-roo ra-ra!'

And laughter, like the cries of ducks disappearing from an early morning misty riverside.

Froggy's bright eyes become dull and tarnished and her wide mouth looks raw and horrible in its gloom. She loses her job because she cannot concentrate and this hurts her more than anything. It was important to her, that job. It was her swamp where she was the queen, serving everyone their food and gathering everyone's stories to her. To make matters worse she finds that she is pregnant. She cannot bring herself to have an abortion. She will keep something nice out of this disaster, she thinks. A baby, all of her own.

Bullfrog is not happy. But, being a quiet man, he lets her work out her problems by herself. He is always there for her though.

Roger starts dating a girl who works in an ice-cream shop further down the stretch. He has had his fun with Froggy and exhausted all the stories he can tell his friends about her.

One day, early in winter, there is a knock on the faded, cracked paint of the Jinnall front door. The frame is blocked by Bullfrog's massive form.

'Yeah?' he growls suspiciously. Not many wadgulas come to his house.

'Is Froggy home?' Charlie mutters, his yellow eyes looking sly.

'What's it to you, mate?' the gruff old man rumbles.

'That's it, Uncle. I'm her mate, see, and I wanted to know how she was goin'. I haven't seen her around for ages.'

'She's not well,' the woman who has come up behind the old man says.

'Well, tell her Charlie misses her company. We had a few good laughs together, ya know,' he murmurs again, edging away.

Then Froggy appears at the window, looking as sad as a wild bird in a cage. Charlie gives her a faint smile and a flick of his fingers before limping away.

The next time he sees her is in the mall where she sits by herself. He buys her a cool drink and a *Dolly* magazine. He enquires politely about the baby and asks if she has seen Roger about money. Then, perhaps afraid of his own audacity he fades away into the murky darkness he likes best. She stares after him and a faint smile lifts her still lips.

Froggy wonders why Charlie spends so much attention on her. He pretty much kept to himself before. But she is flattered and peers at him from behind her long lashes. She gradually gets her old talkative mood back and finds she has someone who really does listen and enjoys her company. Before the end of the month they are seen to be going together.

No-one even saw how it all began but, as they say, that's Charlie's way. Soft-footed and secret, while Froggy becomes her old cheerful self again. And that is when her lover's yellow eyes light up in glowing adoration.

As for Roger he is never seen again. His parents become concerned and eventually his silver-grey Commodore is found down south by the ocean near Esperance. The police think he must have gone surfing, diving, fishing, swimming and been carried out to sea.

Charlie smiles at a glowering Bullfrog who, nonetheless, is pleased his grand-daughter has found a good quiet man.

'I tell you, Uncle,' he grins, 'ducks always fly south for the winter but sly old fox'll always hang around.'

He does not tell anyone how his father went off at 'those black bastards' who must have stolen several of his winch chains.

Spirit Woman

Have you ever heard the story of the Woolgrum?

The wind whispers this to him as George sits on the verandah, his face as cracked and grey as the old jarrah boards. The cold wind that echoes through the leaves with a lost moan. The black silent waterhole that is his nemesis nestles at the bottom of the hill and waits ... forever. A throng of black ducks call out in the darkening gloom, sounding like cynical laughter and somewhere near at hand a curlew lends its eerie, caterwauling cry to the orchestra of the damned.

Night can be a friend blanketing memories but it can also be an enemy conjuring up images that are best left forgotten. Especially at night when the moon is full and as pale as a dead woman's face peeping through the sharp black branches of the paperbarks that tear at the velvet sky.

Oh, lonely life that clasps itself around him with empty arms once so full of possibility and dreams, smothering him in all its banality. Not for him the parties, bridge nights, annual race meets, trips to town and regular meetings of the farmers or Roads Board that made life in the country interesting. He hardly ever moves off the small property he has carved out of the virgin bush and which hugs the waterhole becoming as stagnant as he.

His neighbours think he is a few sandwiches short of a picnic, a few kangaroos loose in the top paddock, and stories are whispered about him on the streets of the fledgling town or in the cool comfort of the town's major building, the pub. He never has any visitors. He is outcast and may as well not exist in the machinations of the District that he once was an important part of – he and his family.

On the marshy ground beside the three big freshwater rivers, it is said you will find the Woolgrum, women whose lower limbs are those of a bullfrog. A Djanak who was lonely for company befriended all the animals so they lived together in harmony. His special friends were the bullfrogs, whom he warned when Yoorn the bobtail tried to make love to them, saying he only did this to eat their young. So grateful were they that they would sing him to sleep every night as they slept with him in his miah. When he left on his travels he breathed on them, thus giving them some magic. So, every now and then, a beast is born among them that is half-frog and half-woman.

How strange! It was a bobtail that brought them together. They had been on nodding acquaintance for a month or two when she came upon him just after he had accidentally killed the slow-moving, blue-tongued lizard.

'Woola! Proper good feed that one, Mister Ellis. Moorditj daadja!' Karlee had smiled. 'Ya cook 'im on 'is back then slice 'im open, ya got like a soup. Good for mandjang and kabarli too.'

She was a mahogany brown with cinnamon eyes and black curly soft hair that fell down her back. Large deep eyes behind long lashes and a shy smile wrinkling up her snubbed round nose. Beautiful! Not tall, nor was she plump. She was like a fragile bird hopping from branch to branch, never still and always alert. Or like one of the small, brown striped frogs that hopped across his lawn after the rains. Her gentle laughter and shy smile were like the sunlight between those branches, dancing over the green grass in pursuit of the little frogs – the whim of the wind.

That should have warned him.

It is a desperate man who seeks the favours of a Woolgrum woman. No pride for a mother to say her son is married to one of these spirit women, shameful for a child to have her mother called one. It is why any who seek these women must do so in absolute secret.

But Karlee was gorgeous, as all Woolgrum women are. And, once captured by the thin intense white youth, she remained faithful. The shadows of Spirits shone from out of her eyes.

'You don't wanna worry what them fellas say, Georgie. They just jealous, unna, cos you got the best property on the river,' she whispered when they lay together at night, his pale stringy body clamped close to her brown one and all his little dreams coming alive in the broken-backed, lumpy bed.

The best property on the river. Was she talking about the rich, black-soiled pastures and sweet clear waterholes, the acres of mystical quiet woodlands where strange birds and creatures abounded and he was friends to all who lived on this land that so ensnared him, the stands of keening she-oak and paperbark that he knew as kwel and mili-mili from the soft words of Karlee Upstone? Or was she talking of her elusive self? She who seemed almost invisible at times, so hidden was her personality and thoughts? She, whom every man secretly desired only because they could not have her. And she knows it so she walks on bare feet, dressed in a simple Mother Hubbard – a veritable queen of her land.

If it wasn't for her he would not have stayed. There was something about her that was the catalyst for all the wonderful exciting things he had seen in his new home. He is a man of books, George is, used to genteel company and London society. He and his brothers and cousins all came out on the boat together and moved into this wild untamed territory – adventurers all. For some the adventure turned sour and they returned to the Old Country or moved back into the expanding main settlement, leaving crumbling buildings and their hopes behind.

But *he* stayed in his slab hut by the wide brown river and the billabong formed by a bend in that river. He let the land sing its lullaby to him. He found beauty in small things: a bird's nest in a she-oak tree, a tiny possum-like creature in the spikes of a blackboy, the brilliantly coloured mountain ducks that seemed to come to the same part of the swamp each year. The shape of a leaf against the sun, the peeling and colour of bark from a tree, the many amazing hues on the multitudes of the birds all made his life special.

And the golden brown eyes of Karlee Upstone captivated him and gave added meaning to life in this new land. Along with her tinkling laugh and the way her lips lifted in a smile as something only she saw as funny made her laugh inside. It seemed to him that her whole inner self was aglow with good humour escaping in muffled laughter, shy smiles and the bright light in her wonderful eyes. *This* is what made her so gorgeous in the eyes of the lonely man.

So he stayed and forgot about his high society companions in far-off London, his enjoyment in that city's libraries, art galleries, museums, theatres and dinner parties. He even forgot about his neighbours, content to while away his time on the land that he thinks he owns but in fact, like a creeper crawling over a rocky wall, owns him completely.

According to the legends of the old ones, to capture a Woolgrum woman you must travel to the place of the three rivers, having been outcast from your kin. To the place where the marshlands lie. You cannot tell anyone why you are going or what for, and you must eat only tjilgi or fish while you wait until the sun's hot breath has breathed enough on the swamp to begin to dry it up. For this is the time the yoorn have their babies and you must find a female in the act of giving birth, throw the baby yoorn on your fire and watch until it bursts.

As soon as this happens turn towards the marsh and you will see the Woolgrums standing in the muddy water, all power of invisibility gone. Throw the remains of the yoorn at the creatures and run towards them fast! If any part of the yoorn touches one of the creatures it becomes wholly human and, there before your eyes, stands a graceful naked female. But you must be fast or else she will slide away under the mud, leaving you with only a memory of her magnificence. She will swim down to the sea and the Woolgrums will never come to that part of the river again.

Then you must start all over when the weather is cold and the spirit women make camp on the shore and then it is hard to find the vital baby yoorn. For it is no use trying to sneak up on their ethereal fires. They will only run away into the water and all you will see are their shadowy shapes – and then they will be gone forever.

If you *do* capture one you must wrap her up in a possum skin boaka and keep her warm by the fire. You must keep close to her for a whole cycle of the moon, never letting her out of sight even for a second. Then she loses all power of invisibility given to her by her Father-creator and she is just like an ordinary woman.

Oh, how George kept close to Karlee Upstone. He couldn't help it, being drawn in by the aura that surrounded her. No-one knew who her father was but her mother was old Jenny who worked for one of the oldest families in the district at Upstone House – hence her name. But there were those jealous of that family's wealth, or perhaps privy to inside information, who dourly speculated as to whom her father might be. As for Jenny, she said not a word.

It doesn't matter to George Ellis. Karlee is the girl who walks along the river and goes naked into the oily black water to capture ducks by swimming underwater and grabbing their feet. She is his Aglaia, Euphrosyne, Thalia – the Graces who look after Aphrodite of whom he has read in his books and to whom he can compare this girl. She has the splendour of a swan about her, and the swan is one of the Goddess of Beauty's sacred creatures. This he knows from his books and learning. He, who is used to ladies in luxurious lace and fine-flowing dresses, gloves on their dainty hands and modesty in their hearts, is not used to this earthy natural display of her brown body leaping from the brown water, laughter and silver drops tinkling all around her.

But, do not be mistaken! It is not a sexual or lustful pleasure that lures him to her. It is more the unknown. The booming or croaking songs of frogs, when there are no frogs to be seen, can be a haunting lovely sound. The glint of firelight on gloomy lonely nights where there is no fire is an ethereal, eerie phenomenon. These are just two of the small but beautiful things he loves about this land – his new home. And so it is with Karlee Upstone.

Her spirit, soul and shadow seem to encompass every-thing this land means to him.

Their courtship is slow for George is not used to the company of women now. Besides, he is some ten years older than Karlee's tender seventeen years. Already the bush he has immersed himself in has rubbed away all the old images of his gay bachelor gentleman's clubs and rules of how to behave. They share each other's knowledge and love of the waterways and he tries to tell her of his former life in London but she just cannot grasp it. At last they share meals together in his kitchen, and then they share the warmth of his rickety old bed that until now has only been a tomb for his desires and dreams.

Her mother comes to visit once and sits in the corner, staring at him with bright black eyes. As black and intelligent as a dolphin's they are, and they spear him with ancient cynicism.

'Nidja wadgula ngitiny kwiyar muking (this white man cold as a frog),' she murmurs and cackles, then spits a yellow stream of tobacco juice into the fire. She knows more than both of them. But she knows her daughter as well so does not worry too much that one of the white men has fallen into the powerful women's magic of her daughter. He should know there are goddesses everywhere. Not just in his books or from his land.

His brother comes to visit him once. His rich and prosperous brother who gave up his farm to become a stock salesman and so is wealthier now than most of his contemporaries and with influential friends. Certainly wealthier than his younger brother who has not developed at all the tract of land given him by the Governor.

'It's time for you to go home, Georgie, old chap. Find a wife. I'll get our cousin to look after the property. He could develop it a bit more,' he says, pompous as usual. He looks around at the dilapidated yards and the encroaching bush. 'This country needs pioneers, George. Expansion, that's the ticket. A land full of opportunity: gold, grain crops, sheep and cattle. A fortune to be made in this young nation and you can be a part of it.'

'It's fine just like it is. I like the way the birds all gather by the waterhole. And I have *two* kangaroos come in now. A numbat and several smaller beasts come in to eat food I leave out for them. Yes, it's fine just like it is.'

'If you don't make something out of it the Government Lands Department will take it off you. All these animals roaming the verandah, George. It looks just like a blacks' camp as it is!' He watches with a bulbous impassionate eye Karlee's progress down to the muddy, reedy edge of the pool. 'That gin looks as though she is about to foal. Yours, I suppose?'

'Yes.'

'Well, there you are then! That's even more reason for you to clear off back to London – or even Perth. This is 1913 after all. We colonials are not *entirely* uncivilised, you know!' he guffawed.

216

'I'd rather stay here if you don't mind. I prefer this place to any other.'

His brother stares long and hard at him, blue eyes as bare as the sky, bewilderment and resentment piercing like sunlight into George's darkened and cosy world.

'You *love* her, don't you. How long have you been like this? God! My brother has turned combo, just like some convict shepherd. Who else knows about this?' he blusters.

'A year. We've been together a year now,' came George's quiet reply. 'And, yes, I *do* love her.'

There are no more visits from his brother. But two years later his cousin calls in to the dark and lonely farm by the river. Nothing much has changed except Karlee has a son and is, again, pregnant. But his cousin is not so worried about that. There are more exciting things to discuss. His fresh face is alight with excitement and he thumps the chair with a pink hand while his corn yellow hair falls over his deep blue eyes in disarray.

'There's a war on, you know. Some of us chaps are off tomorrow, to join up in Perth. We wondered if you were coming along on the adventure!' he cries enthusiastically.

'A war?' George muses. 'Where?'

'England needs us now,' his cousin says proudly.

'Well, who with?'

'Germany, of course. And the damned Turks had the cheek to defy us as well. Damned nignogs! Don't you get

217

the papers out here? It's been going about a year now and we want to get in it before it's all over.'

'I keep to myself now, Desmond. Myself and Karlee. She's all I need.'

'Come on. We've got to do our bit. If Germany wins it'll be the end of us. We'll be a German colony, not British. Anyway, it'll be a laugh and, besides, it'll be good to see the Old Country once again.' Desmond shouts in youthful fervour.

George looks around at the paperbark trees that just now are blooming with their creamy flowers. He can smell the sweet cloying scent from the verandah. All around are trees he has learnt to identify and call by their Aboriginal name: jarrah, marri, mangatj, kardan, wornt. Their twisted bodies resembling arms, legs and torsos, they dance around in the wind – the wind their crooning voices.

He couldn't care less about England. But here – he wouldn't want foreigners coming here and taking him away from Karlee, from their waterhole. His grey eyes gaze at her figure as she walks with Malcolm down beside the rustling reeds.

'Who'll look after Karlee and my children?'

'Don't you worry. Frank'll look after the farm, along with our own. He's the youngest of us all. And, besides, he has a gammy leg so he can't join up himself.'

So, just like that, it is settled and George Ellis along with Desmond Armstrong and millions of others become part of the huge bubbling stew in the cauldron that is Europe. He is overseas from 1915 to 1919 and among the sorry remnants that come stumbling, stalking, staggering, wandering home.

George will never leave his house by the waterhole again. He will never leave Karlee's side, her warm small hands and large black eyes. He loves the smell of the grey, claylike mud and he loves the smell of his woman. She smells of wood-smoke.

When Karlee holds him and her black hair brushes over his face, tickling him, when her warm brown eyes, innocent of all he has seen and only full of her love for him smile down at him, he can forget all about the Somme, Ypres, Passchendaele, Gallipoli as though they had never been. Such is her power that he truly knows he can never leave her.

But the horrors of war have destroyed his young cultured mind. The books he once had taken such knowledge and enjoyment from remain in the shelves unread, going mouldy. Obsessed? Influenced? Most people just think him insane and whisper it is sad to see such a man from such a family squander his life.

The England *he* knew will never be the same again. He prefers to be in his shadowed land, beside his brown woman of the land, where exquisite flowers grow wild and free and every day has a new surprise. His children are a constant source of surprise and joy. He will keep this land and the land will keep him and his children's children.

★

Children born of a Woolgrum woman are not beautiful as she is but they are clever, with excellent hearing and the swimming abilities of their frog ancestors. They are ugly, short and squat, with big heads and wide mouths. Like Malcolm. And Keith and Sabrina. But especially their first-born – sour, angry, black-eyed Malcolm. And they can never have children of their own.

Malcolm, short and squat, sullen, as he realises the prejudices heaped upon him in this life that is not his own but some bureaucrat's up in a place he has never been. Being able to read and write better than most of his white peers, he has always considered himself as good as them. He cannot understand why he can't drink in hotels – or even go into one to sleep. He cannot go into town after dark, is paid less than white employees, is constantly harassed by the police, his 'protectors', and, in a thousand other small annoying ways is made to realise he is a third-class person – not even a citizen in the land that was his grandmother's tribal grounds. Is it any wonder that he grows to hate the white people with an anger that is ugly in its venom? He especially hates the white father who brought him into this world, loved him and taught him to read; taught him he was a human being and then abandoned him to the unfriendly world outside his gates.

If George Ellis had recalled his Greek Classical literature he would have remembered the ugly blacksmith God, Hephaestus scorned by Athene and married to an unhappy Aphrodite whom a jilted Zeus forced into

Hephaestus's company. After she left the sooty, gloomy forge that he adored he married one of the Graces until she too left him to his cave. But all the children he ever sired like Cacus, Periphetes and Cercyon were nothing but monsters.

It is no surprise to the District that at the age of thirty-three Malcolm goes to jail for life, having killed his employer in a fight over wages, although the court saw it as murder. At the time people all over the world are killing each other for different reasons as the planet erupts into mass violence again. But that small death is the most important in Karlee Upstone's life; she will never see her first-born again.

Karlee has already wept tears for her last-born, Keith. Tall, happy Keith, smiling from his wide mouth. Clear-eyed, grey-eyed Keith who was so docile some thought that he was simple, until they saw him in the annual swimming carnival held on the river. He won it every year for four years straight. Then, at seventeen a wagon rolled on him as he was sinking a dam for one of the neighbours. They carried his crushed body back to the slab hut and that's where he is buried. The land has taken his young, precious life – perhaps as compensation for the pain it is now going through. The land of his mother's, that his father loved so well, embraces him forever as his mother can never do again. Instead of his laughter echoing up from the hollow, from the waterhole that was his playground, there is only the crying of the clouds and the lamenting of the trees.

Only Sabrina is left now. Her head is perhaps a little too big and her eyes bulge a little. But Karlee and George love their middle child and only daughter and keep her close to their side.

Sabrina goes to stay with her grandmother, old Jenny, and a few scattered remnants of her mother's kin who make a living collecting mallet bark or skins, or clearing the farmer's property. Anything to keep away from the towns and the clutches of the Aboriginal Department. She meets a handsome youth and settles down with him, as much in love as her mother was with her father. She has her father's brown hair and grey eyes and fair skin. But her spouse is a full-blood Nyoongah, very proud and independent and so she comes under the power of the 1905 Act.

Like sparks from mocking fires, seen but never found, like the shadowy illusive figures of the spirit women rushing to the water and glimpsed only briefly in that fire's flames, the children they were devoted to disappear and fade away. The mocking calls of the frogs down by the waterhole are all that remain.

When this strange Government and all its laws wraps its tentacles around her last and favourite child — and her old mother — Karlee can cope no more. All her magic is gone and she stands as visible as a crane on a rock is to its intended croaking prey. Vulnerable in the bright light that dries up her swampy world. And she is left standing naked and alone while all her world dies around her. It is for George to comfort and protect her in her numbing loneliness, as her life and all she believes in lie like bleached tjilgi carcasses upon the muddy, barren shore of her mind.

But he cannot do it!

All his life George has looked to Karlee as a shining beacon of softly glowing joy. He found her, he caught her. Yet she caught him as well. But when truth bursts in as white and hot as the sun he blinks his eyes and she is gone. Turned invisible again and it is as if she had never been.

He finds her body floating in the murky, dirty pool, not like a maali or a ngwonan. No, not like those graceful black birds but more like a clump of unwanted dead brown reeds rotting in the water.

He knows he can never ever leave this place now. He truly is captured. Her spirit walks beside him, memories sleep with him and hold him in warm smothering arms. The lonely echoes of crying curlew, cackling duck, calling frog, or other sounds from the bush lure him out onto the verandah on cold nights or balmy evenings to sit with ghosts. Sometimes he thinks those sounds are Karlee singing in her low deep voice, or Sabrina laughing at a story told to her, or Keith whistling, as happy as always, or Malcolm's bitter complaints as he tries to understand the world that slowly crushes his spirit.

But they are only djanaks.

Have you *never* heard the story of the Woolgrum?

Walking with Mermaids

Now, the *murbhach* were the mermaids. Sure, and your grandmother herself was of the *Sidhe*, so she was. A little bit of the mermaid in her. They were like the selkies, sitting as they did upon the rocks combing their hair and luring sailors to a watery doom. Their singing would bring on the storms and if any were ever seen then the fishing boats would sail for the safety of the harbour. And did you know that if you were ever blessed with the sight like your grandmother then you would see them in the wild waves galloping around the boat, seahorses' manes white and ragged on the blue-green water, hair flowing ominous and grey across the sky. Manannan himself would be in their midst, so grand was he with his green hair and his face the green as well and eyes that never blinked. Just like a fish he was, breathing under the water. Sure and he was of a race even older than the *Sidhe* they say. And every seven years there was the beautiful sight of seeing the likes of

Tir na n Og and *Hy-Brasil* and other islands from *Tir faoi Thuinn* rising like mermaids, as lovely as mermaids out of the sea. From the Land beneath the Waves the magic would float in the air, so it would, all who saw it never forgetting the magic. And mermaids would call out '*Slan agaibh, mo chridhe*', goodbye, my love. And you know, you will never forget them, my darling son, but will remember them forever.

This is the only story my father ever told of his country. He was not a man of words or stories. But he was a man of the sea and was lost in this dusty ocean, the only ships being the roaring, rattling road-trains that charged past, intent on reaching that far-off city where we all dreamed of going in our own way.

I was always a dreamer, a planner of better things to come. I would sit on the pavement of my father's service station with the sharp scent of petrol mingling with the heat waves throbbing off the cement, the smell of oil and hot engines gagging in my nostrils.

The shimmering sun strutted across the azure sky of my universe, like Shamash, Tezcatlipoca, the 'smoking mirror' of the mighty Aztecs, Amen-Ra, the greatest god of the Egyptians, or other such pagan deities my father enjoyed studying.

Sometimes the rain would come oozing over the red horizon, great purple swirls of shapes and contours that came inexorably onwards like an attacking victorious army, coiling and twisting like mighty purple snakes with black angry heads and vicious tongues flickering like lightning.

My mother and father were a storm. Their bodies twisted in wild passion yet her voice was the quietness almost heard in the eye of a cyclone. My mother brought the words of Abraham and all his kin with her. She walked the deserts of Assryria and Babylon and bathed with Bathsheba in the fountains of the city of David. A thin, dark, silent, godly woman.

My mother was drawn like a bird to a watering hole back to the sad little town of her birth. The Mission and its pious ways could only teach her, not hold her. Nor could the vast city and the promise of good work with good Christian people. Who can say what brought her back to the scattering of derelict houses that made up the town. A whispered song on the breeze. perhaps. And there my father found her, looking as lovely as one of his mermaids. But she was never truly happy here, hiding her disappointment by burying herself in the yellowed pages of her Bible.

My father was king of all the Pharaohs. As big as the sun and just as glorious.

'Well, now, and I wonder what the poor people are doing today?' he'd say with unabashed unoriginality. He'd grin his famous grin, leaning back in his rickety old throne on the dry dusty verandah, savouring his afternoon bottle of beer. 'What we got is not a lot but what we got is plenty,' he'd chant as the dying embers of the sun crawled exhausted over the horizon.

'The people here,' he'd murmur, 'called the sun a woman, a mother. A mother is a better description than the vengeful eye of the Lord, wouldn't you say, Skip?' he'd say to me. Then, almost as an after-thought he'd add, 'Your mum's the sunshine of me life, so she is, the apple of me eye!'

The songs he would sing, hum or whistle were the cowboy songs we both loved or little bits of nonsense that would just spring out of the air at any given time, uninvited and amusing in their ridiculousness.

My old man's a dustman and what do ya think
of that?
He smokes gor blimey roll me owns and wears a
cowboy hat!

My mother enjoyed reading to me every night about her god, a mad, irreverent grinning god, and then we would pray together to forgive our heathen of a father who believed in the fairies and such lies. But she loved him because of his dreams and his kindness, and his clever hands that fixed the engines and brought in the money.

I would watch the huge semi-trailers come clashing and clanking their gears to a grinding, shuddering halt while heat waves flickered off the elegantly painted designs of dragons, damsels, demons that decorated the fronts of their cabs. Then the drivers swaggered in to the old service station for a refreshing wash, a laugh with my father, a huge plate of steak from my mother.

Blue singlets, black shorts, old American-style baseball caps or battered, broken cowboy hats on balding heads, red faces, hairy burnt arms. Sunglasses, loud voices, a multitude of tattoos.

Some came to look at my mother's legs and buttocks as she bustled to and fro with their steaming plates of food. She was a good Christian woman, always ready with a quiet word of welcome and a friendly smile, used religion as soap to wash the little remaining blackness from her mind and skin. And she was dedicated to her husband. But she was, after all, the daughter of old Toby's daughter who herself had been a bit of a looker and not shy with her affections. Some still nodded with lascivious leering memory. Darky girls were fair game, certain men thought. Her own mother had obviously slept with a white man to produce her. They loved a bit of the old heave-ho, didn't they? And she had beautiful legs.

They couldn't see my dreams but I knew this is what they dreamt. All they saw of me as they swept past was a snotty-nosed, dirty, timid little boy with untidy sandy hair and shy, vacant brown eyes. But, besides my father, these men were my idols. They were, after all, the only people I saw. Like sea captains from stranger climes, whose faces had been sculptured by foreign winds, painted by the sun, they came into my life.

But probably the only true friend I had, apart from my father, was old Toby. Old Toby who lived in a humpy by the turn-off to the river. But he and his ways were not welcome at the garage for he was everything my mother had tried to forget.

At times I would creep out to be with him beside his old humpy. He wouldn't talk unless he wanted to. If I pressured him he would retreat into the caves of his jet black eyes and not come out to tell his exciting stories, no matter what the lure. And I would see him savour this very silence because sometimes it's not words but the very lack of them that say the most.

Old Toby was the oldest man in the world. Older even than Methuselah. He had a fine, thick white beard and abundant white curls on his head – which only made his face look that much blacker. But he had taken up with a fair-skinned girl against the Protector's wishes – a quarter-caste in the old terminology, with remarkable grey eyes. Their daughter was wooed by a wandering stockman whose only legacy was a reminder of his auburn hair upon the head of the grey-eyed daughter he didn't know or care he had sired. But the girl didn't want anything to do with her grandfather who brought her up in his own solitary way after her mother died. The missionary tore her away from the cluttered but uncomplicated camp of the humpy and sent her on her way to Jesus.

It was the only time, my father says, that he ever saw the old man cry. As a young lad he had become the old man's friend for it was lonely out here and he liked the silence that wrapped around the old man like flickering waves of magic. And he certainly liked the old man's yarns for they were my bedtime stories sometimes – given by Toby to my father, just for me.

My nickname was Skippy, after the bush kangaroo that my father said I reminded him of, and who old Toby said was my totem.

'Proper cheeky fella, that quokka. One time 'e 'ad one warm thick coat but 'is uncle, that grey kangaroo now, got jealous and tricked 'im out of it so now 'e got only a thin ragged-arse coat. You make sure no-one never tricks *you, koorlang*!'

That was one of his stories. It was one of the last I heard him tell just before he died and trouble came stomping like an army into my tiny world.

They do say the gods are a cruel lot. Even the god my mother hugged to her cotton pastel chest was a god of terrible vengeance. But it was not any god who destroyed my father.

I nestled like a viper in my father's bosom, like the asp that bit Cleopatra. My mother was certainly as beautiful as that Egyptian Princess with her cinnamon-coloured skin and serene grey eyes that shone like the roofs of palaces, and her hair as red as the most precious sunset, a memory never to be forgotten. And her long legs the truckers loved to watch.

Except one did more than watch. One who called himself my father's friend, laughing longest at his silly jokes. One who soon had told enough lies to a somewhat shallow woman, susceptible to the serpent's charm, enough to have those long legs wrapped around his sweating, heaving, hairy back and grey eyes closed in sensual delight as all of Eden burst into fire, the red hair falling like flames, like soft clouds gathering before a storm, upon his grubby pillow in the back of his grimy cab. Like rain clouds touched by the dying hands of Amen-Ra as he died – as even gods can do – as the storm crept quietly over the horizon.

And my father who was not a king, not a god but just a small man with huge ideas, turned to me, young Skip his mate, in times of secrets and times of joy, but also times of need, only to find him cold and stony and alien as I myself struggled with this monumental betrayal, thus leaving my father dreadfully alone. His looks of confusion and my conflicting emotions will shine like a lighthouse within me forever as I watch the ship carrying my father's dreams crack and break upon the dark, storm-ravaged shore. Did not Cleopatra leave Julius Caesar for the arms of Mark Antony, stealing *him* away from his wife? And did she not bring about the destruction of her country by her infidelity?

Perhaps old Toby could have broken out of his silence and spoken some words of wisdom, stopping the destruction before it brought on the decay of all my father thought was his. But he himself was decaying, buried with his memories and stories in the old church graveyard. He was hardly cold in his simple grave before she had gone, leaving her Bible in the drawer beside her bed.

'You ... you knew, Skip? You knew what was going on with that bastard and never even told me?'

The wind whistled like an old crone from the dark tops of the pine trees some enterprising priest had once planted and which now guarded the pioneers' graves.

'I couldn't see you hurt –'

'But ... but ... Well, I thought you was me mate, Skip.'

We were standing so near and yet so far apart, brought together by the ghost of the old man. As we had done every Sunday since Old Toby died. But this Sunday was different. It was the end of one life and the beginning of another.

'You don't see, do you, Dad? This emptiness and this shitty little go-nowhere business. She hated it every second, every small reminder. They wanted her to be a useless boong and that's what she had become in their eyes. Anyone would want to escape that.'

'She was the sunshine of me life, me little mermaid so she was.'

'Aah! You and your bloody mermaids! She's gone – and glad to be rid of us!' My bitter words would have roared in his ears like the cracking of straining timbers torn to pieces on a lurking reef.

'She left me, just like that,' he murmured, dazed and bruised and not understanding. 'All I give her and she took from me and then she goes?'

But she had loved the old man, in her own strange way. It is why she didn't leave until he left this earth. She pretended to bury herself in her Bible but in the end its tales were just stories like the ones the old man had murmured to her when she was a baby – stories about Jezebel, Bathsheba and Lilith, the first wife of Adam. Stories like those of the mermaids in my father's story, who called to young fishermen to come and dance entwined beneath the cold green waves.

'I never thought you'd let me down. You know, if you'd told me what ya knew I could of stopped it.'

My father's face was grey and all life seemed sucked out of him, all the reasons for living. He stood in the smoking ruins of his existence, dreams shattered and scattered around him, and lamented his loss with the wailing wind that sounded so like harp strings vibrating, breaking. It would have been better if he had shot himself. For to live – and, yet, not live – his soul decaying and the light going out of his eyes like the humour leaked out of his ghastly jokes so they cackled and cawed from his lips like crows sitting on the roof of the garage, watching and waiting to peck out all his small triumphs; sitting there watching as the trucks stopped coming for there was no more food, and no more legs to look at, and his gaiety was frightening in its falseness for these big, bluff men of the road.

My father could never understand why I had never told him what I had guessed. He thought he could stop my mother with his jokes and cowboy songs, and he would believe no different. And I could never forgive my mother for living such a lie – her whole life a lie, so no-one knew the truth any more. Her serenity and her calm grey eyes were a lie, her soft words and gentle hands comforting me when I was sad were lies, her earnest prayers were lies. And the love that she gave me and my father was the biggest lie of all.

After all, she had inherited something else from her unknown father – his wandering restless ways. Now she was gone and I could never trust a lying woman again.

I travelled far from my father, sailing like a ship through many storms. I too heard the mermaids singing on empty, lonely, white beaches or from dangerous ruined cliffs. Unlike my father I kept out of their way.

Then into my life there sailed a woman. There is no doubt in my mind she was as beautiful as the moon. Her skin a cardamom brown, her eyes as black as an Egyptian's. Her sculptured legs and full breasts like the masts and sails of fine fighting ships of old. Her teeth as white and shining as wind-taut sails and her proud, out-thrust jaw like the prow of a ship slicing through the water. And her long, black flowing hair that was the crown of loveliness to her and all who saw her.

But it was the mystery enshrouding her that drew me

to her. She appeared one day, like a magic island erupting from the ocean depths, brilliant in verdure for me so used to drifting over the sea. Her hair as soft as fern leaves, as dark as her eyes that were smoking mirrors of cloudy blackness. Her hair had just the faintest tinge of red among the strands – as red as the blood of an eel.

It was the eels who taught humans about the joys of sex, she told me, shown to a woman who bathed in a mountain stream underneath the benign light of Tama-nui-te-ra, the god of the sun. And she told me another story of Hine-I-te-iwaiwa who fell in love with Tini-rau. She turned herself into a half-woman half-fish and swam the currents of the ocean to find her love. They became man and wife and had many adventures, all of which she told me in our bed, her eyes glinting in the lamplight like the lightning of far-off storms. Once this glorious goddess had been known as Hina-uri, the sister of Maui one of the greatest Polynesian gods. She was the goddess of the moon but she had thrown herself into the oceans so she drifted like moonlight on the turbulent water, giving herself to the dangerous attentions of the ponaturi, the water fairies who were always at war with mankind.

The stories she told did not come from dry yellow pages. Like my father's tale they came from her heart and her glow from within during the telling of them was glorious to see. And to hear the whispering of the musical words was as if I heard the *murbhach* singing as she combed her lovely long hair. I would sing her my father's songs and tell her my father's jokes. But it was the few remembered stories of my great-grandfather Toby that snared her soul like a fish on a line. And we swam together in the oceans of her mind.

Sometimes her words would flutter as gentle as birds' wings. I would fly with her out of this world and into one where her aura shone all around me like the rays of the sun and all her faults faded away like starlight. Why! I could almost touch the moon.

But I forgot it was radiant Rohe, sister of the sun, whose elegance was like the soft, mesmerising purple light of evening and whose voice was like the trilling of the birds bidding the sun farewell, who came back from the underworld and caused the death of Maui. Oh yes, even gods, like the sun, must die.

And so too did our love die. The memory of my mother with her lies and crooning songs of falsehood crept with the stealth of a moonless night into the words of my lover. Why could I not believe my Hine-moana, my girl of the ocean? Because every time I looked into her fascinating eyes I saw the ghost of my mother behind them, the residue of her cheating ways and my father's crying soul.

I could turn into a crow, a flapping black moth that shed no light, though my thoughts shone like wet yellow beaks dripping with the blood of carrion, stinking of the odour from all things dead. My mind became a windswept desert. Lonely and dry I wandered, hungry for affection, trying in desperation to hear the sweet songs

236

of her exhilarating stories. But there was only a heavy silence, as complete as when a fierce storm is finally over. I drifted like the *Mary Celeste*, deserted and empty, with unanswered questions floating around me like seaweed.

And she who I loved the most of all had become like an old tramp steamer, her hair as black as the sooty smoke pouring from her funnels, her eyes smoky and aloof. The red in her hair was like the rust marks scarring her battered sides. Proudly she drifted across the ocean currents, as beautiful as a sleeping, dreaming woman, talking to the fish and searching for her man.

Like a drowned doomed sailor I shall walk with the mermaids and hear them singing in the silence with the clarity of raindrops dripping from ferns in the misty rain. I can faintly hear my father singing a mad song as well. Or is it just the call of a strange bird upon the breeze, calling like a siren for all our tiny hopes, like the sun bursting real and red into our shadowed lives and stealing our dreams away forever?

Illusions

We walk up the hill past the old brickworks that nestles at the edge of the park and the noisy, busy Princes Highway. Its towers loom up into the grey cloudy sky, making all who walk near them appear insignificant – ants beneath their overpowering hugeness, the tall stacks emphasising their loneliness. And we walk across the hilly terrain just as big as the smoke stacks in our minds.

My great-grandfather is one hundred and three and, just like one of those towers, looks as though he will never die. He fought in the war to end all wars and it was so horrific that even today a tear will creep from those old dry eyes as he remembers. He has a photo of soldiers silhouetted against a muddy, ruined, insane world of dead torn trees and bloated horses and destroyed buildings, the only living things the men. Every one of them lost in this madness, yet a part of it. And he would always say that one of them was him, a different man each time, and a different story; so the picture became a part of him.

Buggsy, Trix and me walk our way through another war. On the opposite hill are what appear to be flowers.

We think they're flowers anyway, because flowers are beautiful and we need beauty in this new battle we fight. The only other person to be seen on the hill is a photographer taking pictures of the flowing floral pattern. Usually on windy days like this kite fliers swarm the slopes, happy fathers showing their children how it's done.

Trix's father raped her when she was twelve.

Buggsy never knew his father – and I don't think he ever had a mother. He sees where I am looking and says the flowers look like blood spilled on the green tiled floor of his favourite early opener. Then he laughs his mad scary laugh so I don't know if he's serious or not.

My father never recovered from the Vietnam War. Agent Orange made him a very sick man, dying when I was fourteen, coughing up blood as red as those flowers over there. That was the beginning of the alienation I felt for this country. Living in the biggest city in Australia and yet not feeling a part of it, just like Dad.

We often go to the old brickworks. No-one ever goes there. Rather like us, its usefulness has come to an end. But it's a good place to drink and shoot up.

But mostly we like this place because we're all country kids. Here we can smell the grass and feel it beneath our feet. We can hear the bees buzzing among the clover. Birds shoot through the thick heavy air with wild abandon. Insects, too, flutter or dart through the air. Two dancing butterflies drift between Trix and me – not a care in the world.

Trix smiles and says she wishes she was a butterfly, or a bird, and could disappear into that huge hazy sky. She has just done the bizzo so is nodding off even as we walk. Her vague eyes look out over the flowers and she says, 'Buggsy, could you buy me a dress that colour? So's we can look cool when we go dancing?'

And the flowers glare back like nightclub lights.

Buggsy says as soon as he wins the Melbourne Cup.

My dream is to be a muso. It is what I most remember of my dad. The only heirloom he left me is a guitar which I've been busking with since I was fourteen because I like making people happy.

Buggsy says a butterfly only lives one day and can't ever be still or else it feels great pain. He reckons he read the entire *Encyclopaedia Britannica* during one of many times in jail. He could be a teacher if he set his mind to it.

But he's big and frightening to all but his few friends. He's thirty-two years old but looks like fifty, with scar tissue around his eyes. People say he's mean and I've seen him kick a bloke half to death once. But he can sing sweet as a choirboy when he is in the mood.

Trix has worked the streets since she was thirteen, so nine years have left her looking like a faded flower. She shoots up all her money into her veins. She is thin and tired. Pretty once. Her eyes when she's straight are the most glorious blue and she still has a nice smile, not ruined.

Her old clients used to get off going with someone so young but she's too old now and some of her new punters are rough and violent. When Buggsy took up with her he cared about her with all his big heart. In his alcoholic dreamland she is someone real. But he's not very bright and lets his fists do the thinking so more often than not he winds up in jail. Then there is just me to care for Trix and I am not much of a warrior at all.

Once more I look over at the flowers. Some artistic gardener has put them into a whirling pattern, confusing yet beautiful. The white edges keep the hundreds of bright red flowers together – as white as the heroin that courses through our red-blooded veins. And the path of green grass in between leads everywhere – yet nowhere – rather like our lives have done. I can see now the gardener has fenced them off, making them prisoners just as we are. The photographer snaps shot after shot. I wonder how much we could get for such an expensive camera.

They are so alive. Not at all like the dark towers behind us. I feel like rushing down the slope and leaping among them, scattering red petals up into the blue sky in an abandonment of youth. I would laugh and roll among them, crushing them and covering myself in their sweet perfume and I would explore the passageway so cunningly designed.

But we must go on.

Our pockets are full of money, my fingers sticky with red, red blood. An old man thought he'd pick a nice young flower and use it for his own perverse joy. He saw an illusion and had his own dream, but I'm a warrior now and reality hit him like an old brick. Now he lies broken among the brickworks.

Yes, we are the new soldiers, fighting to survive in this grand new country that has left us to rot like bloated horses, not nod gently like the red poppies of my great-grandfather's stories.

It is a story I can never tell the old man.

Confessions of a Headhunter

The unmarked car drew up with a squeal of brakes and a great flurry of red dust. The two men hurried out, one on either side of the youth, while the driver looked around anxiously for the expected crows. But they had been clever in their deception and the only one to greet their arrival at the police station was an old drunk dozing in the sun with his two equally decrepit dogs.

It was certainly the most excitement this small country town had ever had. To think that it was *here* the fiend had lurked, living like a normal citizen, for no-one knew how many months. And it had only been a chance discovery that gave him away. One of those little unrelated incidents detectives dream about that resulted in the capture of one of the country's most notorious criminals.

Although he was not much to look at really, with his washed-out eyes and sandy untidy hair and thin stooped frame clothed in filthy trousers and an old army coat two sizes too big for the shivering, frightened youth.

He held back as the two detectives dragged him towards the door, calling out in a fearful voice.

'No! No, I won't go in there. I know what you bastards will do to me in there!'

But Detective-Sergeant Wilkins had no patience with his pitiful squawking and gave him a shove with his hand that was as big as a leg of lamb, sending the thin Nyoongah youth sprawling through into the empty waiting room. The stark blue walls seemed to glower down at the next victim, wondering what stories *this* pathetic little specimen would tell. They always talk in the end.

The Detective-Sergeant sat down in the chair and with merciless eyes stared at the youth. He had been searching for this one a long while now. He wondered, as he had time and time again, what had made him do it.

I don't know why I did it! Or, I do, deep down, but I can't explain it. And you never would have caught me if not for the one I kept in the cupboard.

Why did I keep it? There was something about the face that I liked. The peaceful look in them eyes that belonged to one of such anger. I mean, he was a soldier, weren't he, and there he stood in the middle of the park – all alone. Looking so proud. And, I suppose because he represented the ordinary Australian. The Aussie Battler, ain't it? There's one in every town, I reckon. And I bet he was the same as all them others with small minds and narrow views and a way of putting a bloke down while pretending to be the famous mate all Australians think they are.

If it hadn't been for him, mate, you never would of caught me. But he wasn't me first old soldier, not by a long stroke of the chalk. There was one in Adelaide I specially remember. One of my first. A general or a colonel or some such thing.

His face was so bitter and twisted that for a moment the huge detective was unsettled. Indeed he had felt uncomfortable in this young man's presence right from the start when they had picked him up in the grey early hours of the morning, pulling him out of his lumpy bed where nightmares should have been his constant companion after all he had done. But his pale eyes were calm as he glared at the men from behind his scruffy blond fringe.

He asked for a cigarette and Detective-Sergeant Wilkins let him light up, although he was disgusted to be in the same room as the youth. But he had to find out. It was best to string him along until the whole sordid story was out and then he could feed him to the gathering wolves. A patriotic man, a lover of his flag and country, a staunch believer in values, he abhorred this person's crimes.

The night was black and crystal clear. Me and my cousin Vinny had just pulled in from Perth and were cruising the suburbs looking for victims when – there he was! Up on a hill, looking down on the sleeping city as though he owned it.

'Well,' I said to Vin, 'don't 'e know this all belongs to Nunga mob over the border. Where are they today? Pushed out into slums most likely, livin' in poverty and Third World conditions on land that 'ad once been all theirs! Just like all over this poxy country!'

Made me wild, ya know! This old man looking so self-righteous. He was everything I hated about the wadgula so, making sure there was no-one about, I crept through the shadows, coming up behind him without a sound like my warrior ancestors did long ago ... then I let him have it with my axe!

Yeah, I know. It was a crude method. I used an axe in the early days until I got more refined and used a saw. What, mate, you never heard of Jimmy Governor and the terror he got up to at the beginning of this century with his axe? Him and his brother Joe. There'll be no statues built to them, I'll bet! Or that fella you blokes called Pigeon who had the whole of Derby shitting themselves. The whole of the Kimberley region. But Joe reminds me of my cousin Vinny.

Yeah, that axe! Noisy! I had to give him a coupla whacks before his head come off. It rolled down the hill and lifeless eyes stared up at Vinny's shocked face when it come to rest at his feet. He shit himself too, the cakey-hole. Nervous as a cat, was Vinny, and twice as edgy. But I finished up curing his stutter, didn't I, with all his nerves jangling away, so there you go! It's a silver cloud on every lining, unna?

★

He smiled then and his whole face transformed. It was easy to see that he loved his cousin. But, as far as Detective-Sergeant Wilkins was concerned they were both as bad as the other and Vinny too would pay for his part in the crime spree that had shaken the country to its very foundations.

Nah, you mustn't blame Vin for any of this. He was against it from the very start, ya know. Why, when I first got the idea in Perth and begun me life of crime, he was against it.

'F–F–F–Fuck ya think ya doin'? F–F–Fuck ya think ya doin' F–F–F–Frankie?' he called out in horrified surprise.

'Gettin' me revenge on th' white invaders, Vin, my cuz,' I whispered as I put her head in the boot of the car. She was only a little one so did not take much effort.

And that was the beginning of the end.

I wouldn't say I was a politician – like say, Pauline Hanson. Now she's a politician and look at all the shit she stirred up with her words. Me, I know I got a cheeky mouth on me. It's one way to survive in this uneven, unfair world. But Pauline Hanson. I believe she would hold me up as a perfect example of the neighbour from Hell.

But I'm just a panel-beater, a mechanic, a boiler-maker. I been all them things. Went to tech and learned all them things and went out into the world to make a name and place for meself. Just like Pauline says we should do. But I found this world didn't want me simply because I got a brown skin. Blue eyes and blond hair like every other bronzed Aussie lifesaver type – but a brown skin not made by any suntan lotion.

It was always the same, the big man inwardly sneered. It always came down to skin colour in the end. He had tried to treat everyone equally in the beginning but later on he realised the boongs would always use that as an excuse. 'You're picking on me because I'm black!' Even the ones who were only a dirty khaki colour – almost white, in fact. It was because they were all drunks and losers, nothing to do with their skin colour, Detective-Sergeant Wilkins jeered, not because they didn't get off their arses and look for the opportunity every Australian had.

But this was too much, this insect rambling on about that fine woman and her fresh ideas that no-one else had had the courage to express. Had this criminal even heard the things she was saying?

So there were certain remarks made and certain places I wasn't welcome. Coppers? You mob seemed to talk to me more than me white so-called mates, who never was around when the real shit hit the fan. Probably because they was too busy dealing and stealing then. The stories I could tell you! *They* were the ones you should of been giving the elbow and the hard word too. Me, I was trying to live an honest life!

You know I was that proud of being a boiler-maker, it being such a hard job to do. But when youse bastards got hold of me and wouldn't believe my first pay packet wasn't money I'd nicked from someone's till I thought to meself, Youse c'n all go and get fucked! I try to do what me parents wanted me to do and you heroes come down on me just for walking the streets with a pocket full of money. So you can take a bow for leading me into this situation I now find meself in.

Not my real parents, of course. I never found them or knew them. That's another reason I'm so twisted up and confused and why I went on this rampage. I'm not your smartest person, I don't mind saying, since education isn't everything. But I'd say it was because I wanted everyone to know me and who I was that I done the things I done. And I was right, unna? Because now all Australia – maybe even the whole world – knows me now!

The youth stared earnestly at the impassive face of his captor. He really wanted to share this feeling with him, Detective-Sergeant Wilkins thought, amazed and sickened. The policeman wanted to know as little about the prisoner as possible. A megalomaniac with psychotic tendencies, probably a schizophrenic. All the detective wanted to do was get this maniac's confession, then go out and capture his mental cousin. You'd have to be mental to stand by and let something like this happen before your very eyes, the big policeman thought.

But I want – I need – you to understand that. If you'd left me and my family alone I would just be another ordinary fella. Who knew what skills my father had that I could of followed. Maybe he was a gun shearer, a stockman, a boxing or footie champion. Hey, let's not forget it was my mob who helped youse dozy lot to build up ya poxy farms. And what do we get for it? Nothin'!

But there I go, rambling again. It's what ya do if ya given the gift of the gab. But I want you munadj to see you can't just go pushing us Nyoongahs around any more. I'm a black urban warrior and there are many more besides me and don't you never forget it!

Yeah, all this hatred the One Party is prophesising – well that's one party this little black duck won't be going to, I'll give you the tip right now! All the farmers and miners running around, like someone just booted their carefully made nest in. Just because some of the old blokes are asking for what is theirs anyway – to share it. This is 1997 not 1897, mate, and if it was 1777 none of you bastards would be here yet and everything would be sweet.

There's a lot of hatred out there, mate. But I've lived with that all me life and I can get on with whatever I'm doing. Land Rights? I wouldn't know what to do with a piece of land if I fell over it, mate. But human rights … you got to have them first of all, unna! I mean, someone calls you a chink, a slope, slant-eye, or a boong, or a coon, or a nigger, a gin or lubra or black slut – what does it really mean, you say. It's only words. But it's more than that. It's another chip off our soul and pride. Hey, I used to fight them at school when I got big enough to punch back. That's where I learnt about racism, along with history, maths and English.

But nowadays I just feel sorry for them. To waste so much energy on all that hatred. Because in the long run, they are just crows ruffling their feathers, cawking away on a fence, the sound of their harsh anger blowing feebly in the wind.

But I was just an ordinary fella trying to make a living and looking for a yorga to make a family with. Thing is, but, I didn't know where I belonged. I was too black for all the wadgulas I met and I never met any Nyoongahs. I never even *knew* I was a Nyoongah until my last years of school.

My mum said I was Dutch-Indonesian and I was that proud of being a New Australian in my new country. I tried to learn all I could about my parents' home and dreamed of going to Jakarta, like all my ancestors on those ships like the *Batavia*. And that Abel Tasman! Why, the bloke who discovered Tasmania might be one of my relations.

So that's why Vinny McIntyre is special to me, I suppose. He's the only relation I know. I seen him in Weld Square, what the Nyoongahs call Beaufort Park, sitting by himself one day. I never would of gone up to him if he'd been in a group. A circle of Nyoongahs frightened and worried me in the early days just as much as it does a wadgula.

Beaufort Park was a big meeting place important for Nyoongahs. It was given to them in perpetuity a long time back by Sir John Forrest or Governor Weld or some such bigwig. It was our own land, can you imagine that? But of course no-one told us, although in a way we just knew and would meet there to see friends and catch up on the news.

How many brothers found sisters, children found parents, nieces found uncles and aunts we will never know. The friends that were made under the shade and shelter of those huge old Moreton Bay fig trees would run into thousands, I'd say. Boys would of met girls on dark nights or grey afternoons and children would of been born. Families. But the trees are all imprisoned behind shaky jails of thin grey poles now. They say they will transplant them like they took my people and transplanted them in fucking settlements and heaped manure on them until they died. Settlements? Concentration camps more better a name for it!

Already some of the trees are starting to die in sympathy of all the hardship. Why move somewhere else so wadgulas can stare at them like animals in the zoo and not know the stories those grey twisted branches carry? So one more piece of Nyoongah history and magic fades away as the tunnel that will go through the park edges ever closer and goes like a bullet through our heart.

*

Detective-Sergeant Wilkins's cold blue eyes burned into the youth and his lips compressed into a thin line. Could it be that this was his pitiable excuse for all the damage he had done. The very fact that he was wandering erratically in the telling of his story gave the man cause for contempt. All this talk about Pauline Hanson and going to school and parks over in Perth, where did it all lead to? Excuses, excuses, excuses.

Made me wild! It was another reason I did what I had to do.

But Vinny had nothing to do with it. All he done was keep a look out and carry the tools.

The first time I seen him he asked for a gnummerai and I says what's that and he says, 'A smoke, ngoonie.' Then he says where did I come from and who was my name, not having seen me there before.

'Wiener!' he roared with laughter. 'Y-Ya don' l-l-look like m-much of a wino to me, bud. Y-Y-Ya don' l-look like no dog n-n-neither so 'ow come ya called w-whiner?' And he laughed and laughed.

Funny thing is, he was younger than me and not all there, ya know. A coupla kangaroos loose up in the back paddock, know what I'm saying? But he was the stronger of us two in the beginning and took me under his wing.

He got a terrible stutter, Vin, and so never spoke unless he had something he really wanted to say. Which suited me and my motor mouth. I wanted everyone to know I was around and never shut up. Get me into trouble sometimes, it would. But all he ever did say was about being a solid Nyoongah. How us mob was all bridarra … mooritj. And he told stories about things and people I never even knew, never mind going all the way to Year Ten in school.

It was Vin told me about Yagan and Domjum, Winjan and Galyute who were our mob, Yellagonga the first Nyoongah to see white men, Munday, Weeip, Mitjigooroo and all the other leaders and all about *our* history. Now, he might not have been much chop at normal things but he was a mooritj artist, the most deadliest artist I ever seen, and he could make paintings just come alive, ya know. Just walk off the paper and punch ya between the eyes with their beauty. And he was a great dreamer and you should never take away a fella's dreams. I suppose he was that good because he couldn't express himself in words like us mob.

He introduced me to the other Nyoongahs that hung around the park and we all had a good laugh about how I thought I was Dutch. That was how I became who I was: Dutchy Wiener.

'F–F–Franz. What sort of N–N–N–Nyoongah name that? They eat f-f-frogs in f-fuckin' France, bud! You ever eat f-frogs,' Vinny said.

'I bet you'd spew if you was given a bardie grub to gnaw on, unna, Vin. Anyway, you can't talk. What the fuck is Vincent McIntyre's tribe, then?' I said back.

'Me? I'm the Black Douglas. A wicked good drink!' he grinned.

And we all had another good laugh at the thought of Vinny's skinny legs wrapped up in a kilt – with him playing the bagpipes.

So I became Frank aka 'The Dutchman'. Made me feel like a gangster, mate. True's God!

I give away me job as a boiler-maker and took it onto meself to look out for me only living relative. I felt like I belonged at last. Vinny, you see, looks a lot like me except he had red hair and green eyes and a Scottish accent and Scottish name. But he had a photo of one woman he said was his mum and I had the same woman in a photo I had given to me when I turned twenty-one so that way we found out we was family. The only family I got. We cried and cried when we found that out, I aren't ashamed to say. But they was tears of happiness, son, tears of joy. I started work as a mechanic and settled down with a wicked looking Nyoongah yorga. I really was happy then. I'd found my place and all the world that I wanted was mine, bud!

Then all that trouble began and I went a bit kartwarrah there!

The big policeman shifted uncomfortably in his chair. He too had a family – almost everyone did, didn't they? The very fact that this insignificant little youth who had run amuck all over the country had finally found someone he could love only made it worse in Detective-Sergeant Wilkins's angry blue eyes. How *could* he understand and

255

forgive this person who had destroyed everything he held sacred? And yet, when the youth's eyes lit up as he talked about his tiny precarious niche in this huge world that seemed to have swallowed him up then spat him out, his captor could almost reach out and touch his soul. But then he shuddered in his white shirt and silk tie as he realised that here, at last, came the confession he had been waiting for, with all its intricate details.

I suppose it was because I'd had enough of all these people telling me who I was and where I could go. I was sick of them having perfect lives and nothing ever touching them that I decided to go on my destructive spree.

You say I took fifty heads? You'll probably never know how many. I bet there's copy-cats out there now and I lost count along the way. But do you understand now why I did it all?

It wasn't only soldiers or men I did. I beheaded women and children as well – as you know.

So now you've finally caught me I can see you looking at me as if I were the worst criminal in all the world. But I'm not ashamed of what I've done. It was my way of getting back at White Australia – at all the pastoralists, miners, the Pauline Hansons of this world, all the rednecks, all the racists that reside in this wonderful country that ever done any of my people wrong. Besides, you mob started it. Or have you forgotten all them cowardly massacres that were supposed to wipe us out?

Well, there you go, ay! I *am* a politician, after all, shooting off a lot of hot air, you might think. But I won't get on my pedestal, if that is what you think I am doing. After all, my victims, that's what they all were doing, unna? Standing on a pedestal. You put them up there, made them special, made them what they were. And this skinny little Nyoongah come along and cut them down with as much thought as if I was having a shit. Frankie the Dutchman. Except I'm a Nyoongah warrior and don't you ever forget *that*.

How come you never caught me? I was too cunning, mate! Cunning as a shithouse rat, that was me.

Night time was the best time, of course. The darker the better, and mostly in some secluded park. Sometimes I'd hang around a day because, of course, they were always there but I wanted to check out escape routes and things. It used to make me wild seeing them all so smug and serene. Sometimes I felt sorry because once they had been famous people, no doubt, and now they stood or sat or lay around in the park. They probably had no family either. It often looked as though no-one cared for them at all. Yeah, just laying around unwanted, unloved, like you say the dirty boongs do all day long, ain't it?

Then, when I figured out me plan and me escape route, I'd get Vinny to drive up in the car, around midnight usually and I would find them in the dark and with the greatest sense of achievement I would take their head. Then into the boot it would go and we were away.

But it wasn't always in some out-of-the-way park, was

it? Sometimes, as bold as brass, I'd take me axe or saw to someone right out in the open. I think that's what got you mob pissed off, unna. That I became so high-profiled. And there was nothing you could do about it!

Take that captain fella. Remember him? He was actually one of the first but there was a reason for that and I can see that there could be no reason for such a heinous crime in your eyes. But there he was, standing outside the bank, minding his own business, with that nasty little smile on his face. It was the smile got me going. That he should stand there smiling after all he had done. Yeah, it's the governor I'm talking about. Governor Stirling, the bastard, who led the attack that wiped out most of my mob at Pinjarra.

Yagan had been a part of that, too. A warrior and a talker, like me. He didn't want any strife with the white man – only peace. If you had listened way back then we would be living in harmony today. But you mob considered us all savage heathens with different blood and different brains. In fact we were the lowest form of human life imaginable, treated like we was troublesome kangaroos. It was you mob who had a few roos loose in your back paddock then, ha bloody ha!

So you cut off his head – and the head of his murdered brother Domjum. You was big on cutting off heads back then, unna. You smoked it and sent it to England and it wasn't found for fucking years, bud. Was it? But our elders brought it back home. After seventeen years of research and searching it was found.

No prouder people were around that day than Nyoongahs, I'd say. Really, despite what the papers wrote, it was a special time for us – especially the descendants of Yagan – but for other Nyoongahs too. He'd become a symbol, you see. The only statue of an Aboriginal in all of Perth, it seemed to me, and he was hidden away on Herrisson Island as though you wadgulas was ashamed of him. Some bastard stole his spear and, once, he was painted white as well. Often some wit would put an empty beer can in his hand or by his feet so he looked like nothing but a drunken Abo. Not one of the few tourists who got lost and stumbled upon him knew who he was. And none of the fishermen cared. Sadly, he stood there forever, forgotten, staring out over his river, proud and brave, watching the city he knew in his heart of hearts would destroy his family rise like the waugal all around him. He dared the white man to come and land in their boats again because *this* time it would be different. That's what *I* reckon, anyrate!

No-one will ever forget the day they dug up Yagan's head where it lay with a Peruvian Indian and a Maori head. Can you imagine the conversations those spirits would have had! Anyway, that was the day Princess Diana was killed. The sky went black with angry clouds and it rained and blew a wicked wind for a week. Sometimes I could almost see the figures of dancing men among the clouds and the cold pellets of rain lashed Perth like a flurry of spears. There was a lot of magic about at this time.

Perhaps Uncle Ken should not have said the things he hinted at, although there was more than one Nyoongah who might have agreed with him. We're the oldest people in this land and our magic and power is an awesome thing. Even me, the Dutchman, a mechanic and boiler-maker and lost soul who thought he was from a different country for ages, a blond-haired blue-eyed fella who grew up in a good Christian home, knew that. As did my mad cousin Vinny, who could of been straight out from the bloody gorbals if not for his coppery skin and proud Nyoongah mind.

In any case, among all that hoo-ha about who was what and which elder had the right to go or not go or who was related to whom, among the world-shattering news of Princess Di and Mother Theresa slipping into the great void, some smartarse stole Yagan's head again. Four hours it would have taken them, the experts say. But Yagan was well made with love and it *would* have taken a long time to destroy him. Some of my victims were hollow inside and only made of the cheapest metal, perhaps parallelling their real lives.

Then another uncle, with typical Nyoongah humour, offered thirty dollars a head bounty for any non-Aboriginal head. Me and my cousin Vinny was just hanging around as I had lost me job. And the dole isn't much really, despite what these politicians say.

'When you got a woman to support, you couldn't feed a flea on the money you get from the dole,' Vinny said.

And I said, 'Here's a go, cuz, let's give it a twirl, ay?'

So I tried out on a little statue of some girl and then I tried it out on Captain James Stirling. And then I thought, why not go the whole cake? Make a statement for once in your life and become a warrior like Galyute and Yagan was.

I must of decapitated ten Queen Victorias, probably twenty Captain Cooks and numerous explorers, botanists, soldiers, founders, anthropologists, archaeologists, men of learning and sundry heroes. I even got Ned Kelly, but he was a hard bugger – in statue as well as in life. All over Australia we went on a head-hunting tour that lasted three months and netted me easily one hundred and fifty heads of various sorts and sizes. And you never caught me. See how simple it was when all you mob thought of me and Vinny as just a couple of useless Abos. When all along we was the greatest criminals this country has ever seen!

There was no point in building another head. Who knew when I would be back to nick it again just as I did the first couple of times. Besides, it is not that easy grafting another head onto a statue, as you probably found.

My biggest coup, I got to say, was in Sydney, where there was a great many statues to be had – so we stayed there about a month. I was walking through Hyde Park one day and there he was. Just as big as life, if you please. Hand flung high as though he was claiming all the land again. He towered above us like I bet he done all his poxy existence. And written in gold all around was:

Born at Marton in Yorkshire
1728
Killed at OWHYHEE
1779
Discovered this territory
1770

The statue was erected a hundred years after his death. But certainly not hidden in obscurity. He was there for the world to see. So I shimmied up the marble pedestal, with a reluctant Vinny's help. Then I climbed up his cold stiff – but black – body till I was perched on his shoulders,

' 'ow ya goin', Cap'n Cook?' I whispers. 'Lend us ya ear a moment, won't ya? Or 'ow about ya 'ole fuckin' 'ead? See, mate. Maaate!' I says as I began sawing. '*You* never discovered this territory. The Eora mob discovered it, ya prick! And all the rest of the tribes. And anyway they didn't 'ave to "discover" it, because it was their land forever. But where's there a statue to them, ay! Where's the monument to Aborginal families that was so destroyed by the arrival of Captain Cook and his mates?'

And that's when I got my other idea.

One day one of the local fishermen went down to Herrisson Island to contemplate life's hazards while he pretended to fish. Costs were going up, unemployment was rife and crime was soaring. Deaths galore by heroin overdose, murders every week, many unsolved. This truly was a rough ride into the twenty-first century.

Even if he lived to a good old age it looked as though he would not enjoy it with pensions being cut, super becoming non-existent and nursing homes being phased out or becoming untenable, uncaring, cruel places. The lucky country? You could keep it!

The eerie grey light of dawn showed the headless forlorn figure of the now famous Yagan. Some white supremacist prankster had made a cement head with low brow and wide flat nose and thick lips – all the stereotyped images of an ignorant savage. And a Nyoongah activist had smashed that head with a sledge-hammer so it lay around the body lookin' like dried-up dog shit or the whitened bones of a dead nation. Occasionally Nyoongahs would mount a guard to protect their statue. There had been huge pomp and ceremony when they brought Yagan's head home and every Nyoongah united in an endeavour to put him to rest at long last.

That day, as the fisherman knelt down to bait his hook he was annoyed to see two other figures down by the shore. So there were some boongs here, he thought bitterly. They'll be along in a minute to bludge some money, a smoke, or some fish. Ever since that Yagan business a man can't have any peace anywhere.

Then the sun crept over the rim of the hills and its golden light made the wide river a purple road to the horizon. Birds began to sing in the trees around about and there was a calm beauty in the air. And there, to greet the new day, were two of the most beautiful statues the man had ever seen. Even he, so biased and twisted in his views, could tell these were made with love, every delicate feature and line moulded with care.

A deep-chested man stood, looking out towards the West, long hair held back with a band and eyes dark with glory. His young woman knelt, dipping a slender hand towards the murmuring water and – now he saw – a boy was between them, holding his father's hand and looking with affection at his mother. Two little girls stood beside him. A perfect statue of ordinary Nyoongahs doing ordinary things and looking out with joy upon the river and land they called their own – a happy contented family.

It had to be quite an artisan, one who was skilled and lived only for their craft. The metal used would have been quite a lot – and it was not all the same alloy but consisted of copper, brass, iron, even aluminium, all melted down and carefully mixed in together. But it was beautiful and no-one had the nerve to order it destroyed. Nyoongah magic was still powerful even as the planet slid towards the new millennium and people could feel an aura, perhaps of the artist, protecting the statues and all who went near to admire them. It became a special place for Nyoongahs to meet. Many good things were done there.

Franz Wiener was given seven years for his acts of vandalism. Conveniently forgetting the atrocious acts that their ancestors – indeed perhaps some of the headless statues – might have committed, some had wanted him put away indefinitely, perhaps locked up in a mental institution.

The nation had, after all, been shocked wholesale at the enormity of this crime. And people needed to be dissuaded of carrying on his work. He had struck the national identity and Australian pride a mighty blow, making people feel weakened and unsure of this country's destiny. Indeed, it was almost as though he had single-handedly murdered the nation.

It certainly did not look good for national pride – or the tourism trade, especially this close to the Olympics – to be confronted by so many headless statues of national figures. It was quite unsettling, in fact.

The new statues reminded everyone of another time, when tempers were less frayed and unbelievable things occurred. Experts said it would have taken the metal of a hundred and fifty heads to make that Nyoongah family. But Vinny McIntyre was nowhere to be found. And as for 'the Dutchman', he said nothing; he only gave a secret sort of smile.

The Poppies Grow in
Flanders Fields

The most wonderful thing about the beautiful surrounds of Surrey Hall was not the magnificent stone stables or the elegant lake. It was the garden which each successive Mrs Crawford had added to over the years to make it the finest in the district – and some would say the state. Certainly people would come from miles around to observe it on Open Day, in horse and sulky or even the new cars that coughed and spluttered their way over the roads nowadays.

Then the hostess of the house would be in her element, smilingly showing her many guests about the gently sloping lawns and the rose garden, sipping iced tea and gossiping to old friends come down from Perth with all the latest scandals. Those who drove between the imposing iron balustrades of the front entrance were all from the very best families in the colony. They had, like the Crawfords, come out in the early days to hack out a living from the wild, tangled bush and become the great people they were today. Their recent ancestors had been daring explorers, risk-takers, opening up the new colony and reaping the benefits of hard work in lonely places. Their daughters went to finishing school in England or France, their sons to the best schools in Perth, some going to Oxford or Cambridge. All seemed right with their world and Mrs Henrietta Crawford's garden parties were the cream of the social events calendar.

But over and above all the flowers in her massive garden – the sweet-smelling roses and lavender, the daffodils, jonquils, bluebells and hyacinths, her daisies, marigolds, foxgloves, violets, larkspurs and snapdragons, pansies, irises and wallflowers – that reminded her of home in England, Henrietta loved and adored her first born, Lionel. And upon him she bestowed all the gifts her happy life could afford.

Lionel loved the garden as much as his mother. He was forever climbing the exotic and glorious giant sprawling trees. He would not fail to pick her a bunch of flowers on special occasions or just because he felt like it.

Old Cudjel was one of the last full-bloods in the district, often seen walking along the road, carrying his spear. He wore a kangaroo-skin boaka over his flannel shirt and trousers but he never wore any shoes on his horny black feet. He loved this country and knew where all the best roots for eating were, and the quandong trees and the few remaining jam trees with their tasty bugs, the yate trees, with their purple sap that was also good to eat.

He and his extended family worked mainly as sandalwood cutters and possum hunters, reaping the benefits of those wild harvests – the scented wood to go to China for sacred joss sticks, the possum skins to eventually adorn rich ladies' clothing. Occasionally they worked on one of several farms round about. But not on Surrey Hall. They were not welcome there.

Old Cudjel's two nieces' former lovers had both been white men so those children were part of the 'half-caste problem' that the gentry at Mrs Crawford's garden parties sometimes despaired of or spoke disparagingly about. The oldest niece's youngest daughter had met a nice, hardworking Nyoongah who had gone to Mrs Bushell's school for half-castes. He had worked as a telegram boy in Perth so could read, write and do some maths, a valuable asset for this curious little hybrid family in the bush.

Another daughter had taken up with a Chinese-Aboriginal man, Jack Lee. He was a great accordion player, even being invited into some of the District halls during the bush dances, so he taught them music. The older niece's son had taken up with an Aboriginal-Maori woman, Biddy Moana, who was a great singer, inheriting that gift from her Maori father.

The children of all the different fathers grew up together in a close-knit, unruly, loud, cheeky, happy family, as was their way. And the happiest and cheekiest of them all was Lester Cameron, the oldest, so naturally the protector of all the others. He was the one who listened most to the old man they called Jerdaluk, grey beard, out of respect. So he knew early in life where to get the juiciest bulbs, when to pick the quandong and how to find the goanna eggs the old man loved. It was grand having the old man who taught them all he could about surviving in the bush and where to gather harvest from the bountiful supplies – if you knew where to look.

And his father, Jacob Cameron, taught the kids how to read and even write. For few Aboriginals were welcome in the little bush schools and even if they were allowed they could not stay long due to their families' itinerant lifestyle.

One week Lester and his cousins Frankie Lee and Morgan Moana came into the small country town which existed only because of the railway siding. They came with a creaking old dray laden with sandalwood which they had been out many months gathering. They were looking forward to spending the money they would get in town on gifts for everyone.

The storekeeper was very fond of this family, not only because of the money they spent in his premises, but because they were a friendly, polite lot. The clan had inherited all their individual fathers' great love of independence and pride. But they were shy of the encroaching white tide that was creeping into their territory so, like the wild animals they knew so well, they kept apart from the wider world.

Which is why the news the storekeeper told them was all that more surprising. Almost a year ago England had gone to war with Germany, he said, and even now Australians were fighting in a place called Gallipoli.

What an incredible adventure! And they were missing out on it. All three, of course, were good shots and young enough not to fear death. The storekeeper said it looked as though it might be over soon, even before Christmas. If they wanted to be a part of it, they had better hurry.

They rode back to their camp deep in the bush and as they sat around the blazing fire that night, orange light flushing their excited faces, the family talked over the merits of going to fight or not. Jacob read out items from the couple of papers they had brought from town. Hopelessly out of date, but telling some news of great battles and amazing things happening in the world far away from their bush.

At last, the old man decided. They should go and visit the world like their fathers before them. *They* would never have been born had not their fathers taken the trip overseas. Imagine the stories they would have to tell when they came back.

They set off for Perth but when they arrived the authorities did not believe Morgan was of fighting Maori stock. They thought he was a full-blood Aboriginal, and full-bloods were not able to join up so he was sent back home. The fairer-skinned Frankie Lee and Lester, with his blond-tinged hair and startling green eyes which he had inherited from his parents, were however deemed quite excellent recruits.

★

Soon the two were among hundreds sent overseas. Lionel Crawford, a few years younger than them, also went. He was an officer, had been involved in cadets at school and shown some competence – and officers were becoming scarce on the ground in the bloody hills of Turkey and now in the muddy red fields of France.

These boys arrived in the bloodiest period of the war as reinforcements to those arrived from the Gallipoli campaign. There was a short period of peace and adjustment when the adoring French women admired the men for their character, general state of fitness and unusual individualism. Many soldiers were heard to boast that the war would soon be over now the Australians were here.

The Somme – more particularly, for Lester and Frankie and Lionel, Fromelles – was the Australians' first major foray into trench warfare. It was supposed to be a surprise as they moved up from the back line. But the Germans were waiting with a sign saying 'Advance Australia – if you can'. And, of course, like every other nation who had tried before them they found they could not.

It was the worst period of the war for the young nation. About seven thousand men in just six weeks were lost as they continuously leapt over the slippery muddy banks of the trenches, staggered through bomb craters or around the wreckage of the countryside or bloated bodies of horses and men, to be hung up on the cruel, twisted rolls of barbed wire in front of the German positions. And, if any made it into the trenches, fierce – almost insane – hand-to-hand conflict occurred. And all to no avail for they were invariably driven back again.

It was said every family in Australia lost some member in that dreadful time. Lester's Scottish grandfather could have related another famous battle where every family in Scotland grieved. But Flodden Field was far from this boy's mind as he floundered in the mud and tried to survive.

Despite the terror their adventure had become, Frankie and Lester still had each other and the memory – that seemed like a dream now – of their beloved bush and close-knit family. But the skills they had picked up in the bush proved useful to them now, and each used his initiative and innovation to survive this gruesome hell.

Of all the men in their platoon only Lieutenant Lionel Crawford seemed aloof. It was not that he wasn't brave, but he had grown up in a world of contented peace and solitude, with nary a problem to darken his horizon, until a gunshot in secluded Serbia had heralded the end of his comfort.

Now an officer, he had been forced into a position that thoroughly dismayed him. In charge of a group of men, some of whom were his friends, others he had known from the district back home, each day he must prove himself to them. Many were older than him, and others cared not for his famous name, or for the acres he would inherit. They had not walked as his comrade in his mother's exquisite garden and spoken of things of mutual interest. They watched him with cynical, amused eyes, waiting for his mistake. Even worse, scornful eyes saw his every fear. Especially was this so with the two natives in his platoon who, in the life they led before, he had scarcely spoken to let alone cared about. The one's almond-shaped black eyes and the other's brilliant green ones held looks almost of pity, and this he hated the most of all.

Then came the day a decision had to be made – by him alone, being the only officer left alive. It was a grey day, with black mud all around. And yet spring had taken hold of this ruined earth, and here and there clumps of scarlet poppies nodded among the carnage. Even a bird or two, amazingly, twittered among the wreckage.

Lionel stood on the parapet, constantly checking his watch, waiting anxiously for the signal to come. A soft voice broke into his thoughts.

'You're not goin' over, are you?'

He looked down at the upturned faces of Frankie and Lester. The others gathered around.

'Of course. The order's been given. Why lads,' he said briskly and smiled, although more for himself, 'it'll be a breeze.'

'They've moved up two machine-guns, Lionel,' Lester said in his soft voice. 'Over there, near that wall. See that tree? Frankie seen the birds gettin' bothered and watched. Them Germans are there now, mate, waitin' for you.'

'I wouldn't go, Lionel. I'd tell them back at HQ things got changed,' Frankie added

His first decisive action in this war looked to be

spoiled because a couple of darkies, one even a Chinkie, was worried about a couple of birds.

'We aren't ornithologists,' he said, snidely knowing this was a word they wouldn't know the meaning of. He heard one of the other men chuckle and felt emboldened. 'We're soldiers and here to do a job. The quicker it's done the sooner we can go home.'

'That'ud be nice,' Frankie murmured. ''ome, sweet 'ome.'

Then it was over the top and the only two men who knew the acute danger they were in hit the mud and crawled immediately to their left to get some cover. In the first barrage half the men went down, Lieutenant Crawford stumbling forward over dead bodies, dodging falling bodies, yelling for his men to follow.

Frankie and Lester began firing at the machine-gun nests cunningly hidden behind the ruined wall. One gunner was hit by accurate fire but the other rained hot lead among the two youths' companions. They leapt up in unison and ran forward, firing as they went. As they got closer each pulled grenades from their belt and threw them as they once had thrown spears at dodging kangaroos. Even as the grenades arced through the air the remaining gunner turned his weapon on this new threat, raking them with a lethal swathe of bullets.

Frankie went down without a murmur to drop into a clump of poppies, petals as crimson as the hot young blood splattering them. But Lester had no time now to mourn. He sprinted to the front where Lionel staggered, disorientated by the noise, still waving his pistol. The trenches in front opened fire. More men fell. Lester bumped Lionel out of harm's way, receiving a slight wound in his arm. Then, in the spur of the moment, he sent a fist crashing into the lieutenant's jaw and hauled the unconscious boy onto his shoulders.

'Back,' he cried out to the remaining men and they tumbled into the trench.

The whole action had taken only ten minutes. They had lost over fifty men. In a short while silence fell over the trenches and the birds began to sing hesitantly once again. The poppies nodded lazily in the breeze.

Lionel never mentioned the assault that could have got Lester into serious trouble. The little charge had caused a diversion which meant the British in the next trench could advance slightly so the disaster was deemed a success. Lieutenant Crawford and Privates Cameron and Lee were mentioned in despatches and each awarded the Military Medal. Not long after Lester suffered an explosion in a dreadful bombardment and Lionel was wounded in the leg. They were both invalided home.

The children in the town soon realised that if one made a sudden noise behind Lester he would shake as in a terrible dance, losing control of his limbs. It was a joke played many times, for children are cruel and care not for stories about the brave deeds of soldiers. He never recovered from seeing his cousin torn apart in front of him, never forgot the sorrow or the shellshock. Sometimes, in the small town he would pass the tall figure of Lionel limping along. He had progressed in life as it was always assumed he would, with accolades and honours bestowed upon him. But the two never acknowledged each other as comrades of war.

The bus is nearly home. The young men seated side by side have hardly spoken a word to each other since leaving Perth, happy in the knowledge that they have no need for conversation at times, sad because they have lost a good mate back in the jungles of Vietnam. And now they are coming home to their grandfather's funerals.

The funeral of Sir Lionel Crawford is to be a fittingly elegant affair. People from stations up North are coming. Motorcades are bringing friends from Perth. People of great importance in the affairs of the world are coming from as far away as Sydney, Adelaide, America and England to see off this famous man. The Governor of WA is to give a eulogy. His grandson has been granted rare permission to come home.

Sergeant Lester Cameron is also coming home to his namesake's funeral. Everyone will be there: the Lees, Moanas, Camerons, all in their various guises of labourers, farm workers, shearers, boxers, sportsmen and women, musicians. He is the only soldier and few of the family have achieved anything like the fame of the man they called Mr Crawford, even though many have worked on his various farms and some in his factories and businesses.

'Funny thing, Lionel,' Lester says. 'Those two old blokes fought in a war just like you and me, same names and everything. Then they die the same time they won their medals. A week from each other.'

'They weren't really friends, though, were they? Not like us. Remember playing in that bloody garden. It went on forever.'

'I was too blimmin' scared of the snakes, there was that many bushes,' Lester chuckles softly.

'They hardly spoke a word to each other all those years,' Lionel reminisces.

'He remembered one thing about that war, Pop did. 'e was always goin' on about the poppies.'

'Yep,' Lionel says. 'That's the one thing they had in common. When the old chap came home he tore up a whole section of the garden and put in nothing *but* poppies. Turned it into a wild place, kind of. Broke his mum's heart, I hear.'

'Remember we used to play there. Cowboys and Indians. You made me be the Indian every time, ya bastard,' Lester grins. 'The poppies that grow in Flanders Fields, ay.'

'Long may they grow there,' Lionel murmured. 'So we never forget what happened there.'

Whanua

The café was full of chattering, giggling people, the clatter of cups and the scraping of chairs adding to the happy hum. In the corner where they met each first Tuesday of every month two young men sat silent, deep in thought. Both were dark-skinned, although one was more a coppery, yellow-brown colour. Both had black hair and eyes, though the bigger darker man had slightly oriental features. The other could be Greek or Italian, quite at home among the many Italians in this popular street café.

'How was New Zealand?' the paler man asked, looking up from the cappuccino he has been studying, but not drinking, as his mate had noticed.

'Not bad, Len. Still full of Maoris, ay!' He gave a deep chuckle.

'Yeah, Perth never changed much, either.'

'Still working out at that butcher's?' the bigger man asked.

Len was furtive for a moment then looked up with a resigned look.

'I packed it in. Those dings are racist, man. When they found out I was an Abo they thought up a way to get rid of me.'

'Ah, bro, it's all in your head,' the big man said placatingly.

'No, Riki, it isn't. Perth's the poxiest city in the country. And you know it. Why else do ya piss off to New Zealand any chance ya get!'

Len's eyes bored into him. He was younger than Riki and always had a fierce temper.

'To see my whanua, man,' he explained gently to the agitated youth. 'My family. Anyway, I only been to Aotearoa the once.'

The older, bigger man had spent much time getting the younger out of trouble, sorting out differences with people Len rubbed up the wrong way. Now it looked as though he would have to do it all over again with his mates at the wholesale butcher's.

'Family ...' Len snorted and looked angrily around the room with bitter hot eyes, searching out trouble.

He stands in the dark hallway. He can smell floor polish and dust and, from what must be the dining room area, the smell of roast meat and cabbage. In the front room he can see through the open doorway where a brightly coloured floral curtain sways in the breeze. The murmur of adult voices discussing his future can be heard.

It was adults who came out to the camp in their shiny black car and put him in the polished interior smelling of leather.

Frightened and confused he can see his mother stumbling about, crying, his aunt clutching his cousins and crying, his uncles arguing with some of the men, agitated. Everyone crying and angry and he, just a little boy of five, afraid and alone, clutching the wooden dog his aunt had given him. Then the whole of his world smothered by dust as the car drives off.

The adults would have told him it was for his own good. A fair-skinned child had no place in a camp full of Desert people. Perhaps it had been his white father feeling guilty and wanting his offspring to have a chance at life. Perhaps someone had complained about the goings-on at the dirty river-camp. But no-one explains. They give him a bag of lollies to suck on and assume he would not understand even if they did tell him.

There are footsteps on the hard wooden floor. They sound loud and harsh in this subdued place. He, who is used to sunlight and laughter and the sound of the river, the sounds of children laughing and splashing in the river, is afraid of this quiet gloomy place. The woman he knows as Matron Bennett fills the doorway with her imposing white starched figure.

'Come along now, Lennard. A nice bath to get rid of all that dust from your long journey.'

The man he knows as Father Benedict comes and stands beside her, smiling down at the child, but the little boy notices that his smile doesn't reach his eyes. He knows he must be careful of this man. He knows these people are his family now – but he doesn't understand why.

'Hey, look,' Len said. 'I'm glad ya back anyrate. We can go to the footy and watch the Dockers wipe out

Essendon next Saturday. It's a home match so we'll shit it in. Let's see if my bro Jeff Farmer can kick another pile of goals!'

'I'm workin' next week, Len. Up in the mines.'

'Oh, yeah, I forgot, ya some big executive now, unna!'

'Just workin' in the mines, Len,' Riki sighed. 'You had a good job at that butcher's.'

'Good job? Bloody dings lookin' down their noses at me all the time. This is *my* country, bud, not theirs! Where do they get off treatin' me like dirt? Anyone 'ud think I never 'ad a fucken brain in me 'ead.'

His voice started to rise, causing startled glances from close-by tables. A waitress standing by looked undecided, knowing these two were regulars of a sort, relieved when Riki glanced across at her with a smile on his rugged face. Then he leaned in close to his friend, a big hand clasping the thin arm gently.

As soon as he came in he had seen that Len was in one of his moods, fiddling with his cigarettes and matches and squirming constantly on his seat. He might have been slightly built but he was all wire and his metabolism churned, burning energy. And he wasn't one to back down from trouble; in fact he welcomed it with a fierce grin upon his craggy face. Riki knew a tornado was building up inside him, likely to spill out and spoil their short time together. He had been looking forward to telling him all about his holiday in Aotearoa but that would have to wait. His mate was in trouble again. Best to sort it out.

'Listen, bro. Keep it down. You don't want the whole world to know our business, ay! What's your problem, bro?'

He sits under the gnarled old peppermint tree in the gravel, hugging his skinny frame and rocking back and forth, tears leaking quietly from his eyes. He has learnt the most important thing is to never show weakness. It is a tough, cruel place at times but is made harder if the other boys realise you are upset. They gather like crows around a dying sheep to cackle and caw and peck out your eyes.

So he hides as best he can in the shade of the twisted tree that has become his friend in these strange days, covering him with shade and the sharp bitter peppermint scent he remembers from the camps. There was one such tree there and he and his cousins would climb its branches being Indians on the lookout for the cavalry, or pirates in the mast of a lurching ship, or just little boys being boys. It afforded them many hours of fun and it is the thing he misses most so he is glad that such a tree grows here. It is the only friend he knows, shading him, comforting him with its pungent, feathery, leafy arms.

And he wouldn't normally cry for he has been here several months now and sees how it must be. But the toy left lying broken at his feet by some bullying boy was the only thing he has to remind him of the camp. It had been brought by his aunt on the day of his departure, given to keep him company on the long journey away.

'What's your problem, bro?' a soft voice murmurs beside him. And he peeps out from behind his fingers, pretending he

hasn't really been crying. He has watched this boy who prefers his own company and admired him from afar for his strength and his standing up to Father Benedict of whom he is not afraid like the rest. He stands apart from the other boys because they are all Nyoongah, often related to each other but certainly sticking together through this time of forced departure from their families. He is different with his stolid nature, solid build, height and Islander features. And he was one of the first to come to this place, the Riverside Home for Half-caste Children, so it is his true home while the others are only here until they can leave or escape.

They know little bits of their people's language to keep them together: kartwarrah, what old Benedict is, silly in the head; djinnabooka, the shoes they wished they could wear in winter instead of bare feet; bridarra, boss, what they all thought themselves to be when playing football; munadtj, police, the most important people in their lives; mooritj, good; moorij yorga, good woman; gnummerai, smoke; kebe, drink. All the important things.

They know little bits of their family history too. Me and Malvin run away this time and when we was in Brookton we found Dad. Pooh! Was we 'appy, or what? 'e bought us this ice cream but then the munadtj come and caught us again. Yoorn! Daddy cryin' there on the footpath. If you name is Boyden then you must know Sally Boyden, my mum. She's your auntie? Well you my cousin, bud. 'ow's it goin'? Old Gecko, they called 'im, well, 'e was the last full-blood Nyoongah in the South-west they reckon. He's my grandfather, bud, Gecko Bailey. That's my name too. Your uncle, you never knew 'im but Dad told me about 'im, they called 'im the Tennessee Kid and 'e was boss, cool! For boxin' there was none could beat 'im but then someone told 'im all about Tennessee and 'ow they string up blackfellas over there so 'e changed 'is name to the Albany Kid cos that's where 'e come from.

They had their little jokes with each other and their little stories that they could poke on cold nights like coals to keep them warm. But he has only his pride at the work he does for Father Kelly in the carpentry shop.

There is only kindness on the big boy's face as he bends down to the dust to pick up the tiny wooden soldier.

'Oh, I see,' he smiles at Lenny and puts an arm around his dejected shoulder. 'I can fix that up, bro. No worries. Come with me to the workshop. Old Father Kelly, he'll let me use his tools.'

'I'll be all right, Riki.'

He smiled then and took a sip of his coffee but Riki could see it was a pale imitation of the generous smile that usually sat upon his friend's lean face. Concern showed in his eyes. He knew Len was a fragile human, swaying from mood to mood; one moment deliriously happy, the next in a deep dark depression.

'Hey, if the Dockers get into the Grand Final how about we splash out on a plane ticket and get a corporate box over in Melbourne with some of the boys,' he said. 'Be choice, bro. What ya reckon?'

'Mooritj,' Len murmured, still downcast.

And when Riki came back he had been going to tell Len all about the amazing time he had in New Zealand.

Tramping through beech forests that were gloomy and sombre but marvellous to him for he had seen nothing like it. The age of the island pressed around him with manuka groves everywhere, karaka trees along the coast with their bright orange fruit, the magnificent kauri of the forests, huge girths and towering trunks, the rimu or red pine, the puriri or New Zealand oak and the rewarewa or New Zealand honeysuckle, the tauhinu a scented shrub that nonetheless grew upon poor soil and the carpets of ferns everywhere, soft and green and feathery, even the punga which grew as tall as a small tree. It was so different from the hot red land he had inhabited for so long. But the beechwood forests had very little undergrowth – none of the wild blackberries that were a pest or the broom bushes – so it was easy to find a camping site.

And he walked on top of his home too, along sharp fierce ridges cutting into the grey belly of the sky, purple shadows peeping out of craggy cliff faces, snow flurries disturbed by the wind and snow-fed rapids raging away down mountainsides. Here he met with some who were descended from the Children of the Mist and he marvelled at their remarkable story. Here he saw a rare kea with its olive green plumage and brilliant vermilion patches under the wings high up in its mountain home. This was one of the highlights of his trip.

But the best part was when he went to his people's marae and took part in the powhiri or welcome, which involved a complex protocol. The manuhiri or visitors must wait for the wero or challenge which the tangata whanua or home people perform to find out if you come in war or peace. At twilight a single fierce warrior advances chanting and shaking a spear, rolling his eyes in a terrible manner but never taking them off the group. It is his duty to lay a fern frond on the ground that the designated leader of the manuhiri – himself in this case – must carefully pick up. It was very important how this part of the ceremony was performed for to disrespect the fern meant war. The manuhiri all moved forward while a single female voice called out the karanga or call of welcome.

Seated, the traditional oratory began, the first speaker being an elder who told of the origin of the world and the tribe's genealogy. Then one of the manuhiri, again Riki, as this was his special day, responded with a little speech about how glad he was to have found his family at last. It was nothing elaborate for he was not that kind of man but it came right from his heart. The people there could see that, could see he respected their tradition and themselves, and they were satisfied. After each speech there was a song, a beautiful lilting waiata from members of the marae and whatever the manuhiri wished to sing after Riki's speech – in this case a few verses of a song from *Once Were Warriors*, one of the gentler songs and done as a type of joke for Riki. And last of all the hongi or rubbing together of noses because by mixing breath the spirits of the two groups harmonise, and the tapu or force that protects the sacred home ground was lifted and he really was home then.

One of his many new uncles was a world-famous wood carver who told him about the totara wood that was of a reddish-brown colour and the best wood for carving. You could tell the tree by its thick fluted bark that ran up the trunk in rough brown strips and its finely fluted leaves. His uncle told him that it was built in a tipua to remind people of the gods. A tipua was a shrine, a guardian of all living things, birds, people, trees, so was a very sacred place indeed. The tohunga would hide a symbol there to make sure the gods stayed there. And sometimes a gecko or little lizard would guard the place, which was usually beneath a tree where lots of birds would come. The tohunga was a wise person knowing of art and lore, a doctor or healer but most of all he was a man skilled in all things religious.

These were all wonderful words from his father's people's language, and special ways they did things, believed in things. For the first time ever Riki thought he really belonged somewhere.

If cooked meat was ever brought into a tipua then the ferns would wither, the game birds would fly away. If someone carved their name or something on a tree in the tipua they would never be able to use that hand again. Trees were living things with souls and you should always apologise to a tree before cutting it down. If you cut a birth tree or other tapu tree down then something would surely happen to you and your family.

Maui was a mischievous god who fished up a piece of land with a magic hook. The North Island was called Te

287

Ika a Maui or the fish of Maui, while the South Island was Te Waka a Maui or the canoe of Maui and there was much rivalry between the North and South Island tribes since the southerners said they were on the land as they were in the canoe. But he was of the North Island so could not agree.

The seven canoes that brought the people from Hawaiki were Arawa, Tainui, Matatua, Takitumu, Kura-hau-po, Toko-maru and Matawharorua and the axes that built those canoes were called Hauhau-te-Rangi and Tutauru.

Rangi was the Sky Father who lay on top of Papa the Earth mother, close together in their lovemaking so the children couldn't get out. Tawhiri, god of the winds and storms held his breath in anger and would not push to help them escape. Rongo, the god of cultivated food, was no use either. And neither were Tangaroa, god of the sea, or even Tu, the most fierce god of war who only drew a little blood. Then Tane, god of the forests, pushed and pushed, like an enormous tree growing and finally light was seen. Tawhiri let go of his breath in anger and storms also were born. Tane made a woman out of clay and from her had a daughter called Dawn Maid who also had daughters from Tane. Thinking Tane was her husband Dawn Maid asked who her father was.

'Ask the posts of the house,' he said and, realising to her shame her father was also her husband she fled to the underworld to be with Papa her grandmother and she became known also as Great Night but rose every morning as Dawn Maid and that was what their surname meant – Te Haeata or the Dawn.

Pounamu and Poutini were twin sons of Tangaroa. Pounamu married Anu-matao, which meant 'the Chilly Cold', and they had four children who became the four main types of fish class. It was shark that was supposed to have swallowed jade so you could find it inside him. The Taramakau River is also called Wai-pounamu by some and it's here great boulders of jade were found. Because greenstone or jade, especially in the form of axes, was very rare and much prized. But nothing was as valuable to Riki Te Haeata than the reuniting with his large, boisterous, sometimes crazy, mostly happy family in New Zealand.

All the good feelings he had brought back from New Zealand with him – the thoughts of the many aunts and uncles he had seen, the marae, the singing and dancing to welcome him, the fishing trips with numerous cousins and the good times in the pubs of Auckland – began to evaporate as he stared at this glum, bitter young man he has known almost his whole life.

'What's up, cuzy-bro? Don't tell me nothin' because I can see it's a big something,' he said softly, oblivious to all the joy this spring day was bringing everyone else in the café.

Lenny glanced up at him. All he had, just as always, was his mate Riki the Maori. Except he was only half Maori.

'So, you a Nyoongah, Riki. Ya doesn't look like a Nyoongah,' Lenny asks as they play down by the creek. Father Benedict

will punish them for not doing their chores when they go back for tea tonight. But Lenny is not afraid of that man now he has his big friend with him. Once, after Father Benedict caned him, Riki just laughed and when the angry man caned him again he just shrugged, but there had been a dangerous look in his eye that warned the Father not to bother him any more. Lenny had been there that day and knew, without a doubt, that Riki Te Haeata was his friend for life. He became the skinny, lonely little boy's hero.

'You an arse-carse, unna,' Lenny laughs.

'We half cast-iron, half solid steel and completely gold inside,' Riki jokes. 'Yeah, I'm not a Nyoongah, I'm Maori,' he says proudly, rolling out the word.

'Can ya do the haka?'

'Nuh. Can you throw a spear? Have a chew on a snake?'

'Nuh,' Lenny says.

And they laugh and laugh, thinking it the funniest joke they have ever heard.

The skinny boy plays an important part in Riki's life too because it is lonely in that Home with its tenuous relationships, people here one day then gone the next. Sometimes Riki wishes he could be more a part of the boys there, play their games, talk their talk and walk their walk. But their ways are not his ways, so he shrugs his shoulders in his 'so-what' style and carries on. But now he has a little friend who admires him, who makes him laugh and forget the lonely life of before. A boy who is as far removed from these Nyoongahs as he is from way up North where they are a different people with different ways.

290

But soon it had been time to leave the Boys' Home and make their way in the wider world. Most of the boys who left returned to their own families. But Len was found a home because he was handsome and a cheerful little chap. He was never more miserable when Mr and Mrs Carmichael took him away to their lovely little house in Mosman Park. Certainly, he had his own room and lots of toys and his own pet dog and as much love and kindness as the Carmichaels could give him. But he didn't have his mate Riki Te Haeata.

Riki had been told once by Matron Bennett that his mother abandoned him because she was too drunk to look after him and his father was nowhere around – a family of no-hopers, as she put in a kinder way. He had come to the Home as a tiny baby and it had been Matron Bennett who changed his nappies, spoon-fed him, tucked him into bed at night and watched him take his first steps. She was as close to a mother as the boy had in his life and strict though she was, even aloof, he loved her in his own way. No home was found for him because he was a restless irascible child, too big and clumsy to be admired by prospective foster-parents, but mostly because they sensed he didn't want to be a part of any family, preferring his own company. Family were for other people, he believed. Perhaps he was like his unknown father, a loner and wanderer. He found it hard to make friends and after Len left he thought, what's the use? You spend time and effort getting to know someone and then they are taken from you.

He grew into a huge man, using his great strength to good advantage, getting a job almost immediately on the mines and making good money. But he too, like Len, had lost something of his childhood. His mother whom he had never known.

It was why Len was drawn time and time again to the hot red sands of the North, hoping one day to bump into one of his mother's relatives and find out who he really was.

Riki was not to see Len for many years and during that time he worked hard, lived harder. Once he went to jail for assault, when he took umbrage against a racist mine worker. A few times he went to court for smoking cannabis but he could always afford to pay the fine. He lived life wild and free and the memories of the Boys' Home gradually faded away like the red dust floating from his car as he drove back up North again to work.

Coming out of a nightclub in the early hours one morning he had literally bumped into a drunk and aggressive Lenny who offered to fight the bemused tall man, for he was as skinny as ever. Riki recognised him then and took him home to his flat to sober up. They had a good laugh about his aggro of the night before and started up almost as though they had not been apart for some ten years.

Whereas Riki put himself into his work to forget, the alienation Lenny felt swept over him even in the nice comfortable house of the Carmichaels. In all those years he had never forgotten his pain and loneliness.

He had gone to a good school and had an interesting circle of friends. It was hoped he would carry on his foster-father's profession and become a lawyer, and he started going to law school. But all his university companions were white people. He only saw his own kind out the window of the bus he took to school, sometimes thinking he recognised some of the boys from the Home loping along the streets, laughing together, gathered together lounging in a park. But because he came from up North he had no-one to stop him in the street or sidle up to him in a pub and ask who he was and where he came from, the key to identity and belonging.

He did not make the arduous journey up North into a strange land. He had felt worthless during his long stay in the Home and believed his family wanted nothing to do with him. Besides, the Carmichaels had been good and kind to him, giving him everything he had wanted. And he had loved them in a way; they had been the only family he had known. He did not know how his people would react to finding out they were related. Perhaps, as had been suggested in the Home and at the Carmichaels, they didn't want to know him at all.

Still, in desperation, he began frequenting places where he knew Nyoongahs would congregate, certain pubs and the hidden places of this sprawling city. He met a few mates from the Home who welcomed him with the sharing of memories and a bottle. They were not his real family but they seemed friendly enough and he did not see it was usually on account of his having money and a flash car. The trickle of their language and ways came back to him and he hugged it around him like a threadbare blanket desperate to keep out the cold. And he didn't lose his skill as a lawyer either, arguing for the rights of his newfound friends when police asked them to move on or tried to arrest them for perceived misdemeanours. He soon had developed quite a reputation as a troublemaker. He gave up going to UWA and sought out new mates who were only too happy to spend his money. And his arguments with the police helped entertain an otherwise dull day, especially if he had had a few drinks.

As he got older he became more bitter, still searching the streets for that elusive answer until after one more drunken incident with the police the Carmichaels washed their hands of him.

'Let him go back to his own people,' they sighed.

But his own people were far away in the red North, not down here in the cold South. Few of the boys from the Home counted him as a friend and so he wandered the unfriendly streets until they delivered him to the safety of Riki who introduced him to *his* circle of friends who genuinely did like the younger man for his bursts of warmth and his ability to make them laugh. He found Len the apprenticeship in Giotti's and got him a flat to make a home of his own, knowing this was an important step in the pathway to independence. He arranged the meeting that became so important for the both of them, in the café each month, their time to be together.

★

In a North-west pub some years back Riki had met a Maori even bigger than himself, covered in tattoos with a grizzled grey head. Cynical black eyes observed him drinking alone before the giant ambled over.

'Haere ra,' he grunted, inviting himself to the table.

'G'day,' Riki grunted back.

These were blunt, uncomplicated men who loved a smoke, a bet on the horses, a beer or two, a good feed and a good party. They were honest in their own way of thinking and stood for none of what they perceived as foolishness. They were not so great on emotions though so it was not until after many an awkward pause, a few grunts, some occasional bursts of laughter and finally joyous acceptance when they realised their surnames were the same that the two worked out they were father and son.

It was true, Riki, discovered, his mother was a drunk. But much more than that she had been lively and fun – and beautiful. The lonely Maori youth a long way from home, Hemi, his father, had been reminded of his own feisty people when he met her because she had an opinion on everything and was not afraid to express it. More often than not Maori people in the city scorned Aboriginal people for losing their land and sinking into abject obscurity – or so it seemed to that warrior race. But they were wary of the power old elders possessed in the country and they could relate to the stories about the stars and the trees or the birds which were similar to their own.

And his mother had all of those things: power, love of the land, ties to the land, a great sense of humour and dignity, a huge spirituality and lots of stories. People called her a useless drunk.

'But they didn't know her,' the giant murmured as he brought another jug of beer. 'Besides, what harm was there in a drink or two?'

He stayed with her only for a month or two anyway before his restless soul urged him to wander on. She would not leave the safety of her family to venture out into an inhospitable world. She was quite young herself then so why would she do that when she had a loving father, doting mother, a younger brother and sister to look after. So what if they lived in a dusty camp on the outskirts of town. They had the creek for water, a giant peppermint tree for shade.

Hemi had never known he had a son but, as soon as he saw Riki, he recognised not just himself but the woman he had loved as well for a brief time. Anyway, she had given his son his surname and there weren't many Te Haeatas in Australia, his father joked.

But plenty back home in Auckland, he said and explained about the whanua and how important it was.

'You should go home to see your people. I know they'd be happy to see you,' his father said.

And before they left he gave Riki a list of names and addresses of family to visit. 'Don't worry about your mother,' he said, 'she's probably dead by now anyway.'

It was the sort of honesty he expected from one of

his kin. After the big man bid him good night at the pub door at closing time he sensed he would not see him again any time soon either, but he was disappointed nonetheless at the thought of never meeting his mother, especially after he had spent all afternoon and long into the night talking about her.

'I met this woman,' Lenny whispers at last.

She worked in the butcher's as well, at the front desk and he thought she was one of the relatives who worked for Giotti and Sons, Wholesale Meats. But she was stunningly beautiful with luxuriant curly black hair and cheeky shining black eyes and he was just as good as any Italian, he thought. After all, he was one of the best apprentice butchers in the business, he had been told. But that still didn't stop him thinking the other butchers mocked him behind his back.

It didn't take him long to find out she was Nyoongah like himself. It was her ambition to be an actress or maybe even a model one day. She brought light and laughter into his life and made his job not the burden it was becoming. He told her his idea to start up an Aboriginal restaurant using bush tucker. To this aim he intended to do a chef's course the following year.

They shared their dreams with each other in their lunch breaks, then he got up courage to ask her to a movie and then, on a regular basis, to dances on Friday nights. It was not long before they became lovers. And soon after that she took him to meet some of her extended family. And this was the greatest joy of all for the child who had been torn from the bosom of his own family by the starched officials and put into the Home. To finally belong to a family – and, soon, start up a family of his own. He knew without a doubt he would be the world's best father and his kids would want for nothing, having their father's wisdom and love to carry them along life's rocky roads.

At the barbecue held in his honour, so all her family could meet the man who had stolen their favourite sibling's heart, he had fitted in perfectly. They were pleasant people, some of the boys going to private schools, her father high up in the Aboriginal Department and her mother something important in Education. Never had he met such a family and he was excited that he would be a part of it.

But there was one old woman who watched him all afternoon, with shrewd dark eyes, a quizzical look upon her weather-beaten face. Sometimes, in the middle of a laugh or when he hugged Narrissa he would catch her studying him and it made him uncomfortable.

Towards evening, standing by the barbecue, alone for the moment, while Narrissa was seeing a brother off and the rest of the family were relaxing inside while the younger children took over the yard, running and shouting in play, he had an image of his own childhood days. They had been snatched so quickly from him, but he had the feeling he would recapture all that fun once more – with Narrissa.

'It's good to see Narrissa found 'erself a good man,

unna,' a voice broke into his thoughts. The old woman stood beside him, looking up at him, a gentle smile on her face. 'Proper cheeky woman, that one!' she chuckled. 'Excuse me, Lenny, but I never caught ya other name.'

'It's Carmichael,' he said, looking down at her.

'Oh,' she muttered. 'Don't know no Carmichaels. Where's ya from, coorlung?'

'My mob from up North. Carmichael is my adoptive parents' name.'

'Ooooh,' she murmured. 'You don't know 'oo ya mob is, then?'

'They come from Jabbitty Creek, far as I know. Somewhere out past Derby way.'

'I thought so,' she said. 'You been seein' Narrissa long, Lenny?'

'Couple of months,' he said warily, wondering where this conversation was leading. He heard the insistent whine of mosquitoes buzzing over by the fishpond and thought he should take Narrissa home soon. She was susceptible to mosquito bites and they could cuddle up in bed and discuss the wonderful evening they had had. He wished the old woman wasn't there.

'You can't see 'er no more, Lenny.'

He looked down at her, in a daze.

'What?'

'You can't be with Narrissa, Lenny. She's your cousin. You mob the same mob. 'er dad come from Jabbitty Creek too. That man inside, he your uncle, Lenny. Me, I'm your auntie.'

It was as though a house of bricks came tumbling down, each brick a dream. There was Narrissa and him, arm in arm, strolling along the sunset beach; there he was, holding their first child, she looking up with rapturous face; there he was in his new car picking up his children from school; there was him and Narrissa, close as skin could get, making love in their bed at home.

It wasn't as though cousins didn't go with cousins in Nyoongah society. Sometimes it just couldn't be helped, not knowing who was who in the incredibly complicated family trees each family had become. But this was a respectable family and they would not be happy knowing that a law had been broken, moral as well as skin law. Especially, he could see the look on Narrissa's face if she found out and knew how devastated she would be, how ashamed.

Shocked, he had left through the side gate so as not to see Narrissa. Let her aunt – *their* aunt – tell her if she dare.

That was the real reason he had not gone back to the butcher's. The one piece of happiness he had truly found and felt at peace with had been ripped as cruelly away from him as had everything else.

Riki can think of no words to comfort his distressed mate. He cannot really comprehend the deep tear that has ripped Len's heart in two. It was just not in his nature. He punched him softly on the shoulder.

'I met this woman too, man,' Riki said. 'A Maori princess. She's a Nga puhi so if our two families get together I'll own half of Aotearoa, man. If I marry her it'll make me a prince,' he laughed.

'Stay 'ere, you can be King bloody Billy, bro. King more better than a prince,' Len gave a faint smile.

'We'll have to get you over to the land of the Wrong White Crowd, Lenny. Find you a Maori missus.'

'Yeah, I'd like that,' Len said, sensing it would never happen.

'She'd bounce you all around the bedroom, you're that bony. You don't have to worry about her eating you,' Riki continues to joke.

He can laugh, Len thought sadly. His world didn't just crumble around his ears. He has a whole new world now. Sensing things were changing and knowing that Riki had always preferred his own company even in the Home. Knowing that soon he will leave Perth and Lenny and go over to his precious new country and new family and Len will become just a distant memory. The thing was, he thought, I still look up to him, still need his comfort and kindness but he doesn't need my laughter any more. He has found a whole tribe of fellas with bucket-loads of laughs between them. What would Len do in a strange land surrounded by strangers? Wasn't that what he already existed in – and had done almost his entire life? He can just remember a drooping old tree with pungent leaves and his cousins climbing in the knobbly branches and his aunt calling out for them to come and have a feed.

'Well, I'd better go. I've got a long drive in front of me tomorrow,' Riki said and stood up, stretching. He gave the skinny shoulders a brief squeeze. 'I'll see if I can't find you a job up North with me, Len. Keep an eye on ya then, ay!'

'Rightoh.'

'Till next time then.'

As the two head out of the café, each taking his own path, they know that even friendships can come to an end. They are not boys any more but men, and each can sense that the bonds of friendship are starting to fade away, as did the memories that once plagued them so. And yet the Boys' Home will remain forever a mountain upon their horizon. As does the almost forgotten touch of the mother neither of them ever knew.

67 Yagan Way

He sits in the kitchen, waiting. Rays from the sun creep through dirty windows, caressing his russet hair. Outside, birds flutter and swoop in joyous abandon as they sense spring is in the air. This is an old suburb, well established and full of history. It is filled with trees as well and large quiet blocks of land are home to masses of colour and flocks of birds. Next week it is officially spring but the robin red breasts and wrens outside the window do not know that. They simply seem content to begin nesting.

Their cheerful tunes penetrate the gloom of the kitchen. He rocks backwards on the rickety chair, throwing a small rubber ball against the far wall so it bounces back into his knobbly large hand each time. Once he saw a movie where the hero did just that, continuously bouncing a baseball against the wall to relieve the boredom of a POW camp solitary cell. *The Great Escape*, that was the name of it.

But there is no escape for him here.

Occasionally he will toy with the package wrapped up neatly in front of him. He touches the string, spins it around idly. He will not open it, though. That is not part of the game.

At last he hears footsteps on the cracked cement path outside. A soft sliding footstep as someone glides through the front door then stands there, allowing their eyes to become accustomed to the dark interior of the house. The silhouette is smaller than he expected. A hood is pulled down over the face so it is in shadow. The figure moves closer to the table. One black eye catches the sunlight as it looks down at the parcel, the other is hidden by the shadow of the hood.

'You're late,' he says.

'Could be you're early,' comes the soft reply as his guest sits down.

'Let's get on with it!' he says sharply.

'What's the hurry? You got somewhere to go?'

They stare at each other a moment across the dusty space. A wren sends its musical call spiralling into the silence.

'So, you got a name?' his guest inquires at last.

'Just a number not a name,' he half-sings in his rusty raspy voice, a slight mocking smile on his lean tanned face.

'I went and broke my mother's heart,' his guest half-sings back.

'I see you like Hank Williams too,' he says after a pause. Trying to get to know the mind of this person before him.

More staring. Then a small hand snakes out and runs fingers over the brown paper of the parcel. Such delicate fingers. The black intense eye glances up across at him and he returns the scrutiny impassively.

'Nothing's been opened. You can see for yourself,' he says.

The figure leans forward to pick up the parcel. The baggy black t-shirt falls open at the neck.

'You're a girl,' he says astounded, seeing the beginnings of her small brown breasts snuggled in the blackness of her clothing.

'So what?' she says angrily.

'I didn't know the Burrell mob had girls running around doing their business.'

'Yeah? And you're the best Choko could send, are ya?'

'I'm over twenty-one,' he says with that mocking smile.

Of course, in these days that's a big thing – to be over twenty-one. But no emotion comes over the girl's face as she deftly unwraps the package. The paper conceals a flat wooden box secured with a brass clip. She hands it to him. 'Be my guest.'

He spends only a second admiring the beautiful wooden lid with its fine grain and polished deep colour. He wants to finish this. He has done it before and Choko has promised that, for him, this is the last time.

'A Studebecker 957,' he says in awe when he has opened the box. 'Straight from the Czech Republic.'

'They must want this done properly,' she says, equally awed, though trying not to show it.

They both stare in fascination at the handgun before them. He looks up at her.

'My name's Roydan.'

'Jan,' she replies, not looking at him but at the weapon.

He picks it up, clicking open the chamber with a calloused thumb. He taps the single bullet out onto the scarred table. Its gleaming fat little body spins around, catching a part of the sun with its silver metal. The nose is as black as Jan's eye. A tiny cross is carved delicately upon it.

'Ramsley hollow point. They *do* want this done properly. What did Mervin do to piss off Choko?' Roydan says, slipping the bullet into the gun.

'Same thing. Turf penetration,' Jan mutters.

Before, at the beginning of the century, each gang had known its own place. There were the M'bros, the Spider Boys, the KGB, the various bikie gangs and other smaller gangs. Violent incidents had occurred, several people being killed or maimed, but mostly each gang kept to themselves. Then, about 2009 – after the last great police strike when law enforcement all but disappeared off the streets, the real drug wars had begun. Convoys of cars or bikes would roam the streets with boys carrying every conceivable weapon. They were out to cause maximum mayhem to anyone who got in their way of making easy money.

The emergence of the Master of Chaos and his highly sophisticated net of international and interstate gangsters was newsworthy for the local people living in an increasingly violent, unsettled world. It was no longer just groups of bored schoolboys gathering in the park for a bit of devilment on a Saturday morning; the immense loads of cocaine, heroin, ecstasy, crack, ice, speed and newer drugs required gangs and leaders who thought quickly on their feet and were prepared to take risks and be brutal.

Other things were happening as well: terrorist attacks, wars, petrol prices going through the roof; house prices skyrocketing. In a few years – after the first terrorist attack in the city, that surpassed even the most bloody gang confrontation – the city began to empty of normal folk just trying to get on with their lives in this new crazy world. Besides, there was no more water, no jobs and people were fed up with the violence. They poured into the new emerging metropolis of the blooming desert up North where there was plenty of work and plenty of water. And, with such an efficient National Reserve Army – in response to the invasions on Australian soil, every eighteen-year-old was now required to do three years' service and be on standby for the next seven years – there was very little crime rate.

Or people moved down South, setting up peaceful enclaves to work the land, each with their own minister and council and defence. Many, it is true, controlled by fanatics or cultists, but all were productive and most of a benign nature. It helped having the huge desalination plants in several of the coastal cities that had been in danger of being deserted after the floods of 2011.

But the city itself, the once proud emblem of an easy-going, tolerant, perhaps somewhat dull and slow State was reduced to ruins. Many suburbs were left to rot with absentee landlords not having a hope in hell of getting their rent from the gangs who lived there. Of course the more enterprising leaders began buying up houses at reduced costs. Soon whole suburbs were owned by a particular gang and gang law prevailed. Other suburbs were peopled by those who could not leave the city; they were not members of any gangs and so became dependent upon said gangs for protection.

The gangs themselves never ventured beyond the limits of the city. They had no need to. They were princes in their own world. The two kings were Choko Peterson and Mervin the Mad. They were continually at war, trying to build on their fiefdoms. Once, vicious battles had occurred with many dead. Now, each leader sent one of their best warriors into a safe zone to settle differences. It was better this way, they decided.

'You done this before?' he says.

'Course,' she says brazenly, but bites her lip in a nervous gesture.

'Then we'll do the normal thing, ay. Paper, stone, scissors – best out of three games.'

'Yep,' she says and settles down to play. And, like the time before, she wins the contest. She holds the gun in her hand, its cold casing burning her warm yellow palm.

'What's to stop me shootin' you in any case?' she says at last. 'Then just walk out of 'ere.'

'Oh,' he murmurs, pretending surprise. 'I didn't tell you? I'm Roydan the Knife.'

From nowhere, it seems, a slender throwing knife appears in his hand. It glitters in the sunshine like a snake's eyes then it rests on the table, just by his fingertips. A mocking smile flashes across his face and his almond eyes glint with a sure knowledge.

'You could try. Dozens have. But I'm still here. Besides, you know we're being watched.'

'Yes,' she whispers. 'The Wah Jook mob. This is their land.'

The Wah Jook (Wah as in 'was' and Jook as in 'look' – a Wah Jook person was the last look you had in life, being the joke among the other gangs) controlled the suburbs along the coastline from Freo to Scarbs. Unlike the Asian, Lebanese, Italian, Islander, African or other gangs who only relied on loyalty to individual leaders the Wah Jook were all related by skin and blood, their ancestors being the first nations in this place.

At the same time as the gang violence was escalating at the turn of the century, these people's ancestors won a significant Native Title claim, giving them the rights over all parks and Reserves over the whole of South-west. The elders took this win seriously and soon many Nyoongah people were employed in restoring the mighty Derbal Yarrigan, known as the Swan River, back to its former glory, and in caring for the sick land. Tree planting schemes were set up, for the gathering of bush tucker and medicines. Once their young had been in as much danger of self-destruction as the other youth of this city – perhaps more so. A great apathy had enshrouded these peoples; they believed there was nothing for them in life unless they took it themselves. So they did, and Perth quickly gained a reputation of being the crime city of Australia. It didn't help that the other gangs were happily pushing their drugs onto the Nyoongah youth so they needed to steal more for their habits. It had soon become a vicious circle but this momentous win in the Federal Court would enable the Nyoongah elders to at last rein in their youth by giving them something to be proud of and to live for.

To start with, they stopped taking or selling drugs. Various youth leaders led the way by showing their peers there was a better life than imitating either the foreign gangs or the white people who trespassed on their soil. Athletics, swimming, basketball, netball, football, rugby union, even soccer and cricket stars emerged from the new youth, often whole teams to give the youth something positive to barrack for. They began to expend their enormous energies in less incriminating ways than stealing cars or doing raids or robberies. Artists' workshops and theatre or film groups started up in great numbers, spreading the word of their proud heritage; authors and songwriters and business men and women, lawyers, teachers, doctors and scores from other trades emerged from the new class and the Nyoongah people of the South-west were once again in control of their destiny.

Then the end of the world began as the new empires started taking control over the old. The city disintegrated in a series of violent incidents, not least the blowing up of Parliament in 2016 on the fifteenth anniversary of 9/11. But the new Nyoongah leaders held firm and, as others left the city in droves they moved in, buying up whole suburbs when possible.

Now, so long as they were left alone, they would bother no-one but simply get on with their highly profitable business of being toll collectors. If they were crossed, as once or twice they had been, then the ensuing war was swift and brutal. They controlled the boats that went in and out of the beaches and harbours or marinas. Gangs not liking this monopoly had intervened. The battles had been long and hard and fierce, but in the end the rest had left the Wah Jook alone.

'Neutral territory,' Roydan smirks. 'We come in, do our business, walk out.'

'One of us walks out,' she says, then puts the muzzle to her head and pulls the trigger. 'Your turn.' Her voice is flat and cold now it has begun.

'No-one gets the blame.' He carries on, spinning the chamber and repeating what she just did. A tinny little click crashes around the expectant room. 'The winner goes back and that's the end of it. No blood on the streets. No flames as we yell out, "Burn, baby, burn." Bit boring really –'

'Do you know Halsey De Souza?' she says, breaking off his ramble.

'Yeah, I know Halsey De Souza.'

He watches with interest as she pulls the trigger. But there is no fear on her face, just a blank acceptance that what might happen will happen. She hands the Studebecker 957 back. He tosses it to and fro between his hands, scarred and cracked. The tip of his little finger is missing. It truly is a beautiful gun, a piece of sheer workmanship.

'So ... Jan. Not much to know about a sheila who might kill me. Jan who? How'd you get mixed up with the Burrell mob? They a bloody crazy mob. If you'd taken up with Choko we might be cruisin' around in some flash car, set up in one of the Northbridge penthouses. I'm known as a bit of a ladies' man, meself,' he grins.

'Mm ... hum?' she murmurs in a non-committal tone, her black bright eye watching him. Perhaps the faintest smile on her brown lips.

Her eye is as black as a bird's, he thinks. Like that little blue bird now singing outside the dirty cracked kitchen window. He rubs the gun up against his ear as though cleaning out wax then pulls the trigger.

'Yeah. You could of asked Halsey about that,' he says, handing her the gun. 'Boyfriend of yours, was he?'

She doesn't reply. Just puts the gun to her head.

'Let's pull the trigger four times in a row without spinning the chamber,' he suggests.

'Sick of my company already? Well, you don't smell so hot yaself, bud. When did you last go near water?'

'Water? What's that? Can you drive it? Because that would be no use, there not being any petrol left either –'

'Why not six times? That would be a sure result,' she breaks in on him again.

'Take away all the fun,' he says.

'Halsey was my brother,' she says. 'Not my bro. My true brother.'

'So you're Jan De Souza.' He ponders the implications. 'Pleased to meet you.' He smiles and pulls the trigger, then hands the gleaming weapon to her. His oriental eyes watch her without emotion. 'Good mate of mine, was Halsey. But he screamed too much when we killed him. It took him a long time to die.'

'I heard about that,' she says softly, then pulls the trigger. 'Two,' she says.

This time it is his turn not to reply. He pulls the trigger.

She holds the gun in her hand, looking at him.

'You loved it, every minute, didn't you? Torturing my brother. You used a blowtorch on him, they say. They say he looked like he'd been cooked in a volcano.'

His hand strays ever closer to his reliable knife. This is a corrupt, evil world and there is no place for mercy or for any relaxing of the vigil that has kept him alive these years.

'So is this why a girl like you got involved in this business? Revenge on her brother. Don't you think with all that's going on it's a bit ridiculous to top yourself over a brother as useless as Halsey. But, no, you find out it's me comin' over from Choko's side so you decide to have a go at knockin' me off. Is that it?'

'No,' she says and fires the gun into her head. 'Let's pull the trigger twice each time now.'

'I've got to stretch my legs for a minute,' he says. 'Good morning, Sunshine. How's your day?' he sings as he gets up from the table.

She watches him from under her hood suspiciously, her whole small body tense.

He walks over to the window, limps more like it. She sees now that one boot is thicker than the other.

'You've got a club foot,' she remarks mildly.

'Yeah, I use it to beat my missus once a week!'

'The last bloke I shot had a club foot too, and a terrible stutter. Thank Christ he only lasted three turns, it was agony trying to understand 'im.'

'Is that right,' he murmurs and comes back to sit down.

'I've never met a Chinaman with red hair before,' she says.

'Me dad's Irish – and my mum's Vietnamese.'

'Red Roydan,' she breathes.

'That's me. Heard of me then?'

'Apart from killing my brother how many *have* you killed for Choko?'

'Hundreds,' he grins mirthlessly.

'And you got a club foot?' she giggles. 'I reckon you a big bullshitter.'

'Well, I'm Irish. With a touch of the Blarney.'

'You're touched all right. And not by no Blarney

neither,' she laughs. And suddenly her hard face is just as small and soft and delicate as the rest of her.

'I'll tell you this for free. I've killed a coupla blokes with club feet too in this game. It must be all the rage over your side of the city. Sending out defects. Because I've killed a one-handed bloke and another only had one eye.'

'So 'e was pretty 'armless and the other one kept an eye out for ya.'

'I should shoot you just for telling bad jokes,' he says. Then pulls the trigger twice in a row. Click, click the hammer goes on empty chambers.

'So he only had one eye, did he? Was it like this?' Jan asks and pushes back her hood.

Her hair is short and curly like a boy's and her features are from her Filipino father. She would be quite pretty except for the livid purple scar that covers the top of her face. Where her left eye should be, is a puckered ugly hole. No wonder she wears that hood, he thinks as he involuntarily rears back in shock.

She glares at him brazenly, her ruined face there for him to see.

'Nice, isn't it? Win Miss Bloody World do you think? So, in your respected opinion Mr Hoppy, do I register as a defect in ya mind, or what?'

He can only stare at her in silence, still getting over the horror of her damaged face, but seeing the delicate beauty there in the rest of her face as well. Unfortunately, he thinks, she is the prettiest opponent he has ever encountered – and one of the funniest. Certainly she has no fear like the others and this is what he respects and likes about her the most of all.

'So all the people you've killed are pretty useless aren't they?' she says, her good eye staring bleakly at him. 'As useless as you are with ya gammy leg and big mouth. All you can do is knife someone when they are tied down or watch them shoot themselves. Why, I bet ya don't even care if ya die yaself, ay, mate? I know I don't.'

She pulls the trigger, then stares down thoughtfully at the barrel of the gun. She looks up at him again. 'You know the name of this 'ouse? We're at 67 Yagan Way. Right in the middle of Wah Jook country. Yagan was a great warrior who fought battles for 'is land, for 'is people. Like what we do 'ere, unna. Except we fight other people's battles and those people don't give a toss if we live or die. They'd prefer we died actually. We're no good to their oh-so-perfect lives, haven't you figured that out yet.'

She raises the gun to her head then places it in her mouth and sucks on the long hard thin barrel, her one good eye challenging him to answer, to say she is wrong. She takes it out and looks down at it again.

'What about your brother, Halsey?' Roydan says at last.

'My brother Halsey was the most useless of all, trying to play each side against the other, you gotta have brains for that. Yagan, now! 'e 'ad brains dripping out of his 'ead, mate. It was Yagan tried to make peace between the white man and the Nyoongah. But they shot his brother Domjum and then shot 'is poor old dad Midgegooroo. So Yagan went wild, killing whitefellas until, in the end 'e was killed by someone 'e thought was 'is mate. Bit like what 'appens nowadays, wouldn't you say?'

'There's a lot of killing,' he has to concede.

'Not in Wah Jook land,' she counters. 'I reckon Yagan's spirit is 'ere today, watching over us. I think 'e wants there to be peace between us. Everlasting peace, now *there's* a thought,' she murmurs almost to herself. 'Quiet and dreaming for ever more.'

'What about your brother, Halsey?' he says again. 'He'd of wanted you to live and me to die.'

'My brother!' she cries, coming out of her reverie. 'Who do you think did *this* to me? My lyin' rotten mongrel dog of a cowardly brother, mate,' she hisses, touching her scar. 'It's a cruel world. We're better out of it.'

She raises the gun once again and presses it to her temple.

'Wait,' he pleads. 'Don't. Not yet. I have to know … I … I never knew that about Halsey. A cheat and a thief, yes. It's why he died. But to hurt a woman, a girl, like you … Why? Tell me why. If you're going to die, tell me why.' His voice is sing-song, but this time there is no joy in it, or in the smile upon his ravaged face.

'It's a cruel world,' she repeats. 'But tell me this, what could Mervin and Choko do to us out here in Wah Jook land?'

'What would *we* do in Wah Jook land?' he counters, unprepared for her change of topic. 'They're watching us, you know.'

'I know,' she smiles. 'I saw them as I came here today. They thought they was hiding and from you they were but my name ain't just Jan. It's Jandindi, which means moor hen. My grandmother comes from the Wah Jook people. Me – and my friend – would be welcome 'ere, bud. Even if 'e was a big flash lady killer full of the Blarney and with a hairy red arse and a big mouth full of rotten teeth and bad songs,' she chuckles.

He stares across at her and the thoughts begin to swirl in his head. He does like her, he acknowledges to himself. He has heard the Wah Jook are a kind and caring people and, now he looks closely at her, he can see the Aboriginal features on her face. They would accept her as one of their own and it is known that they care especially for any of their lost children coming home. A small but genuine smile begins to grow on his face. This time it is answered.

'Just walk out and start a new life? Be nice. Could you do that with me?'

'Yeah, you did me a favour if ya topped Halsey. If ya didn't, I could still get on with ya. After we wash ya in the sea,' she grins.

He knows now for certain. He is sick of all this killing. The needless killing. And that – just possibly – he has someone now to live for. He leans back in the rickety chair and raises his hands behind his head as he

318

contemplates this new life. He stares at her face and looks past the horrible scar into her soul. He thinks he can see a light shining there. He can hear birds carolling in the trees outside. It is, he thinks, a most glorious day. The first day of a new, long and prosperous, happy life.

She points the gun at him. He freezes. The knife is too far away. Tricked at last – by a tiny one-eyed girl who will kill him for something as trivial as murdering her moron of a brother.

She points the gun at the light bulb and pulls the trigger. There is a roar that deafens both their ears and the glass shatters. A hole appears in the ceiling and all the birds in the garden chatter in fright and swoop to the sky in fear.

They stare at each other for a very long while, realising how close they had come to their dreams being snuffed out just as they realised them.

'Time to go home, sport,' she says, pulling the hood over her hair and reaching for his hand.

Deserts

Have you ever walked out into the Australian desert? All alone, letting the awesome emptiness seep right into you, through you, until it seems you are part of that arid landscape, a miniscule particle of dust in that mighty space. Trees, shrubs, clumps of spinifex and the ripped ragged outlines of craggy rocks break up the frightening horizon that emphasises the emptiness. But it is a desert all the same, and it can fill you with a great sense of wonder or it can kill you.

She had deserted him.

When he came back from a week away up the country checking on the fences he found an abandoned house with the wind whistling a lonely meaningless tune as it blustered through the open door and played among the rafters. Heartless wind, it did not care for his misery as he sat on the verandah and looked out over the red distant horizon.

He had called her his oasis in the desert. A man needs a camel to cross the desert, he had explained to her, but camel and man need water. You give me shelter from the stinging desert sands whipped up by the wind, he had told her. At night when she held him in her arms all the troubles and fears of the world had gone away and he had felt small and safe, like a bilby crouched in its burrow beneath the sands.

How could two people so different have met, then fallen in love so completely that to be apart from each other was an agony? She, small and round with a pale face fringed by strawberry red hair, her eyes a soft luminous brown, tinged with green. He, angular and awkward, with unruly brown hair, green eyes flecked with brown. Her parents owned a rare books store. Her family were academics, with sisters and brothers in universities across the land. He was from Alice Springs, not knowing his father who was, possibly, a ringer on one of the stations. His mother lived in town. Her friends were Moselle and Fruity Lexia and any strange man who would be her friend for an hour or two.

But he had loved his mother with all his heart. It had been Charlie who had sat beside her as she slept off her drinking, protecting her from predators who slunk among the spinifex like dingoes after a bleating defenceless sheep. When she was sober she taught the boy all she knew. And Jenny Sutton knew a lot that her mother and her mother's people had taught her. They borrowed Uncle Jimmy's old Landrover and drove out past the MacDonnell Ranges, that beautiful line of hills made famous by Albert Namatjira and others. She would sing songs to him in the language she only just remembered and pass on the stories she had heard as a child. She taught him how to survive this harsh environment and to love it as she did.

And what wasn't there to love about this place? Cool, secluded waterholes with fresh water and soft red or white sand beaches. Stunning gorges of crimson, orange and purple rocks. Ghost gums with pale trunks. The myriad of small things that make an empty desert alive: kangaroos sheltering from the sweltering sun, little lizards basking in the sun, tiny delicate tracks across the sand. And, most important of all, the presence of spirits watching over him and his mother wherever they went.

Unseen tracks crisscrossed this desert. Tracks his mother's people had walked for eternity. That power could not be described easily – or learnt easily. But Charlie Sutton, the son of an unknown ringer, whose mother was the daughter of an unknown station owner's son, even he could sense their power.

In town it was all around them. They slept in its warm sand at night; they ate of its animals when they were hungry; they admired the artists who sat with them in the river bed and painted its beautiful colours in all its many moods, often just from memory; and they sought its solitude when they needed a true friend.

But he was fair-skinned so some in town despaired at seeing a young boy (who was mostly white after all) wasting away his life with the drunks and no-hopers of the Todd River bed. Wheels were placed in motion to save him from the desert that would become his life. A life where there was no hope except turning to alcohol, as his mother had done, or to sniffing petrol as so many of his peers were doing, and then onto an early grave. They did not see his great love for his mother, nor her love for him that bloomed as beautiful as any flower after the annual rains turned the desert into a mass of brilliant hues.

These kind-hearted people sent him to a Catholic College far away down in Adelaide, the City of Churches. He was only seven years old. He was never to see his mother again. He was in a new desert now. A myriad of people and houses but a desert just the same, empty of love and laughter and a life that held any meaning for him. In school he was much admired by his peers for his quick mind in the classroom and quick feet on the track and football field. They did not know of his sleeping in the sandy river bed or his drunken mother singing songs from half-remembered aunts and uncles or, more usually, from her favourite group The Eagles.

These boys from well-to-do homes from the well-designed suburbs of Adelaide could not hope to understand the incredible landscape of his childhood, where trees and rocks and sand stretched endlessly and there were more birds than people.

He missed his home dreadfully and often cried himself to sleep at night. When he discovered an exit to the roof this became his special place where he would lie on the hard red tiles and stare at the array of stars.

A little girl lived down the street. The adults, being great friends, often invited each other over for dinner parties or intellectual conversation. Sometimes they would see a show together. One family had several children, the other only the boy, and often they would hire one babysitter for both families. So the youngest girl became the playmate of the lonely boy, pining for his mother and his great gorgeous desert. She soon became more than a sister and a playmate. Gradually she took the place of his mother and his memories of her land, and he would protect her as he had his mother.

Time passed with the cycle of seasons. And one night his mother was murdered, after being raped.

He was not told of this fact for they thought him too young and, as the years passed, he became immersed in the offerings of city life. The desert and his mother faded slowly from his memory. He walked the streets with pride, Jillanne by his side, and went to the theatre with his affluent family. He was no longer alone and the little boy who had crept out onto the roof was just a memory as well. He rarely looked at the stars.

The courtship of Charlie Sutton and Jillanne Ferguson was not long for they had known at an early age that they would be together forever. They had taken part in the obligatory parties and barbecues and day trips to the beautiful Barossa Valley to sample the wines. Now it was the overseas holiday after school and then marriage; life would be almost complete. A university degree to follow, to make his family proud. As they walked together of an evening she would excitedly make plans for their future. This was the boy who had carried her all the way on his back when she fell off the swing and became concussed; the very boy who once had fought two bullies who had tormented her, without fear. Her Charlie had shown nothing but consideration for her.

They were in love then and he was her whole world. At night he would sing to her:

I want to be with you in the desert tonight
With a thousand stars all around ...

And he would chuckle softly and wrap his strong arms around her, pulling her against his warm body.

During the Adelaide Festival one night, having a quiet drink at the Fringe Club, he was approached by an elderly Aboriginal woman. There had been several Aboriginal shows on that year – a play, a dance theatre, some painters from the Western Desert – but he had not had time to see any of them. It was one of the painters who approached him now and, after a period of studying him obliquely from shy eyes, came up and hesitantly asked if he were not from Alice Springs.

'Once,' he smiled, still full of good thoughts about the play he had just seen. He was a friendly youth and the Festival was a time to meet people from all over. Actually, he cared no more for Alice Springs these days than he did for one of the quaint little German towns in the Barossa; it was just a place to visit and enjoy as a tourist.

'I know *you*, Charlie Sutton,' the old woman smiled back, sure of herself now in this strange city, and glad to meet a friend. 'You know me? I'm your auntie by skin. Your poor old mum, she had same grandfather as me. You same as your poor old mum. Same eye, same hair, everything.'

And there it was. In that crowded place he was told the truth about his mother for the first time. He was greatly ashamed as well as shocked, and the old woman sensed it, placing her hand gently on his dejected shoulder. The excuse that he had been a little boy and the onus lay on the people who had adopted him to tell him did not work. He was a twenty-four-year-old man now, married and the controller of his own life.

The old woman spoke to him in a quiet soft voice and, when Jillanne came bustling across from her friends, quiet eyes studied her and a black hand caressed her reluctant one. She was no part of this woman's world.

There was no university degree after all. They left just after the Festival, back up into the dusty dirty heart of this huge continent. For him it was a return and for her an adventure.

At first she found some pleasure in Alice, working in the library. She thought Charlie could use his education to get a job in the town and perhaps help his people that way. She did not see that he had lost so much in Adelaide: his identity, his sense of place. And, of course, he had lost his mother whose memory was everywhere he walked in this strange – even unfriendly – town that he now called home once again.

He was unhappy, saw the drunks and heard the shattered remnants of fights at night, the odd scream or angry shout, reminding him how and why his mother died. In the daytime he heard the crooning, remembering the songs his mother once sang. He tried to make acquaintance with the singers of the songs but he knew he had no real family up here. Even though the old ones were polite to him and talked fondly of his mother, there was a gap between those of this desert culture and he who had gone to the city.

But Jillanne had left so much to be with him and, he reminded himself, she was the one he protected now. He had left one woman before. He would not leave this one. So he got a job on the Roads Board. At least sometimes they had to go out of town to work on the highways and tracks.

Then, another discovery added to their troubles. Jillanne discovered she could never have children. Her womb was dry; nothing would ever grow there. This devastated her, coming from a large friendly family. She had wanted just such a family herself. But for him, who had *never* had a family and had wanted above all things to hold his children as his father – or even grandfather – had never done, it was a catastrophe from which he never fully recovered, although he did his best to hide it from his wife.

After eighteen months in Alice Springs he had had

enough. When Jillanne came home one day she was greeted with the news that he had taken a job as a station hand. He smiled at her, saying it would be an adventure. And he was happy for the first time since he'd been a little boy, travelling from bore to bore, checking water and fences and the state of the cattle. She came with him on the first few occasions but her face burnt in the sun and she was uncomfortable. She hated camping out when it was a necessity and not the fun thing it had been down South. The glare of the fierce white sun hurt her eyes and the flies got in her mouth, the sand in her hair. The spinifex was prickly, and there were scorpions and spiders and snakes as long as two metres. Even an oasis might dry up eventually.

The blue sky goes purple in the evening and there is the short, sharp cry of a bird sending the night down. Insects flutter in the cooling air and a vast emptiness fills him. She, who came from a world of books and writing, did not even leave a note. His heart aches for her. The two women he had sworn to protect are gone. Only swirling images remain, like the particles of sand in a fierce storm – a storm that can blind and cause you to wander lost, in great fear, until death arrives.

The desert is still all around him, watching. It has been here forever and its people have walked upon it for thousands of years. But it is a desert all the same. It can fill you with a great sense of wonder or it can kill you.

The Window Seat

First of all she took his seat. He had specifically asked for a window seat and there she sat, lumpy and black, big battered hat pulled down over her head, impassive face looking out the window.

He wondered for a moment whether he should complain like he had once at Kojonup when an Aboriginal woman sat in his seat. Immediately she had argued, telling him he was a racist; that she was picked on because she was Aboriginal. Her strident voice went up and down the bus, causing people to turn and crane their heads while he stood there in embarrassment. It had not helped that a couple of cheeky young relatives of hers, no doubt noting his discomfiture, were giggling among themselves from the back of the bus. Finally, under much protest, the driver made her go back. But each time she passed on her way to the toilet or to get a glass of water she let the bus know what she thought of him, and all the way up the highway he could hear her whining voice complaining to those at the back what a mean person he was and what a cruel country this was. It was a very long journey.

This one would be even longer because he was going to Port Hedland. He decided to avoid any unpleasantness and sit in the aisle seat. Perhaps she would get off soon anyway. But he did it with obvious bad humour, throwing his bags around and jabbing her accidentally on purpose with his elbow as he dropped angrily into the seat.

A murmur of protest was all that came from her and then she seemed to hunch into herself and stare harder out the window. He considered it a small victory.

Eventually it was time to go. The bus was surprisingly full for this trip since many people took the plane these days. There were about a dozen backpackers off to see the wild red North and several dusty-looking characters presumably heading home after their visit to the big lights of Perth. And this old Aborigine.

He noticed with disdain that several backpackers were Asian, almost certainly Japanese and, as always, he felt anger towards their grinning faces and excited chatter. His father, who had been on the Burma railway, had instilled in his children a smouldering hatred towards the Nips. In the Cassidy household there was nothing 'Made in Japan' – and there never would be. But here were the descendants of those who had tortured his dad, killed his dad's mates, laughing and joking in barbarous language and walking happily in his country as though they owned it.

Perhaps, he thought, they did. The Chinese certainly looked like owning it soon enough. Everything you bought nowadays came from China. Good Australian companies employing honest Australians were going under as cheaper – even, he had to grudgingly admit, better – goods came on the market. Companies were employing Filipinos and other foreigners over local lads. Every week another boatload of refugees washed up on Australia's shores or another boat was captured stealing Australia's fish. The Indonesian President and the Malaysian President were running around telling Australia what to do. Had the Malaysians forgotten the crisis in the 1960s with the Communists when Australian troops had come to their aid? Now, it wasn't the Communists but the Muslims, and they were becoming a regular pain in the arse, Jim Cassidy thought.

But the people he hated most of all were Aborigines. There was a group now, as the bus drove through Midland, sitting where they always sat. Dirty clothes, untidy hair. Some already with a bottle in their hand at this early hour of the day.

Two men hugged each other in unrestrained delight. A younger man helped an older, probably drunk woman stagger to a seat. There was much good humour among them. One lout waved cheerfully to the bus, another came to attention and saluted it, much to the amusement of the others. Then they were gone.

He caught a glimpse of the old face beside him out of the corner of his eye. A faint smile creased the placid features. It must be her relatives, he thought scornfully.

The bus bounced along with the usual jokes from the driver and the promise of a video later on. This was a long trip; all day and all night and half the next day with stops in between. So everyone was prepared with books to read and pillows. He had a pillow and an excellent mystery to get into. He usually tried to initiate a conversation with his companion on long trips but he wouldn't speak to this thief of his seat. Hopefully, he thought again as he turned to the first page of his book, she would get off in Geraldton at least, the first major stop. Maybe even Carnarvon. There was a terrible problem with the natives there, he knew, the whole town being one big violent camp, he believed.

The backpackers were excited this early on and there was much moving up and down the aisle to converse with friends they had made at the hostel. Whenever the Japanese smiled at him he pretended he didn't notice but he smiled once or twice at a couple of young girls who by their accent seemed to be Swedish. One was the stereotypical blonde-haired, pert-breasted beauty; the other a slimmer brunette. At the next stop he'd get to know them better. Perhaps they were going to Port Hedland and his job as a Customs officer would no doubt impress them. He could show them the sights and they could show him theirs. He giggled to himself, the mystery forgotten for the moment.

'Excuse me,' the soft voice came from beside him.

The old woman was getting up, but not looking at him, her face in the shadow of the battered cowboy hat she wore.

With very bad grace he put aside his book, stood and

let her squeeze past into the aisle. She was a big woman and overweight so she moved slowly. He looked after her in annoyance. The bus had just left Perth city, wending its way through the Swan Valley with the beautiful Darling Ranges on the right. If she can't hold her drink why sit by the window in the first place, he thought crossly. Probably she had realised that if she sat by the aisle she could easily have fallen out of her seat, being inebriated as she was. But if she fell asleep against him or, even worse, vomited on him he would have her thrown off the bus.

She came lumbering back down the aisle and he pretended not to see her for a moment, leaving her standing in the aisle. Another small victory.

'Thank you,' she murmured as she wedged herself into her seat, then resumed looking out the window. He didn't bother to respond.

At the first stop he made a beeline towards the two Nordic beauties but there was a language barrier so they spent their time in inanities with much muffled giggling on the girls' part. They had met several such awkward Australian men on their three-month tour and, besides, they both had boyfriends at home. But flirting was a fun part of their holiday so they giggled at his funny accent and discussed in their own language his various merits or demerits.

He was tallish, but bony, with a prominent Adam's apple and, although he wasn't all that old, he was already going bald. He had a nice smile but crooked front teeth.

His eyes were a soft luminous brownish-green, the nicest feature about his lean face.

He saw the old woman hobble off by herself to the corner of the shop to sit in the shade, patiently waiting for the journey to begin. Three Japanese tourists approached her and it appeared the youth was asking if he could take her photo with the two girls. Whether she really wanted to or not, this is what happened, the two smiling girls on either side of her stolid figure. They then all bowed to her and went into the shop, chattering away.

The bus moved on. He sat thinking about his job and the promotion he had just got. He looked forward to working at Port Hedland Customs where a lot more was happening. He felt he could play his part in the defence of Australia, just as his father had done. And, he too, would be taking a stand against the Asian Invasion, searching for boat people or poachers.

Video time and he was disappointed to see the movie was about a redneck school amalgamating with a Negro school and the problems that caused the local football team. Not only did he not understand the rules of gridiron but he thought Denzel Washington a much over-rated actor. Why couldn't they have a movie about an Australian football player hero? He decided to have a snooze. If Lady Muck wants to go to the dunny she can just cross her legs and wait, he thought vindictively, snuggling into his pillow.

When he stirred from his doze they were pulling into Geraldton. They would eat, change drivers and some of the lucky ones might scrounge a shower. He hoped the old lady would get off the bus but she didn't. Several of the dusty characters and the two Swedish beauties did. In their place three Aboriginals, neatly dressed, dark and shy, got on. One stopped beside the old lady and spoke softly in their language to her. She nodded, giving a gentle smile.

He wasn't hungry and, neither it seemed, was the old woman. After a brief stretch of the legs and a disappointed farewell to the two laughing Nordic princesses, he got back on the bus and read steadily away. His companion did not even go for a walk but stayed in her seat.

Off again, night creeping down over the landscape, a bright red sun illuminating the horizon. Soon they travelled in their own little world – muted lights, cheerful conversations and the smells of stale chips, stale bodies, cool drinks, the musty carpet. He could smell her now, as no doubt she could smell him. But she had a sour, oily smell.

The other video came on – an American comedy that was mildly amusing. The occasional smile flitted across the old woman's face and he wondered if she actually understood the story, for it was different from anything she would ever have experienced, surely.

Then night fell with a swoop, the video ended, most people settled down to sleep and there was just the hum of the air-conditioner, a whispered sentence once or twice and the bouncing wheels of the bus thrumming on the asphalt of the never-ending highway. The old lady pushed her hat down over her face.

Sometime late at night they pulled into Carnarvon and, sure enough, the only people to crowd on were five Aboriginal youths with their canvas swags. Three looked as though they had come straight from a Station with their big hats, cracked boots, checked shirts and faded jeans. Two stopped beside Jim Cassidy.

'Hey, look out! There's Auntie Nancy there. I thought she was in 'ospital.'

'Yeah. Must of taken 'erself out, ay!'

'They probably got sick of 'er. Cheeky ole woman, Auntie Nancy.'

'Make ya laugh but,' the other chuckled and they made their way up the aisle.

In the early hours of the morning, as the sun spread red over the eastern sky, promising a fierce hot day, he awoke from a fitful sleep. Somewhere among his jumbled dreams he had been with both the Nordic beauties, whose names he still did not know, and in another he had seen the old woman's face for the first time when she turned and looked at him. He could not remember if that was a dream or not.

She was lying against him, as he had dreaded she would, her hand resting on his knee. Abruptly he shoved her away but she only settled more into her seat, her hat slipping further down her face. He would like to make a fuss but there were too many Aborigines on the bus now who would side with dear old Auntie Nancy and it would only cause embarrassment to him. Stiffly, he got to his feet, wending his unsteady way to the toilet.

Back in his seat again dour thoughts assaulted him as he squirmed about. The window seat allowed one to use the actual window as a rest and so as a general rule was more comfortable than the aisle seat. He thought how unfair it was this person had taken his seat and spoiled his whole trip, just as the woman at Kojonup did all that while ago. The South Africans had a good idea, with their apartheid, he grumbled to himself. Best to be seen but not heard in the case of the black races, except maybe in singing which, like sports, they were good at. But the Australian blacks were the worst of all, not even being really good singers. They were drunk and lazy and, unlike his father, had not joined up in hordes to defend their country. They were thieves and gutless violent parasites, destroying the good name of Perth. And now he'd had to endure one all the way to Port Hedland. He glanced over at the sleeping form spitefully. Just a waste of space, dead drunk to the world.

Only after arriving in Port Hedland was it discovered the old lady, known among the North-west Aborigines as Auntie Nancy Eaton, had died in her sleep. Really, she had not been well enough to travel but she had not wanted to die in a strange place surrounded by strangers so had checked herself out. All the long journey her eyes had devoured the beauty of her country and she had been content.

Jim Cassidy was devastated. He had sat and slept next to a dead person, God alone knew how long. Everyone was sympathetic towards him, the Japanese especially so, possibly something to do with their religion. There were murmurs of condolences, little gasps of shock as the rest of the travellers learnt of the drama. But deep down inside Jim knew that he'd had mean thoughts about this person and her kin while she lay there dead beside him. Perhaps if he had been friendlier he might have sensed her distress. They could have got her an ambulance and she would be alive now.

As for Nancy Eaton, her spirit lingered after her body departed. The other Aboriginals gathered in a little knot sensed it and held whispered conversations. Soon all the North-west communities would know of her passing. But they would know she was happy, that she died at peace, for this truly *was* her land.

Author's Notes

Stolen Car

I wrote this story after my first experience of police 'justice' on the streets of Perth, before my novel *The Day of the Dog* went into more detail, and it pretty much sums up the life I then led. It describes people I know or knew well, including my foster brother David Wallam. It was after publication of this story in *Aboriginal and Islander Identity* that Jack Davis became interested in my writing.

Dead Dingo

This is one of the first short stories I ever wrote, when I was seventeen. It won a national short story competition, giving me the clue that fame and fortune could be made from writing, not fighting. I had recently read the novella *Wildcat Falling* by Mudrooroo (then Colin Johnson), whom many say influenced this story. But in fact it was a visit to the zoo, just as the protagonist makes, that caused me to think about the different kinds of incarceration we put upon ourselves and others.

Sandcastles

I wrote this story on a wet and wild afternoon at the West Australian Institute of Technology (WAIT) where I was doing an English degree. My best stories – or my favourites, if you like – have all been written in a torrent of energy, as was my first novel. They seem to hold the raw feelings that make the story great – or work – for me. But this story holds a precious memory for me – a day in Albany when I was seven or eight and my brother and father intended going to a secluded spot for a picnic at the beach. I had just met my neighbour's kids and decided on the spur of the moment to stay with them, which was a big mistake as they turned out cruel as only children can be. I had thought there would be many more times to visit that beach, but it was not to be. My parents divorced soon after. I do not have many memories of my father and this would have been a good one, I'm sure. Coincidentally, there were some kids from an Aboriginal family on the beach that day with whom my brother played, including making a sandcastle.

The Storm

This is just a nice short description of how man is powerless against nature. As a short story, I feel it fits in well with the genre, not having many characters, but each character having a definite story. I had not long finished working on the wheat bins at Miling at the time, so no doubt that town was in my mind.

It's Only a Game

This story was a commissioned work, the theme obviously about football. But I decided to have a go at comedy for the first time and I believe it worked. I think the best humour is tongue-in-cheek. If I were going to write a serious story about football, I would write about my beloved East Perth team, the Mighty Royals. But in fact I grew up in a family dedicated to Rugby Union, and one of my first unpublished novels which I wrote in school – *The Rise and Fall of Mulga Black* – is about an Aboriginal Rugby player possibly being chosen for Australia, even before the remarkable Ella brothers.

Ghosts of a Form Present

One of my favourite stories, this is another commissioned work, the theme being the millennium that was on its way out. Once again, I drew upon a Creation story in writing this, but the story is actually about the passing of the old Perth I once knew into the modern, unknown world it had become, especially for me.

Dead Roses

This was a commissioned piece, and it is one of my favourite stories. All the chosen authors for the anthology were given two paragraphs of text relating to Sydney which had to be incorporated into the story somehow. In my case, I turned the first and last paragraphs back to front. Naturally, I did not live in Sydney at the time, so I thought up this town. Most of the places in my stories are imaginary, but all are located in my beloved South-west. This story was also only my second attempt at a murder mystery.

The Island

I not only write commissioned works but I also write for fun, or because I think up an idea. The first version of this story I wrote when I was at school, when I did not know much about love, but this version was written many years later. The island in question was Carnac, where we had recently gone on a school excursion, and you can see I enjoyed it so very much that it stuck with me, for I have never been back there since. In the later story I developed the characters more, and made them and their story more complex.

The Lilies of the Valley

This story was written as a commissioned work, the theme given being 'a harbour' – which I decided to interpret as 'a safe place'. The safe place here is the hotel where all the various protagonists work or get together. The version I originally wrote was much longer than what was published. It went into more detail about the relationship between Lyndall and the detective, and also the relationship between Lyndall and Yveline, whom I have turned into one of my more devious characters. And my previous ending had a further twist than ended up being the case. So I was disappointed that my story had changed so much but I still feel it has merit. And Lyndall,

Rags and Sharkey are three of my favourite characters, although I do think that the story of Yveline somehow became lost in translation. I based this story on the Song of Solomon from the Bible, and originally the way that the girl thought her thoughts was in verses from this beautiful song, but in the version that was anthologised that also was cut out and fell onto the editing room floor.

Chains around My Heart

The theme set for selected authors when this story was commissioned was food, so once again I used my imagination to develop an unusual story. In fact, in all my writing I endeavour not to choose the obvious path. I try to give my readers something to make them savour the characters or the situation. My story was not chosen for the anthology, but I still had a lot of fun writing it.

Spirit Woman

In my short fiction I draw on a lot of the wonderful Creation stories of the South-west Nyoongahs. This story was influenced by one of them. I believe very much in the spirituality of my country and am awed by the age it has been here, and I often use a Creation story as a metaphor or when describing some character.

Walking with Mermaids

There was a competition a few years back to write a story in the vein of James Joyce. The first prize was a visit to Dublin to see where he had set his fantastic stories, none of which unfortunately I had read at the time. But Ireland is a place I'd always wanted to go, being partly of Irish descent myself, as well as Scottish – and having made most of my white characters Irish as well, since the Irish have had a similar history of invasion and alienation by the British as the Aboriginal people have had. I did not win the competition, but this was my effort. It is a story about people telling lies. The Maori girl was based on a friend of mine whom I had always promised to put in a story.

Illusions

This story was commissioned by the *Sydney Morning Herald*, which sent out to authors a selection of photos to write about. I cannot remember the exact photo I chose, except that it included a field of flowers, but I am sure you can imagine what it looked like when you read the story.

Confessions of a Headhunter

I first thought of this story after viewing Captain Cook's statue in Hyde Park, Sydney, and made it all up in my head on the long walk back to Glebe where I was staying, whereupon I actually wrote it down. A lot of stories I actually don't write down, but just leave stewing in my head until they gradually fade away. There was a lot of activity at the time in Perth concerning our great Nyoongah hero Yagan, and thus the idea was born. When I read the draft to Sally Riley she said, 'Don't give that to anyone else. It's mine!' And so she turned it into a great little film that won several awards. Like a few others, this story was written fast, so it's raw – and because of that it is still one of my favourites.

The Poppies Grow in Flanders Fields
There have been many Aboriginal soldiers who have fought in wars in which Australia has been involved. This recent story acknowledges all of them. As with some of my other work from the past few years, this story had to be of a specific number of words, as I was entering it in a literary competition. So a lot of self-editing was required to prune it down – which I think makes it much tighter than some of my earlier work.

Whanua
This is a story about gaining and losing families – a theme quite close to many Aboriginal hearts, I fear, due to the practices of various Protectors of Aborigines over the years. But it is also a story of friendship. I have long been fascinated by Maori culture, and this plays a part here too.

67 Yagan Way
I have recently branched out into futuristic themes, yet still keeping a link to the present and the past because everything ties together and 'history repeats itself'. This story is influenced slightly by an American story I read in school many years ago. The theme was gangs and their practices. But there the similarity ends.

Deserts

I wrote this story in 2007 for a competition, the theme of which was 'Deserts'. My entry, however, was not only about the actual desert landscape but also about how a life, too, can become a desert. Once again my themes were of alienation in one's own land and loss of family. I didn't win the competition but this story remains a favourite of mine as it was the one that got me writing again – at least for a short while. And it allowed me to introduce a dear friend of mine – although only in the context of the story, as she also left my life, which become a desert again for a brief time.

The Window Seat

In 2006, I decided to enter many writing competitions with my stories and poetry to see if I could win some money, which was not in great supply in my life then. I wrote a few stories as a result of this. Some were themed, but most were simply stories I tried to craft with little twists in them, although Jeffrey Archer I am not. I did not win any money, but I had a lot of pleasure creating the characters and situations. This story is based on an incident I witnessed on a TransWA bus at Kojonup several years ago when there was a mix-up with the seats.

Glossary

NOTE: This glossary contains words from the Nyoongah language, contemporary Aboriginal English, colloquial Australian, Maori and Celtic.

baandji (also bunji) – looking for sex, as in baandjiman, or conning people with promises of sex, also as in baandjiwoman

bardie grub – succulent grub found mostly in balga trees (i.e. 'blackboys' or grass trees) but also in jam trees

black velvet – derogatory term for Aboriginal woman, especially in the context of being a sexual partner

boaka – kangaroo skin cloak worn by South-west Nyoongahs

boong – derogatory name for Aboriginal

borrie – a picked-up girl, borrowed, and therefore not worthy of serious attention

bridarra (also birdiya, boordiya) – the boss, i.e. good at whatever that person does, as in 'bridarra footy player'

combo – derogatory term for a white man living with a black woman

cooda (also coodah, cood) – mate, friend, brother (it's
a word from the people around Carnarvon that has
come down to Perth)

coorlung (properly koorlang, koorlong) – child

coorlunga (properly koorlangka, or even nobaratj)
– children

ding – derogatory term for an Italian

djanak (sometimes spelt djenak) – evil spirit, the dead

gidji-ing – ketj or kitj is a spear, but a gidgi/gidgee
usually refers to a fishing spear

gin – derogatory term for a young girl (from the Eora
word tjin meaning girl)

gnummerai – cigarette

gorbals – a tenement slum in Glasgow, Scotland,
now destroyed with the residents mainly moved to
Castlemilk

humpy – shack

kabarli – old woman

kartwarrah – literally 'head bad' i.e. a crazy person

koorlang – see coorlung

kwel – she-oak tree

lubra – now a derogatory term for an Aboriginal
woman, originally a word from the language of the
Eora people

maali – swan

mabarn – magic man, witchdoctor

mandjang – a man who is sick or not well

manuhiri – (Maori) the group of people gathering to
meet the village's occupants (often nowadays tourists);

coming into a Maori marae is full of ceremony and
tradition, and the manuhiri play a part in that

marae – (Maori) village, settlement for a particular tribe
or family

mili-mili – paper

monaych (properly manadj or munadj) – black
cockatoo, and so a name used to describe the police
who once wore dark navy blue uniforms

moony – sexual intercourse

moorditj daadja – from moorditj meaning good or
strong and daddja meaning meat, so good meat or
good meal

mooritj – great, wonderful, nice or pretty, as in 'he's
my mooritj man'

moorook – sorcerise, or put a curse on someone

munadj – see monaych

ngoonie (ngooni, ngoon) – brother, sometimes used as
friend

ngwonan – black duck

nignog – racist term for any black person

Nunga – used to describe Aboriginal people of South
Australia

nyaandi – marihuana or hashish, possibly an Eastern
states word

Nyoongah (also Noongar) – South-west Aboriginal
people, the Bibbulmun tribes of Western Australia.

the Protector – the white man who was in charge of
all Aboriginal Affairs in the early days; often an
autocratic, bullying, interfering bureaucrat

Selkies – (Celtic) creatures of myth in Scottish and Irish waters which are half seal and half human, or seals in the sea who shed their skins when they come briefly onto land to dance and play

smack – heroin

tuppy (djapi) – a vagina

tjilgi (also djilgi) – freshwater crayfish smaller than the darker marron, often a greenish colour

unna – meaning 'is that so?' or 'this is the truth, isn't it?'; a Nyoongah expression

wadgula – white man

waiata – (Maori) a traditional song, usually one of welcome or love

waugal (also wakarl, wagyll) – sacred water snake, the Creator of land and laws in Nyoognah culture, also meaning a carpet snake, none of whom were destroyed or hurt by Nyoongah people, especially if they were blessed with purple eyes

wilgie (also wilk) – red ochre used for ceremonial dancing (or corroboree) purposes

Winny – Winfield brand of cigarette

woola – an expression of joy, a shout of praise, as when a goal is scored, or at any momentous news or event

yella fella – derogatory term for mixed blood person

yok – wife

yoorn (also nyarn) – expression of sorrow

yorga – usually an unmarried female, or other female

Acknowledgements

I have already acknowledged many people in my dedication but I would like to thank Patrick Gallagher of Allen & Unwin for first publishing my novel *The Day of the Dog* and setting me on the path to creative writing. Alan Alexander at WAIT from whom I learnt a lot as my creative writing teacher. The late great Jack Davis and also Ken Colbung for their support, as well as Robert Bropho of Guildford. Jim Welsh at Guildford Grammar School for his support and my good friend Jimmy Holland who was a pupil there – as well as Maurice McGuire, Shane Kickett and Brian Blurton.

And, as is the case in the best Oscar speeches, I cannot go without thanking my mother and her glorious man John who have been such a great support and inspiration to me, sharing my love of books and good old movies and wonderful jazz and blues – all of which make up an important part of me.

Publisher's Note

Earlier versions of some of the stories in this collection have been previously published as follows:

- 'Dead Dingo' in *Aboriginal and Islander Identity*, 1977; in *Stories from Three Worlds*, ed. J.A. and J.K. McKenzie, Heinemann Educational, 1978
- 'Stolen Car' in *Aboriginal and Islander Identity*, 1977; in *Paperbark*, ed. Jack Davis, UQP, 1990; in *Brief Encounters*, ed. Barbara Ker Wilson, UQP, 1992
- 'Sandcastles' in *The Dwarf: selections from the McGregor Literary Competitions, 1978–79*, ed. Noni Braham, Darling Downs Institute Press, 1979; in *Personal Best: thirty Australian authors choose their best short stories*, ed. Garry Disher, HarperCollins, 1989; in *The Penguin Century of Australian Stories*, ed. Carmel Bird, Penguin, 2000
- 'The Storm' in *Aboriginal and Islander Identity*, 1979; in *Laughing Cry: an anthology of short fiction*, ed. Faye Davis, Mary Dilworth and Jennifer Kemp, Gooseberry Hill Press, 1984

- 'It's Only a Game' in *The Greatest Game*, ed. Ross Fitzgerald and Ken Spillman, William Heinemann Australia, 1988
- 'Ghosts of a Form Present' in *Millenium: time-pieces by Australian writers*, ed. Helen Daniel, Penguin Books, 1991
- 'Dead Roses' in *A Corpse at the Opera House: Crimes for a Summer Christmas,* ed. Stephen Knight, Allen & Unwin, 1992
- 'The Island', *Southerly*, 1993/4
- 'Lilies of the Valley' in *Harbour*, ed. George Papaellinas, Picador (Pan Macmillan), 1993
- 'Spirit Woman' in *Influence: Australian Voices*, ed. Peter Skrznecki, Anchor, 1997
- 'Illusions', *Sydney Morning Herald*, Dec/Jan 1998